LOVE ON THE LINE

A Great Expectations Love Story: The Graykens, Book 2

LAURIE LEWIS

Love on the Line

A Great Expectations Love Story:

The Graykens, Book 2
By Laurie Lewis
Copyright ©2019 by Laurie Lewis
ASIN: B07NLFN3QM
Published 2019 by Willowsport Press,
an imprint of JATA Inc.
Mount Airy, MD 21771
Cover design by Sheri McGathy
This page has been designed
using resources from Freepik.com
www.laurielclewis.com

DEDICATION

Dedicated to Chris and Dana Heisler,
who shared their story of love and faith,
and whose battle with leukemia
inspired many elements of this story.

"I can do all things through Christ
which strengtheneth me."
Philippians 4:13

FOREWORD

"Whenever love is on the line, we'll always choose us." It was an easy promise for Matt and Mikaela Grayken to make. After all, Matt fell in love with Mikaela the first time he saw her across a room, serving her cancer patients, and Mikaela crossed an ocean to find Matt's birth sister Kate, whose stem cells could save his life.

That's the kind of love they've built.

In their quest to defy the limits of Matt's health and return a bit of the good they've known, they embrace grand, miraculous opportunities. But these opportunities threaten Matt's health while also entwining the Graykens in the lives of complicated people. After all they've faced, outside influences challenge their bond, testing the promise they made—to choose each other when love is on the line.

Love on the Line, Great Expectations Love Stories: *The Graykens*, Book Two, is the highly anticipated sequel to *Love on a Limb*.

CHAPTER ONE

The organist played "Pachelbel's Canon" as Matthew and Mikaela Grayken exited the chapel from their vow-renewal ceremony. Mikaela's mile-wide smile beamed like a first-time bride's, sending a tinge of guilt through Matthew over the contractual circumstances and hurried staging of their legal courthouse ceremony five months earlier. With her reassuring hand in his, Matthew led his best friend and champion down the aisle and past the small group of applauding, backslapping guests. Simultaneous cheers and dings of texts from Mikaela's military family also sounded as they witnessed the livestream of the event across the globe.

The festivities drew a crowd of curious D.C. strangers huddled outside the doors, dressed in Christmas garb and carrying presents and holiday arrangements. Their smiles and applause extended the Graykens' triumphant bridal exit yards farther, into the lobby where the wedding trappings eventually became diluted, merging into the normal hospital scenes of worry and illness. A med tech pushed a cart bearing the symbol for radiation, and the truth of their circumstances slammed Matthew with brutal irony, reminding him that at only twenty-nine years, he was a human mass riddled with acute myeloid leukemia, or AML, a patient whose existence could likewise be measured in terms of half-life and rates of decay.

Mikaela seemed to read his dimming smile. With her left hand still securely holding his, she touched his hollow cheek with her right, bringing his worried gaze back to her steadfast, love-filled face. She mouthed, "Merry Christmas, Mr. Grayken, I love you," strengthening his faltering courage.

Burton, the octogenarian volunteer charged with ferrying Matt to and from the ceremony, was waiting, but not with a limo or a horse-drawn carriage. With a wheelchair. More sobering to the groom was how relieved he and his jelly legs were at seeing that chair.

She squeezed his hand. "One short reception and it's go time," Mikaela said, her smile and touch restoring his courage. "I completely love you, Mr. Grayken."

She leaned down, brushed back a stray hair from his dwindling collection, and kissed him while Burton adjusted his foot rests. Matthew met her kiss and whispered in his thickest Irish brogue, "What if I tip Burton here a hundred spot to wheel us into a taxi headed for the nearest airport. I have a platinum credit card in my vest pocket. You name the place, Mrs. Grayken, and we're there."

Mikaela's first reaction was a brief look of sympathy that shifted into the oddball humor that dragged Matthew from almost certain death to hope. Her face twisted and wrinkled in exaggerated thought as she weighed his proposal. "Hmmm. . . tempting as that is, I hear they pull off a world-class magic act in the Arminger Cancer Wing, and I've already made reservations for two in room 625." She raised one eyebrow and sent a seductive glance his way. "I think you'll enjoy the private party I've arranged for after the guests leave."

"Puttin' something special in my IV bag, are you?"

"Oohhh . . . I need to add that to my list."

A smile doubled the wrinkles of Burton's saggy cheeks as he looked back and called for the wedding guests to take the elevators to the sixth floor. When the elevator doors opened, Mikaela said, "I'll be in soon," and gave Matt a final kiss before leading the group to the visitors' lounge, where the caterer set up food for wedding guests and transplant department staff.

He reluctantly let her go, forcing her hand to withdraw from his, a millimeter at a time. She held him in her over-the-shoulder-gaze until Burton wheeled him around a corner and into the care of the medical staff, who were prepared to end his temporary reprieve and begin his transplant preparations in earnest.

He was soon back in his bed, surrounded by IV poles and machines once more. He closed his eyes and replayed the ceremony to ward off the invading fears. For twenty minutes, standing in his tux instead of lying in pajamas or a gown, he had felt reclaimed, somewhat like himself again as he watched Mikaela walk toward him. By the end of the ceremony, she was nearly holding him up.

He looked upon his withered body. Arms that had once steered kayaks through raging currents could now barely get a glass of juice to his lips without spilling half its contents. And his legs . . . He wondered if he would ever run or swim or climb stairs, let alone conquer a mountain as he once had.

A donor had been found. A sister he never knew. Kate's arrival from Ireland was greeted like the discovery of the Holy Grail. He didn't mean to sound ungrateful, but the expectations and hopes of his family and friends were crushing him. *But what if Mikaela's love, Kate's DNA, and the medical staff's efforts, aren't enough to heal my ragged body? What if I die anyway?*

The sweats began again as his anxiety ramped up. He needed Mikaela, and then, like an answer to a silent prayer, the door swished open, and relief poured through him at the thought of *her* arrival. "Mikaela," rushed from his lips as he turned, seeking her face, crying out her name, more for comfort than as a greeting.

"Sorry, Matt. I'm afraid it's just me," said the sixtyish hospital chaplain who had performed the ceremony.

Matt shrank into his pillow, embarrassed by his show of emotion.

The chaplain slowly moved near his bed, filling the uncomfortable moment with chatter. "Mikaela asked me to tell you she's hurrying back to you, but there's so much food set up in that family waiting area that she's making the rounds to every nurses' station and hospital room on the floor, inviting everyone to enjoy the Christmas buffet."

Matt balled the sheet fabric in his trembling, IV-poked hands and smiled at the wonder of his wife. He looked at the door again, willing her to appear.

The chaplain patted his stomach. "I grabbed a quick bite, but before I head home to my family dinner, I wanted to thank you for including me in your wonderful day. It was an honor. I've never seen a couple deeper in love than you two. You're truly blessed to have found each other."

"Yes. We're very blessed," Matt repeated in a monotone. He knew that his mood was spiraling into a nosedive and that he'd failed to pull out of his emotional descent in time to fool the chaplain. Worry appeared on the chaplain's expression, and Matt knew the clergyman picked up on his somber mood. Matt adjusted his position in the bed to buy a few moments as he pulled himself together. "I'm sorry. I'm just tired."

"That's understandable. You've had a busy day."

The chaplain was as bad at camouflaging his worry as Matt had been. Instead of leaving, the pastor pulled a chair near Matt and sat. After a brief silence, he said, "One of this past year's resolutions was to read all the works of Charles Dickens by the end of December. I won't succeed, but a few lines have stayed with me and made me think. Like this one from *A Tale of Two Cities*. 'It was the best of times, it was the worst of times.' Ever heard that one?"

Matt closed his eyes and huffed a sad chuckle.

"I imagine the miraculous circumstances surrounding this transplant opportunity, with all its hope and unknowns, must feel a little like that."

Matt's eyes burned at the man's correct assumption. "You believe in getting right to the heart of the issue, Pastor Carnes?"

The chaplain shrugged and smiled. "Let's just say I had a feeling you might need to talk."

Matt wondered if his mood and concerns were as transparent to everyone else. "It's not just the transplant. It's . . . it's a lot of things."

The chaplain settled back into the chair and folded his hands in his lap. Matt could see the clergyman wasn't going anywhere, leaving him two unpleasant choices—sit in awkward silence or speak to the man, who gazed at him through eyes filled with unconditional love.

"Whatever we discuss . . ."

"Stays between you, me, and God."

Again, twisting the sheet fabric provided a needed distraction. "Today should be the happiest day of my life, but I can't help wondering if meeting Mikaela was the worst thing that could have happened to either of us."

There was a momentary hitch in the chaplain's breathing before he answered. "I saw how happy you two were today. You clearly love Mikaela, and she clearly loves you."

Matt didn't question their love for each other. He questioned the rightness of it, and he stated his case softly, almost whispering the agonizing words, as if saying them delicately would lessen their pain.

"A young, vibrant, joyful woman is bound to me, a man who may be dead in a few weeks, or worse, to a man who might survive to be an invalid and burden to her for years. Look at what I've put her through. What I'm about to put her through. How can such selfishness be called love?"

"Are you implying that love is only love if it's easy?"

Matt's mouth hung open for a second as he pondered the question. Knowing he'd lost that point, he bit the side of his mouth and turned away from his guest to stare out the window. "I wasn't honest with her. When I proposed to Mikaela, I told her I wasn't looking for love, that I just needed a qualified caregiver and a companion to share my last days, but I lied, because secretly, I was already in love with her. I had been from the first moment I watched her caring for her patients at the clinic."

"I imagine she knew that. She did agree to marry you on your terms."

"Because I needed her. She was too giving to deny my request. I told her I needed a wife with the legal authority to speak for me when I no longer could, to prevent my parents from assuming guardianship of me and forcing me to submit to hopeless treatments."

"And yet, here you are, willingly submitting to every Hail Mary treatment medical science can pull out of its sleeve and doing it of your own free will. The reversal in your position was because that legal contract turned into real love."

The chaplain's knowing smile coaxed a sad chuckle from Matt, who nodded involuntarily as he felt the impact of the statement. "Yes . . . it most certainly did."

"Of course, it did. If Mikaela felt burdened and wanted out of this marriage, it seems all she had to do was let the cancer take its course, and you'd be gone in short order. But she didn't. Instead, she listened to a hunch, a heavenly whisper of sorts, and contrary to the formidable opposition of your parents, she took a long-shot gamble and left your bedside to follow that hunch across the ocean to Ireland, to find your sister, the last member of your birth family, so she could ask her to be the donor to a brother she'd never met. And why? Because *Mikaela* also wants more time with *you*."

"There's more to the story, Reverend. A miracle of sorts had already occurred, sending Kate to America before Mikaela arrived. My sweet wife flew across the Atlantic to find an empty house. She flew back, believing she had failed in her quest, and then she found out that Kate was already here."

"Just imagine . . . Remember all that when you worry that your meeting Mikaela was the worst thing that could have happened to *her*. Now tell me why you say meeting her might be the worst thing that could have happened to *you*?"

Matt blinked and raked his fingers through his thinning hair. "Because loving her makes me afraid. More afraid than ever before, because I now have more to lose than ever before."

Matt turned his head to hide the moisture welling in his eyes. He felt the chaplain take his hand, and lay another hand gently upon his shoulder as he began offering a whispered prayer, pleading with God to heal Matt and grant the couple more time. When he said amen, both men's eyes were reddened and moist.

"Matt, I do pray that God spares you for many years, but don't let your happiness depend on the *amount of time you have* but on the *quality of the love you give*. Yours isn't a marriage based on selfishness or deception, Matt, it's a marriage that's been blessed to evolve beyond its initial restrictions of sickness and impending death."

The chaplain squeezed Matt's shoulder and stood. "I meant every word I said in that service today. What you two have is unique and beautiful. Don't doubt yourself or withhold any part of yourself, just because you had a complicated start. Embrace what you have now. Lean on the Lord and build from here. If you do, I promise you that regardless of how much time He's allotted for you to be together, whatever time you do have will be exquisite and enough."

The chaplain's prayer and challenge replayed in Matt's head long after the clergyman exited. *Lean on the Lord and build from there. . .* Matt hadn't given a lot of thought to God or godly things until he met Mikaela and her unapologetic faith. His parents took him to church as a young child, made sure he received his First Communion. After his first diagnosis of cancer, their Sunday prayers took on a new intensity, becoming daily, even hourly petitions. Once he was in remission, prayer and church were relegated back to Sunday worship and then primarily to holidays, like a tradition that accompanied pulling out his mother's lace tablecloth and her mother's best china.

His acceptance into the St. Andrews Academy for Boys meant religion was a part of every school day, but the prayers and hymns floated around him like sweet familiar air, rarely becoming part of how he saw himself. Until his second bout of cancer, when he allowed anger and frustration to overwhelm his faltering faith.

Faith in God was innate with Mikaela. She couldn't live without it. She *chose* not to live without it, and Matt had been the grateful recipient of the optimism and hope her faith brought her. But she could only run along behind him and cheer him on for so long. At some point, he needed to propel his own faith on. He knew that time had come.

With his peace somewhat restored, Matt surrendered to the overwhelming fatigue creeping into every muscle and dozed off as he waited for Mikaela to arrive.

"Hello, Sleepyhead," she whispered, adding a lingering kiss. "Your guests would like to say goodbye."

Slender, regal, delicate, she was still dressed in the long, white garden dress that served as her bridal gown. Even Matt could see a special glow in her. He marveled at how she reminded him of one of the calla lilies in her bouquet.

In every way that mattered, she had been his wife for months, but it was clear that the morning's chapel ceremony was more than just a Christmas gift to his parents and Mikaela's military brothers and their families, who had missed the couple's courthouse vows. This was the wedding Mikaela had longed for.

A few guests filtered past the door to offer parting hugs and prayers for the coming battle. Matt's adoptive and only parents, Donovan and Catherine Grayken, arrived after Mikaela, with Kate, his newly found sister. His seven loyal friends pulled up the rear. All seven were members of the Dead Virginia Presidents group, or DVP, an adolescent society formed during the groups' highbrow prep school years. These loyal seven migrated to D.C. to fill prestigious positions in commerce and government. To Matt's delight, they still gathered weekly to celebrate and support one another in anything from Thursday night poker games to medical testing to save one of their own. Matthew loved them like brothers.

"PJs, Matthew? Already dressed for the wedding night?" teased Matt's best friend, Daniel Lebed. "You know, my PR firm just got a retired quarterback a couple mil in mattress endorsements. I could make you a star."

Kate moved between Daniel and Matt. After a dramatic toss of her dark waves, she spread her arms wide. "Stop it," she teased in her rich Irish voice. She jutted her face near Matt's. "I may have only met my baby brother a few days ago, but he's my kin, blood of my blood, and I can assure you that not even your fancy advertising agency can afford exclusive use of a Fitzpatrick's mug."

She looked sheepishly at Donovan and Catherine. "No disrespect intended, Mr. and Mrs. Grayken."

Gray-haired Donovan, Matt's proud adoptive patriarch replied, "None taken. If anything, I think we've added additional value to Matt since we adopted him and made him a Grayken, so I agree, Kate." He turned to Daniel. "I'm afraid you'll have to look elsewhere for your pinup boy." He raised his pants leg a few inches, revealing a bony, woolen-socked ankle, which fueled the revelry a moment longer. "I, on the other hand, could be persuaded to entertain an offer."

While the group roared, Kate moved to Daniel, who discreetly slipped an arm around her waist, drawing her near. The couple returned to the DVP group, but Matt's eyes remained on them. He was surprised to see this romantic development between the pair, but he saved his questions for later when they were alone.

One by one, the rest of the DVP men said their goodbyes to Matt, receiving hugs from Mikaela at the door until only Daniel and family members remained.

Donovan helped Catherine with her coat before wrapping his Christmas scarf around his own neck. He laid a loving hand on his son's leg, but his glance moved between Matt, Kate, and Mikaela. "So, everything begins tomorrow, eh?"

Matt yawned and leaned back into the mattress. "They'll begin administering drugs to lower my immune system. I need to be near zero to give the transplant its best chance of success."

"And, Kate, when is your surgery to remove the marrow?"

Matt turned to Kate and found her staring at him, her expression a mixture of sorrow and confusion. When her eyes met his, she snapped out of her daze, shook her head, and excused her fog as fatigue.

"And what was the question?" she asked Donovan in a voice strong and bold. "You were askin' about me and my contribution to this process? Well . . . I may not have to undergo surgery to be Matt's donor."

Donovan's eyes crinkled in wonder. "Really?"

"It's true, Da." Matt yawned and closed his eyes.

Mikaela closed the door behind the last exiting friend and joined the conversation. "That's why Kate is our miracle. If all goes well, the meds they give her will cause her body to overproduce stem cells that will spill out into her blood. Then they'll collect her blood, separate the stem cells out, and give them to Matt."

"My part's easy," Kate added. "Lots of blood draws, but no surgery."

"And then we wait," said Catherine.

Matt nodded. "And then we wait."

"And pray," added Donovan. "God's got a hand in this, Matthew, from Mikaela's coming into your life and then her instinct to fly to Ireland to seek Kate, to Kate's having already been cleared to donate to your twin brother in Ireland, and on to her recognizing you on that YouTube video and heading here to find you. Yes, I just have to believe God's in it and that He still has work for you to do. You're going to be fine, Matthew. Just fine."

"Thank you, Da." Matthew liked the math of his father's faith, where one plus one plus one equaled a miracle. He saw no good that could come from challenging it.

Catherine Grayken leaned close, tucking the blankets more snugly around her son's shoulders. "I was just curious as to whether you've discussed the *contingency* plan with Mikaela?"

His brow wrinkled as he decoded the cryptic message. And then he understood.

"I can see that you haven't, but surely you will, won't you?" Her voice rose, both in pitch and intensity.

"I . . . I don't know. I haven't decided. I've asked too much of her already."

"But—"

"Not a word. Promise me."

Matt could imagine the machinations going on in her mind as she sought for a way to keep that promise and still convey the secret to Mikaela.

"Not a word. Not a picture nor a text nor charades nor anything else. Promise?"

Her body visibly shrank in sorrow. "All right. I promise."

He shot his mother a wink. "Are you heading back to New York tonight?"

Catherine craned her neck back in shock. "Of course not. Didn't Mikaela tell you? We're staying at your house until we know you're faring well."

Matt chuckled and raised his arms as high as the wires and tubes allowed, inviting his mother's embrace. "Thank you, Mother. I love you."

Her hug was long and strong despite her almost seventy years. As she withdrew, her hands framed her son's face. "You're my bonnie boy. Always will be, even when you're a gray-haired old man."

Matthew leaned into her caress and kissed her palm. "I'm happy to be your bonnie boy."

With a final kiss and a smile, Catherine gave Kate a parting hug before moving on to Mikaela with wide arms. "You made me the happiest mum in the world today. I couldn't love you more."

"And neither could I," said Donovan, adding a hug of his own. The door shut behind the Graykens, leaving only Matt, Mikaela, Kate, and Daniel in the room.

Matt turned his attention to the remaining two guests. "Kate . . . Daniel . . . is there something I should know about you two?"

Kate shot Daniel a confused look that was matched by his own. "Whatever could he mean?" Daniel asked as he wrapped his arm around Kate and kissed her. "I think he's delirious."

Kate kept a straight face and nodded. "Totally seein' things."

"Then I'm seeing them too," Mikaela said. "When did this happen? I just introduced you this morning."

The couple shared a searing smile. "Not exactly," Daniel began. "Matt asked me to help Kate settle in since you were busy here with him. We've shared a few meals and talked every night until past midnight."

"We just clicked," Kate said.

Daniel underscored the comment with another kiss. Kate pointed to a smudge of her lipstick on his mouth, dabbing at it with a tissue she pulled from her purse.

Mikaela linked arms with Kate and smiled. "I think I'm owed some details."

"Uh . . . me too," chirped Matt.

Daniel rocked back on his heels and pulled on his ear. "Well . . . this is awkward."

Matt pointed to a chair by his bed. "Let's have a chat. I am after all, her only blood kin—"

"And as *your* only blood kin," said Kate, as she extricated herself from Mikaela with a wink and a smile, "we're going to leave you to rest and build up your strength."

"But we're still on the 'cleared-to-enter-the-inner-sanctum' list, right, Mikaela?"

Mikaela chuckled. "Yes, Daniel. You're both on the short list of people who can visit Matt during his immune suppression. His immune system 'knows' you from spending way too much time with you, Daniel, and it knows Kate by blood. You'll have to take some precautions because you can still carry pathogens in on your clothes, hands, and breath, but if you're healthy, you're welcome to visit."

Daniel gave Kate a waltz-twirl and dip. "Did you hear that, Kate? We're in!"

He released Kate to Mikaela's waiting care and turned to offer Matt a final goodbye. His expression sobered as he gripped Matt's hand. "Seriously, man. You've got this. *We've* got this. You and me and the DPV guys have shared everything since prep school—first pimple outbreaks, first kisses, mono." He laughed. "We're still here for you. The vow still stands."

"Like Washington and Jefferson,"

"Our lives and sacred honors . . . and anything else you need."

"I know, brother. Thanks, Daniel."

Kate leaned over and kissed her newfound brother's cheek. "I've lost one brother. I'll not lose another. My little stem cells are hankerin' for this fight." With a wink and a squeeze, she grabbed her coat and moved back beside Daniel.

Daniel opened the door for Kate. "We'll give you two newly-weds some privacy and continue this reception at a club where we plan to dance the night away. Party on, you two, and feel free to have an extra pudding delivered to the room on me. My treat."

Laughter danced from Mikaela's lips as the door closed behind the couple. "That's some team you have."

"The best." Matt studied his wife as she came his way. Her dark hair was softly twisted into a loose bun, while loose tendrils swayed along her cheek as she moved. His heart ached to hold her in his arms and press his body to hers.

"Leukemia doesn't have a chance against us."

"Because of you, Mrs. Grayken."

Mikaela responded to the change in Matt's mood from playful to serious. "What's the matter, Mr. Grayken? You can tell me. It's just those of us on the first string now."

Matt shifted an inch to the right and patted the narrow space on the left, inviting Mikaela to lie beside him. "I love Daniel's silliness and Kate's tough-girl talk and even my parents' blind faith, but what I love most are moments like this. You and me. Talking truth. Facing it together." He kissed her hair. "You are my strength."

"Forever." She linked her hand in his and held their clasped hands up. "Like this."

Matt looked at the suitcases sitting in the corner of the room. "You don't have to stay here. I'll be okay at night."

"I know you. You won't want to be a bother, so you'll be slow to call for meds or help. You'll do better if I'm here, and I'll sleep better here than I will at home, calling the nurses' station every hour."

"The blessings of marriage."

"The blessings of marriage to a cancer nurse," she corrected, adding a kiss on his nose. "There's still something else. What's really going on?"

"This is the first stretch of alone time we've had since you returned from Ireland. I suppose I'm still processing everything."

"I wondered about that. You've found a sister but you've discovered that you've lost a twin brother and your birth parents. Then we staged a quickie wedding, and you're prepping for a bone-marrow transplant. It would be a lot for anyone, even without all the added family drama."

He mentally checked off each item on Mikaela's list, but none of them hit at the core of his concerns. As the silence grew, Mikaela raised up on an arm and peered into his face. "Are you having second thoughts about the marriage? There are no refunds, Mr. Grayken."

"None needed. Yours is the love I'm one hundred percent sure of." He tightened his weak arm around her, but she resisted his tug for a kiss.

"Meaning what?"

Among the new details he was processing about his birth was the ugly truth about his adoption. "I was always fine with being adopted. My parents made me feel special because they told me that from all the children in the world, they chose me. But now I know that they didn't just choose me. They bought me."

"Don't say that. Their attorney made unscrupulous arrangements to get you, but the Graykens didn't know it. They just wanted a child, and your birth mother couldn't take care of you."

"Money was exchanged, Mikaela. I was ripped from my siblings for a price, to balance the family budget. It's not the rosy story of love I was told all my life."

Mikaela gasped softly and pressed her cheek to Matt's chest. "Do you doubt the Graykens' love for you?"

Matt didn't need to think about the answer. "No. If anything, they'd smother me with their love. But knowing your married birth parents made a choice to keep your twin brother while taking cash in exchange for you . . . It shatters something inside a person."

Mikaela sat up and leaned over Matt. "Their choice has nothing to do with you and who you are, and everything to do with them and who they were. Let it go for now, Matt. Save that fight in you for the real enemy we're facing. I'm not trying to dismiss or trivialize what you're feeling, and I'll help you find someone to talk to when you're ready, but for now"—she took his hand in both of hers—"this is who you are. Half of *us*, two mighty warriors poised for a cancer fight, and we're pretty amazing."

She smiled at him until he was unable to resist the magic of her optimism.

"Mr. Grayken, I promise to fill every shattered crack in you with so much love that you'll feel whole again. And I'm sure my brothers and the entire Compton clan will be delighted to squeeze into whatever nooks and crannies remain. How's that for one crazy family?"

"I'll take it." He pulled her close, not only needing to hear her words of love but to feel the warmth Mikaela brought to him, body and soul.

She popped back up with a childlike grin. "Speaking of crazy families, would you like to open our wedding gifts?"

"Is that what those packages are?"

"Uh huh." She sat up and dragged several large bags over to Matt's bed and sat in the chair beside him.

"Who gave us those? Everyone knows we've been married for months."

"The smaller bag is from me. It's packed with movies and

games and puzzles to keep us entertained during your isolation period. Wanna see what I picked?"

"Maybe later. What's in the shiny black bag?"

Mikaela tipped her head and offered him a sideways glance. "It's from Daniel and the boys. My guess is that we'd do well to save whatever's in there for when we're back home and alone."

Matt lowered his voice and partially closed one eye. "I like the sound of that, but I think I at least deserve a glance."

Mikaela did the honors, peeking at the contents of the bag, offering dubious glances and winces along with the occasional wide-eyed approval.

"Just tell me if any of the contents include slinky attire," said Matt.

With half-dollar-wide eyes and lips pursed in whistle mode, Mikaela said, "That's a big yes."

Matt wriggled into his mattress and clapped. "You did promise me a private floorshow."

"I did at that. But I doubt it would stay private for long. Once you get a glimpse of this negligee, your heart monitor is going to go berserk, and then several brawny nurses will barge in here with a crash cart. But it's your call."

Matt laughed and felt the earlier heaviness slip away. Mikaela had restored him once again. "All right. I'll wait. What other wonders did we get?"

"The big bag is from my brothers. They all pitched in."

"Oh, dear. What is it? POW gear to remind me of my place in the family?"

Mikaela shot him a scowl. "I have no idea, but it's heavy, and they said I had to follow the instructions on the card."

"Okay. I'm game." Matt used the bed control to elevate his head while Mikaela opened the envelope and read the note.

. . .

THE SILVER BOX is for Matt. Hand it to him and read this after he opens it.

SHE OBLIGED, and when the paper was removed and the box was about to be opened, she read:

CONGRATULATIONS ON DARING to marry our sister twice. (Just kidding, Mickie.) To be a warrior, one should look like a warrior. All our prayers are with you as you battle your enemy. We never leave a man behind. We are with you. Every step. Every day. Love, George , Thomas, James, John, Abe, Franklin, Dwight, and the entire Compton Clan.

MATT OPENED the box and pulled out a flak jacket with Grayken embroidered on the pocket, a pair of Oakley aviators, and a small pocket Bible. Stuck between the pages was a chain from which a set of military-style dog tags dangled, bearing the initials CC. "What's CC mean?"

"The Compton Clan." She squeezed Matt's shoulder. "It means you're in. You're one of them now."

"I don't have to worry about being turned into a martial-arts practice dummy for marrying you without prior permission?"

Mikaela's smile spread across her face. "I think they're saying you're safe now."

Matt clutched the tags in his hand and swiped across his eyes. "Tell them thank you."

"Let's show them." Mikaela helped him try his gear on and texted a photo to the family with this note.

. . .

LOVE YOU ALL! *Video chat tomorrow at 11:00 a.m. EST. Does that work for you?*

HE TOOK a deep breath to calm his emotions. "Please tell me the rest of the gifts are boring chip and dip sets or a punch bowl."

"I doubt it. There's one more package from my family. The tag reads, *For Mikaela, but have Matt open it while Mickie reads the card.* That hardly seems fair."

"No pouting, lady. Hand it over. Rules are rules."

Matt gave the small cube-shaped box a shake, offering a quizzical expression. "Any guesses?"

"Anything is possible with my family. Just rip it open quick like a Band-Aid. I'm sure this is going to hurt my funny bone."

"Very well." Matt flexed his aching fingers and slowly ripped the white wedding paper, revealing a decorated box. He kept his hand poised above the lid and said, "Start reading."

MATT,

We hope these come in handy during your weeks of isolation. Make Mikaela watch too. Perhaps you will succeed where we have failed.

Love,

George, Thomas, James, John, Abe, Franklin, and Dwight

"WHAT IS IT?" asked Mikaela, whose efforts to steal a glance were being thwarted by Matt as he looked at her with an open mouth and expression of horror.

"If what they're implying is true, I may have to rethink my proposal."

"No way. There's no prenup. You're stuck. And what crime are my brothers reporting to you anyway?"

He held up a DVD. "Have you seriously never watched any of these classics?"

Mikaela sucked in her lower lip and shifted her eyes left and right. "They're space movies about war."

"Space movies? These represent the fundamental battle between good and evil. They're iconic—"

"Fine." She bit her nail and frowned. "Is this gonna be a deal breaker?"

His mouth shifted as he thought. "The marriage can be salvaged if you agree to watch every episode in order, start to finish."

She rolled her eyes. "That's asking a lot, but . . . for the sake of the marriage." She extended her hand to shake on the deal, and he tugged on it until she moved the presents to the floor and lay back down beside him.

The moment grew tender as Matt ran his fingers up and down over her arm, feeling her warmth beside him, finding peace in the steady rhythm of her breaths. Eventually, even that amount of exercise tired his weak arms. He was struck by a moment of self-pity, which he tried to push away, dismissing it only far enough to shift into an honest melancholy. He laid his arm across his forehead and stared up at the ceiling. "We'll give it everything we have and delay it as long as possible, but we know, in the end, that this cancer is going to win."

He felt Mikaela flinch beside him. "Everyone dies, Matt. No one knows when or how. We could ski that Swiss mountain you talk about and get swept away in an avalanche. You could get run over while crossing the street to buy flowers from Gino. I could choke to death on a forkful of bangers and mash."

"Highly unlikely."

"Just saying." She rolled onto her side and wove her arm between the tubes and wires until it rested across his chest. "Maybe we should look at our situation as a blessing."

He shot her a dubious glance.

"We know life is short. That every day is a gift. Some people live a hundred years and never figure that out. We have an advantage. Let's just live what we know."

"Make every day a gift? Haven't we been doing that with the Christmas tree you put up in September with the ornaments from places we've been and things we've done?"

"But maybe we can do more. Live with a purpose bigger than beating cancer."

He lifted a tube and looked at her. "It's a hard thing to ignore, Mikaela."

"We're going to win some innings, and sometimes when we enter the ring, we're going to get pummeled, but let's strap on our gear, ready to play our best game, every day."

He threaded his fingers between hers. "You're mixing metaphors."

"You're changing the subject. I'm just saying, if death is going to shave off some of our time, let's not give him one minute more because we surrendered."

"Deal."

"Thank you." She snuggled close, pressing her forehead against his cheek. "I got worried when I heard you and your mom discussing a contingency plan."

The comment shocked him, leaving him without a reply as he anticipated the possible follow-up question he was also not prepared to answer.

"What contingency plan? What were you two talking about?"

He shushed her and kissed the side of her mouth. "Not tonight, okay? Can you trust me on this?"

"No secrets, remember?"

"It's not a secret. It's just a matter of timing."

Mikaela laid her head back down, and Matt thought of little else but the contingency plan as he held her close, drawing strength and courage from her as he waited for the nurses' arrival and the prep to begin, knowing that his body's response to the transplant protocol would determine if and when he would have the time to share the plan at all.

CHAPTER TWO

She peered through the dim light at the fourteen-by-twenty-foot suite that would be their home for the next few weeks. Its blue and white striped wallpaper and art prints of landscapes on the walls made it feel less sterile. The area had two obvious sections. The half nearest the outside window had the functionality of a typical hospital room. Matt's bed sat near that window, giving him a rather lovely view of D.C. from his sixth-floor perch. A sleeping chair was rolled in for Mikaela and positioned by the window. The closet, small bathroom, a wall clock, and a wall-mounted TV were situated directly across from the bed areas for convenience.

The other half of the room was set up like a small efficiency apartment. A door in the center of the glass wall overlooked the nurses' station. Curtains could be drawn for privacy or opened wide when monitoring was critical. In the corner to the left of the door sat a small dining table, four chairs, and a small kitchen sink.

Matt's diet was now being carefully controlled to avoid

food-borne bacteria, so Mikaela either ate in the cafeteria or ordered an approved tray for herself. A sofa and armchair filled the corner to the right. Both were angled toward a credenza, above which a second flat-screen TV hung. A bookshelf, complete with a few novels and games, rounded out the furnishings.

While the space provided a more welcoming environment for patient and guests to relax together, the decor did little to camouflage the wires, IV poles, and chirping machines, constant reminders that this was, indeed, a hospital room.

Mikaela hoped Matt would embrace the ideas percolating in her mind. She believed working on these projects together would energize Matt enough to keep him from climbing the walls or escaping over the next few months.

Matt stirred, and she leaned close to greet his first glimpse of this important day. "Good morning, Mr. Sunshine."

He stretched and scowled as his IV pulled tight. "Good morning," he groused back before reclosing his eyes.

"It's almost seven. And guess what? We got almost four inches of magical Christmas snow."

"Nice. Is it game time?"

"I'm afraid so, buddy."

He gave his hip a compassionate rub. "Bone marrow biopsy."

"Yep. They'll extract and test your marrow, and then they'll administer a high dose of chemo followed by lots of blood draws to check your cell counts over the day. It'll give them a better idea of how much chemo you need to get to near zero immunity."

He forced a smile. "How sick am I going to be at the end of the day . . . on a kissable scale of one to ten, where one means I'm still okay for lip to lip contact and ten means you'd rather kiss a wart hog?"

Mikaela hovered over his face. "Let's just say I think I'd better get my kiss now."

Their kiss was soft and sad and sweet all rolled together. It ended when a masked and gowned tech with sympathetic eyes knocked on the door and entered with a gurney. Dr. Marcosky popped his head in a moment later with two nurses in tow.

"I guess it's go time," Matt said to Mikaela. He looked over his shoulder at the doctor. "Left or right hip?"

Dr. Marcosky's bushy gray eyebrows rose. "I'll let you choose. I just wanted to check in and make sure you were still planning on showing up for the after-Christmas party in the Interventional Radiology Suite."

Mikaela gripped Matt's arm protectively while maintaining her ruse of calm confidence. "He'll be there," she said, adding a squeeze on his arm.

Nurses hurried to detach or transfer IVs to make him mobile, and within a few minutes, Matt was gone. Mikaela knew the biopsy wouldn't take long, so she quickly showered and redressed in clean jeans and a tee, twisting her long, brown hair into a loose bun which she haphazardly clipped to the top of her head. She was already manic about washing her hands, a gift from her nursing training and from caring for Matt, but that proclivity toward sanitation was amped up by degrees as Matt prepared for near-zero immunity. She didn't dare pick up a cold or other illness now.

She brushed her teeth, waiting for the door to open any minute, and when it didn't, she paced and wrung her hands while checking and rechecking the clock. She thought about Matt, a man who asked a stranger to marry him to prevent his adoring but desperate parents from assuming responsibility for their failing son's healthcare. He knew their love would compel them to try every treatment imaginable to save him, even at the risk of prolonging their son's suffering. Now here he was, submitting himself to whatever the doctors suggested, because he wanted more time with Mikaela. It was the greatest imaginable act of love and one she promised to never forget.

She let out a long, low sigh when the door opened and the gurney arrived. "I was starting to think you might have run off with the anesthetist."

"If not for you, I might have. She gave me the good stuff."

"No pain then?"

His eyes fluttered open and shut. "Just a little."

She could tell by his reaction that his pain level was worse than he was admitting. His left hip was sore, and his already weak body seemed fully spent. She worried how he'd tolerate the long day of testing that still lay ahead.

A powerful chemo drip was begun, and nausea set in hard and fast. Defeat began to show on his face as the first half-hour blood draw was taken, so Mikaela made use of her nursing "peer privileges," grabbing a ginger ale and a ginger lozenge from the department's supplies, to lessen his nausea. She knew he needed something more, a distraction, to get him through all the draws and analysis to come, so she revisited an earlier topic.

"Can we talk about your contingency plan now?" she asked as she tucked his blankets more tightly around him.

Matt closed his eyes. "I don't want to talk. You talk. Tell me about your plans for our bigger, more purposeful life."

She didn't press the matter though the topic of his contingency plan nagged at her peace. She wasn't certain the timing was any better for a conversation about her future plans either, but she forged ahead anyway. "Okay," she said as she gently lay beside him so their faces were mere inches apart. "I have several. Would you like to begin with the small ones, or should I jump ahead to my whopping big ideas?"

Furrows appeared along his brow. "Small. Definitely small."

Mikaela stroked his thinning dark waves, and Matt leaned into her touch as she began. "I'd like to paint the kitchen a butter yellow, like the kitchen where I grew up. It always felt so cheerful and welcoming. I think it will give us a fun project to do together when you're released and on medical house arrest," she said, trying to make light of the weeks of transition time when his hampered immune system would slowly be reintroduced to the world. "What do you think?"

Matt's eyes remained closed, but he offered a modest smile and nodded. "Sounds good."

"Great! On to idea two. I know our backyard is small, but I think we could have a really productive garden if we build some raised beds. I saw some DIY plans for a tiered bed designed to double your growing capacity. I thought we could make two, one for vegetables and one for berries." She received some thoughtful brow wriggles, proof that Matt was at least listening. "Is that a yes?"

"Are you handy? Regrettably, I'm not."

"That'll be half the fun. We'll learn together."

He shot her a dubious glance.

"What could go wrong besides wasting a little wood?"

"Electrocution, maiming, amputation."

"Fortunately, I'm a nurse. I'll patch us up."

"Do the big whoppers involve demolishing walls?"

"No. Totally different topics."

"Good. Then, I'm in on boxes."

"Perfect! I'll start ordering the kitchen paint and the materials for the beds so we're ready when you get home."

He took her hand and squeezed it tight.

Mikaela's head lifted in worry. "Is your pain level up?"

"No. I'm just bracing for your whoppers."

"Relax. These are totally in your wheelhouse of talents."

"Proceed."

"I love how your company makes peoples' wildest dreams come true, but not everyone can afford a pricey Great Expectations adventure, and most people's dreams are more basic and immediate than a safari in Nairobi or a hot air balloon tour of Europe. Remember how it felt to pay off those families' medical debts? You were so sick, and yet I've rarely seen you happier. I want us to do more of that kind of work."

"*We*, as in you and me?"

"Yes. I know we can't fund it all personally, but I'd like us to put in the seed money and solicit donors and benefactors."

Matt motioned for his water cup, and Mikaela gave him a sip. When his dry mouth was soothed, he laid his head back down and asked. "For medical bills only?"

"For whatever our clients need. You'd be amazed by how little it takes to make a difference in most peoples' lives."

"Has some agency contacted you?"

"Personal knowledge." She cocked her head to the side and smiled. "Do you remember who you married? The girl who made the budget work by shopping at the downstairs thrift store, remember?"

Mikaela noticed the blush tingeing his pale cheeks. He closed his eyes and said, "I'm sorry. That was thoughtless of me."

"You are anything but thoughtless. You've been a bit preoccupied." She kissed his cheek. "A few thousand dollars could fund many people's dreams. Imagine launching a single mom's home-based business, funding a grandmother's flight to see her first grandchild be born, or buying a car for someone so they can get to work? But some people's dreams don't even require money. They need access and manpower, which is what you and Great Expectations specialize in, like giving someone the chance to sing on the stage with their favorite musical artist or providing transportation for a disabled person to visit the Grand Canyon."

Matt leaned forward. "Could you raise my bed a little and hand me my tablet?"

Mikaela saw the small wrinkle form between his eyes, a sign that he was thinking about something. Grateful that his mind was occupied by anything other than his pain, she gladly obliged. The IVs and monitors proved so gangly that Matt handed her the tablet and began dictating ideas back. "You know we've already done things like this. We helped a family take their disabled daughter to the New7Wonders of the Modern World, and we arranged for a man to be an extra in a Broadway musical."

Mikaela's happiness soared at seeing how engaged he had become. "That's why I know we can do this."

A nurse came in and drew the next round of blood for testing, and Matt barely registered her presence as he focused on Mikaela's idea. The fatigue in his voice was apparent, but he carried on, asking questions and adding comments.

"There's a lot we'd need to discuss. How would we solicit clients? Who would screen them? Who would get the donors? A commitment like this could require year-round planning and fundraising, which alone would be a fulltime job. We'd need a staff, and that means salaries and benefits and oversight. We could attach it to Great Expectations. I could speak to Ben about setting up a humanitarian division."

Mikaela had hoped Matt would offer to involve his company in the project. "Do you think Ben would support the idea?"

"I handed him the president's chair, but I'm still the CEO. I think the Great Expectations staff would eat up an idea like this."

"But I'd like us to be involved."

"You can be as involved as you want, but you'll be pretty busy if you decide to return to work or apply to medical school."

Mikaela felt the first of several elephants enter the room. She sat up and faced Matt, who now had her full attention. "I wanted to talk to you about that. I don't want to go back to the cancer center. I just can't . . ."

Matt laid his hand over hers. "I understand. Believe me. I get it."

"Thank you. And I'm not thinking about med school right now either. Maybe someday. Just not right now. Another opportunity has presented itself and I'd like us to consider it."

"Another opportunity? I thought that last one was the whopper."

She drew a deep breath and considered how best to deliver the news she'd wrangled from her former boss at the Baltimore unit of the Prospect Cancer Treatment Center. "This is *the* whopper . . . another way to help people medically." She backed the story up to sell it to Matt. "A few days ago, I received an envelope from Dr. Gorman. Inside were letters from the families whose medical bills you paid."

He touched her wrist. "*We* paid."

Mikaela smiled and took his hand. "Okay. *We* paid. The letters were filled with gratitude, explaining what removing that financial burden did for them, both financially and emotionally."

"We asked to remain anonymous."

"They still don't know who paid their bills. The letters were sent to The Prospect Cancer Treatment Center, in care of the financial services advisor, who chose the recipients. She forwarded them to Dr. Gorman, and he sent them to us."

"Okay then." Matt waved his hand over his medically tethered body. "We wondered how people who go through all this manage to drag their bodies to work to pay the bills. Or worse, what happens if they simply can't?"

"Exactly, and I think that's why Dr. Gorman sent us the letters, to prove how critical this kind of help is to people." Her barely there smile slowly spread across her face, mingling with a hint of pleading. "What if we could help people avoid life-crushing medical bills? Or catch illnesses earlier in families who can't afford to see a doctor until their health is already compromised?"

Matt's brow narrowed. "I know that look, Mikaela. What have you agreed to do?"

"A committee has been fundraising to provide mobile medical clinics to serve the uninsured and the underinsured in the Baltimore/Washington corridor."

Matt's head shot up. "And?"

She shrugged. "When I heard how they were struggling to get financing . . . what I mean to say is, I told Dr. Gorman I needed to speak to you first but . . . but I'd like us to chair the committee."

"Mikaela . . ." Matt's head dropped down on his pillow. "What's really going on here?"

"Just what I said. We can do a lot of good for so many people."

Not only did Matt not offer a response, he laid his forearm, across his eyes as if to shut Mikaela out. Her heart sank. It wasn't like him to turn away from a challenge or a chance to do something good. Mikaela realized that, instead of inspiring him, she had overwhelmed him and drained his hope. She lowered her head and clasped her hands. "What was I thinking? I'm sorry. I shouldn't have brought this up now. I hoped it would give you something to look forward to, but instead, I've added to your stress. Let's change the subject."

But neither of them raised a new topic, and a quiet discomfort settled in between them as Matt not only retreated from the conversation, but from Mikaela as well.

THE WORLD not only felt dark, it looked dark with his arm pressed over his eyes, and with the darkness came an end to talk of changing the world. Mikaela was tentative and shy as she lay down beside him in his imposed silence. He knew what Mikaela's manic need to be busy was about—what it was *really* about, even if she didn't. Mikaela was spooked by this round of cancer.

When they were home, she fought the monster's physical threats by grinding the contents of their fridge's vegetable bin into a protein-packed smoothie Matt lovingly called sludge, and she fought the fear the cancer brought into their world by creating hope, one memory-filled ornament at a time. But now they were in a new ring, this hospital, and the fight was out of her hands. If she couldn't battle Matt's leukemia, she'd seek a new adversary—kitchens, vegetable gardens, poverty, and the health of people she might actually have a chance of making well. Yes, for the first time since he'd met her, Matt knew Mikaela was afraid.

He thought about the contingency plan. It hadn't occupied a minute's thought until Mikaela, whose love, along with the tales of her large, close-knit family, caused him to reconsider his jaded opinion of domesticity. Mikaela's was altogether a different kind of love than any he'd ever experienced, and not just because of the physical elements of marriage. Mikaela's love was soft but strong. Encouraging and leading rather than pushing. A safe partnership. She would be a wonderful mother someday. His heart ached at the thought of her happiness lying beyond his life, in a life without him and with a man who could grant her greatest dream—family.

As he saw it, the drama and intrigue surrounding his own life and parentage were enough to make anyone question their worthiness to influence another human. The Graykens loved him. He didn't doubt that, but their smothering love had made them so possessive that Matt ran away from them rather than submit to more of their intrusiveness. On the other hand, and from what he had recently learned, his birth parents were a step above algae on the ladder of parental evolution. He considered a question from college psych. Which force was more defining in a life—nature or nurture? Matt wondered whose example was imprinted upon him? And could overcome both their examples?

Questions bombarded his peace. Was he a good husband? Was he able to give Mikaela what she needed? Could he build a good family? Could he guide a child? What was fair to Mikaela, and what was an added burden? His mind swirled with the chaos of it all. And the bigger question, could he love and leave another person behind? The topics made him flush hot with panic.

He peeked out from under his arm and saw Mikaela biting her nail in worry. He lifted his arm from his eyes and slid it under Mikaela. "I'm sorry I overreacted."

"No. You were right. I don't know what I was thinking. I'm sorry."

"Does Dr. Gorman know what we're already dealing with right now?"

"Some. Not all this. I've been thoughtless."

"I don't think that," Matt muttered in a weak defense of his wife. He shifted to his side to look at her. "But I think you're in denial, Mikaela. I might get better, and I might not. We might get our lives back, or we might be looking at a very different life, or you might be looking at a life alone again."

"How can you even say that?"

"Because someone needs to. I think that's really what all of this is about. In some corner of your beautiful, brilliant mind you don't even want to admit to, you feel a need to prepare for that eventuality. To have something meaningful queued up and ready to fill your life in the event the worst happens, and I want you to know that I get that. I understand, and I want you to have a fallback too."

"No." She stood abruptly. "I wanted this for *us*. Not for *me*."

She began to cry as the tech came in for the next blood draw. With a quick turn to hide her eyes, Mikaela slipped into the bathroom, her one place of solace, and prayed to know what to do and say. After they were alone again, she slipped back over to Matt's bed and took his hand. "Please forget what I said about projects and plans. I have terrible timing."

Matt cupped both of her hands within his. "I want you to listen to me very carefully. All right?"

She wiped at her eyes and nodded.

"I love you, Mrs. Grayken. More than words or gestures or love songs can express. And why I love you is because you are the most unselfish, giving person I know. So I don't question your motivation or your timing. I know you think this project is good, and it is. Here's the part I really want you to hear without rushing in with debate." He drilled his gaze into hers. "I think you know I'm right. That even though you don't want to admit it, my wise, savvy, loving nurse/wife knows there's a chance our life together will be short. Inside each of us is a piece of divine understanding that prepares us to live on when we can't imagine why we'd want to. It helps us find an emotional scaffolding to cling to in case our very worst fear comes true. I think this project, along with your family and your faith in God, is your scaffolding."

She lay back down and buried her head in his chest. "I know you married me, at least initially, to avoid all this"—she waved her hand around the sterile hospital room—"and now we're here, with you in pain, spending too much time as a patient instead of at home. I'll never forget that you're putting yourself through all this for me."

"For us."

"For us . . . I know this is hell on earth for you, but please promise you won't give up without talking to me, because I'm not giving up," she said.

"I promise." Matt raised his tethered arm in a show of proof. "See? But I do want you to have something else in your life besides sitting here with me."

"Like the contingency plan?"

He quickly squelched the idea and said, "Like those whoppers on your list."

She brightened and snuggled close. "Thank you. I think it'll do us both good to have something else to focus on, don't you?"

"Absolutely. Let's take a little nap, and then we'll brainstorm a list of potential donors."

He had barely closed his eyes when his lunch tray was delivered. Matt looked at the offering on his plate and scowled. "You should get some real food."

"I'm prepared to suffer by your side."

"I appreciate the loyalty, but I'd prefer to have you recon the cafeteria and return with the scent of pizza on your clothes."

"Are you sure you can handle the temptation?"

"I could use the excitement."

"In that case, I'll try to rub up against a strawberry too."

"Take your time. I plan to get a nap in before the blood-suckers return."

"Will do. While I'm out, I'll call Dr. Gorman and tell him you're on board to lend *limited* support on the mobile clinic project. I'll be back within a half hour."

Mikaela cupped his face in her hands and kissed him soft and long before leaving the room. Matt forced two bites of his lunch down before fatigue won. His brief rest ended when Daniel arrived carrying two bottles of root beer. "I'm afraid this is as exciting as it gets for you, my friend."

Matt offered a sleepy smile and pointed to the side table. "Thanks. I'll save it for later. Where's Kate?"

Daniel pulled a chair up close to Matt's bed. "She's here for her appointment to rev up her stem cell production."

The weight of Matt's gratitude and indebtedness pressed upon him. "How is she, really? We've barely had any time to talk. She's been through the ringer, losing the brother she knew and loved, and then coming here to meet a stranger who shares her blood, looks like Hugh, and needs her help." He closed his eyes and groaned. "I'm worried about her."

"She's definitely your sister. Same hard head. Same mulish obstinance. No wonder I'm smitten. You've trained me too well." Matt managed a paltry attempt at a laugh. Daniel leaned closer with worry on his face. Placing a hand on Matt's shoulder, his voice was thick with concern when he asked, "How are you doing, pal?"

"Just tired. This is the easy part."

"None of this looks that easy. Where's Mikaela? How's she holding up?"

Matt had no glib comeback, but neither was he going to admit that he and Mikaela were having a tough day. Instead, he focused on how forgiving she'd been over his mood and how willing to make things right between them. He smiled at the blessing that was Mikaela. "She's great."

"What else is going on with you two? I see that ornery grin on your face. You and Mikaela didn't actually"—his eyebrows wriggled—"have a wedding night here, did you?"

Matt wriggled his eyebrows weakly in return.

"No!"

"Hey, my single friend. I told you marriage was grand."

"Nah," Daniel protested. "Really?"

Matt shook his head and laughed. "Moving on."

"Please. And don't get too attached to my prized action figure. We DVP brothers worked out a plan to keep our Thursday poker game on schedule. Gunther will teleconference you in. Kate will sit in for you to hold your cards, and you call the plays by phone."

The news touched Matt more deeply than Daniel and his DVP brothers could have known. Maintaining this whimsical piece of normalcy, poker with school chums who bid with action figures, felt like an anchor in a constantly changing life. "Just keep that medical drone at the ready. If I win, I'm coming for it."

"I'll trade you that drone right now if you'll take my next meeting." Daniel sat back and slid down into his chair, rubbing a hand over his face. "I'm sure you've heard the news reports about Bennett Sadler, billionaire heir of P&S Med Tech?"

"I take it Sadler is the S in P&S."

"And Bennett is the a-double-s of the company."

Matt laughed. "Refresh my memory. I've been off-grid for the last week."

"Bennett inherited the company from his father this summer, and his first order of business was to increase the cost of a heart medicine tenfold. He became an overnight pariah, albeit a stinking rich pariah. As if being a heartless deathmonger wasn't enough, he hosted a weeklong holiday bash on his yacht, which he anchored off Catalina, only he didn't bother checking the IDs of his guests. One was a minor, and her father is a captain in the Coast Guard."

"No, no, no." Matt lay back and laughed.

"All true. You can't make this stuff up."

"So how many counts was he busted on?"

"Seventeen, in categories from serving alcohol to a minor to drug violations and on to a kidnapping charge that won't stick but will fuel a tawdry news cycle for a few weeks."

"Be glad you're not his attorney."

"Ha! I've got it worse. Our firm handles P&S's PR, and guess who's been assigned as Bennett's new PR rep?"

Matt pressed his lips together to keep from laughing. "Oh, dear."

"Yeah," Daniel replied with enough dripping sarcasm to fill Bennett's yacht. "In short terms, I'm assigned to babysit the creep and keep his proverbial nose clean while resurrecting his image. If I can't, the board of directors will vote him out and start a fresh ad and PR campaign with another company."

"It sounds like you'll be busy. Kate will miss you."

"Kate has volunteered to draw some sketches for the P&S campaign. She can't work for pay because she doesn't have a work visa, but she can donate her skills, and I could use a fresh perspective on the loathsome Bennett Sadler."

"I don't envy you."

"Any chance Great Expectations has a high-profile project that could use a very generous benefactor?"

Matt thought back to the earlier conversation he'd had with Mikaela. "I might actually. Not with Great Expectations. It's an initiative to build more mobile health clinics to treat the poor and the underinsured."

Daniel slid forward and leaned close. "Something medical! This could be perfect."

"It's Mikaela's new pet project. Well, Dr. Gorman approached her to head it up."

"Oh, man. Like you two don't have enough going on."

Matt wondered what Daniel would think if he knew what else they were planning. "We discussed involving Great Expectations in some way, but she's got other community assignments for my company. Maybe there's a way your loathsome Mr. Sadler could fund Mikaela's mobile clinic project."

"I like it!" Daniel's phone buzzed, and he checked the text. "Kate's ready. I'll tell her I'm in here."

"Funny that she didn't just plan to visit me."

Daniel set his phone down and looked at Matt. "You two do need to talk. I think seeing you, looking so much like the brother she buried . . . It's hard for her. It'll work itself out. She wants a relationship with you, but it might take time to make your own memories together."

The door opened slightly revealing Kate's tentative face. "Is poker an element of this visit?" she asked in her thick Irish brogue.

"No," said Daniel as he rose to kiss her. "But I did explain to Matt that you're going to help us keep his skills up during convalescence."

Matt noticed how she furtively glanced his way and then shifted her gaze elsewhere. "I may need a pledge that you're not Daniel's hired gun, luring me in to steal back his favorite pilot action figure."

"I assure you, I'm not. But your toy's future may be more secure if I play your hand outright. I daresay I'm quite adept at the game."

"*Toy*," moaned Daniel. "You wound us."

"You have no idea how deeply." Matt pretended to stab himself in the heart.

"I believe you boys have just validated my point."

The tech arrived again, and Kate used the opportunity to excuse herself.

Matt called after her. "Wait. Daniel, could I have a moment with Kate?"

Daniel shot Matt a warning glance, but Matt ignored the call for patience and pressed Kate again as the tech finished the draw and left. "Just five minutes. A brother and sister chat."

Daniel squeezed her arm and slipped out of the room, leaving Kate awkward and unsure.

"Please. Just sit and let me get to know you, Kate. I want us to be close."

She slid into the chair and grew uncharacteristically quiet. "I've read all about you. I feared you were a shaper."

"A shaper. . . My father used that Irish slang for someone, but I don't recall what it means."

She covered her smile with her hand. "Snooty and pompous. I'm delighted to know I was wrong."

"No one really knows anyone else until they've shared time together. I'd like us to share a lot of time together. You're an artist. Tell me about your work. How did you get started?"

She shrugged. "We lived in a section of town where old buildings were being renovated. Sheetrock scraps were easily available, and the children would gather them up and use them to sketch chalk pictures on the sidewalks and roads. People thought I had a gift for drawing, and they started hiring me to draw on their store windows for holidays and the like. It just grew from there."

"Daniel told me some of your murals are in Irish castles now."

She blushed. "A few that were converted into inns. Working in such beautiful buildings was the curk." She translated for Matt. "A lot of fun, and it bought the biscuits."

Matt laughed aloud. "Mikaela's going to walk in and find me converted back to my Irish roots. And now I hear you've volunteered to help out with Daniel's newest campaign?"

"For a time. Daniel's a corker." She looked back at the door as if hoping it would open.

"He looks out for the people he cares about. Like you do." Silence followed the compliment, and Matt asked, "Tell me about Hugh. It must be hard seeing me when I look so much like someone you're grieving for."

The heel of her hand wiped across her eye. "I admit, this whole thing has sort of taken my breath away. He was so strong and handsome, but the leukemia hit him hard, and faster than we expected. We had everything set up for the transplant, and then, as Providence would have it, he was struck down in a motorcycle accident the day before he was to be admitted."

Her sorrow was thick and heavy. Matt tried to segue into a new topic. "What was he like?"

"Ahhh . . . he was mad as a box of frogs, always up for fun."

"I can tell you two were very close." Matt felt a twinge of something akin to jealousy at the bond he missed out on sharing.

"We were friends and allies. Our da was a hard man. He'd just as soon batter ya as share a kind word. I gave as good as I got, and I paid for it, until Hugh outgrew me and stood by my side."

Our da. . . Matt's real da too. He shivered at the thought of the beast who fathered him and the siblings he had not been privileged to know. "I'm sorry your lives were so hard."

"I imagine being an only child, as you were, brings its own hardship. And don't fret for us. Da eased down those last years before he passed. Mother soon followed."

"How old were you when . . . our mother passed?" For the first time, Matt considered the woman who birthed him and gave him up, as his mother.

"I was twenty-two and Hugh was seventeen. Mother had been worn down and ill for some time, so I was already more like a mum to him. He was a good lad. We had what we needed."

Matt felt his mouth quiver as a picture of Kate and a young man that looked like him stood against the world. "I think I would have loved taking my chances with you two."

"You'd've loved Hugh." Kate wiped at her eyes again. "But I don't know if I could've handled the two of you." She laughed sadly. "There's no good in pining for things that aren't. Life has a way of working itself out. And here we are now." She dug a tissue from her purse and wiped her nose. "I assume Mikaela told you how you came to leave us and be with the Graykens?"

Matt ached to understand the day his desperate birth mother handed one of her newborn twins over to a nurse the Graykens' attorney hired to carry the child from Cork, Ireland, to New York. A sick queasiness hit him as he pictured his father negotiating the reimbursement for "expenses" incurred during the delivery. As far as Matt was concerned, he had all but been sold.

"That sour expression you're wearing is all too familiar. I saw it on Mother's face for years, and on mine and Hugh's when we were told the truth. I'm sure we'd've fared all right if you'd've remained with us. I think that's what tortured Mother. She forfeited the opportunity of knowing you. Instead of fighting Da, she let her son slip away, along with the promise a new babe always brings to a family."

Matt felt his own eyes sting. "Thank you for telling me that."

"Don't be too bitter at her. She was a very poor woman with a maggot of a man. She grasped at the only straw held out to her. She knew you would never want for love or material things, and the arrangement made it possible for her to keep a roof over the rest of our heads during very lean years. In some respects, I suppose I should be thanking you."

Matt waved the comment away with a huff, but the emotion in the room remained thick and heavy.

Kate sat back and sighed. "Hugh always hoped to meet you someday." Her eyes began to twinkle, and a smile stole across her mouth. "But I'll tell you this, Matthew Fitzpatrick Grayken, he'd for sure've gotten you out of that three-piece suit and onto a Harley."

The comment broke the tension in the room as they each surrendered to its humor. Daniel poked his head in. "All right you two party animals. You're having fun but the nurses are giving *me* the evil eye. I think they want you to rest, Matt."

Kate stood, but not before Matt took her hand. "Thanks for the chat, Kate. Could you tell me more about Hugh and Mother next time? And did you bring any photos?"

"Aye. There's a few on my phone. Next time, okay? You rest now."

"I love having a sister. Thanks for saving my life."

A tear shone in her eye. "We've got a fight ahead. No time for getting soggy, love."

She straightened and once again became tough-girl Kate as she turned back to Daniel, who returned the conversation to the previous topic.

"Tell Mikaela we need to meet to discuss that mobile clinic opportunity. I'll take the idea back to my office. Tell her to consider it as good as funded."

"I will."

As Daniel and Kate left, arm in arm, a new peace settled over Matt. He was anxious for Mikaela's return so he could tell her about the funding for the mobile clinics. But there was more he longed to tell her. His chat with Kate put to rest the guilt that gnawed at him over using his newfound family member as his donor. She was no longer a stranger with the power to save him. She was his sister. A sister who admitted that he had been loved and missed by his mother and siblings.

And while Matt didn't regret being adopted by the Graykens, it healed some open wound inside him to know that his birth mother did regret surrendering him. It changed how he felt about himself somehow and how he felt about his potential to be a father. How had Kate expressed their mother's feelings over giving Matt away?

She forfeited the opportunity of knowing you . . . she let her son slip away, along with the promise a new babe always brings to a family.

Matt didn't want to forfeit any more opportunities or miss promises intended for Mikaela and him. No matter how this fight with leukemia turned out.

CHAPTER THREE

Mikaela refused to surrender to the difficulty of their situation, but Matt's insistence that she face the future realistically challenged her draining optimism. She was not naïve about the protracted battle that lay ahead. Her work at the cancer center had exposed her to the roller-coaster ride of hopes and disappointments that accompanied the fight with leukemia, even for those fortunate enough to find a bone-marrow donor. Matt needed hope.

She thought about the tree in their living room at home. How each specially selected ornament chronicling the milestones and memories made during their five months of marriage had given Matt visual proof of the value of his life. As he watched the tree fill, from September on, with reminders of experiences shared and those to be shared, his will to fight increased, carrying him on to where they now were. They needed a new focus. A new plan.

She slipped into the gift shop to find a funny card to cheer Matt up. An after-Christmas sale banner hung in the window, and hoping to find more ornaments for their tree, she grabbed a basket and perused the remaining inventory. Hanging from a stand by the register were car air fresheners, and a silly gag idea formulated, aimed at giving Matt even a momentary laugh. She selected a humorous card, placing it and the gag gift in her basket as she moved to the tree and the discounted ornaments.

Two chestnut-toned wooden boxes sat on a nearby shelf. Their tags read, "Amish handicrafts. Hand-carved in Lancaster, Pennsylvania." She thought about their trip to Lancaster a few weeks ago, marveling over how much had happened in each of their lives since that day.

Her eyes moved on to the tree bedecked in child-themed ornaments. She fingered all the balls and stars lettered with the words, "Baby's First Christmas," and felt her throat tighten as it always did over that surrendered dream, destroyed by rounds of chemo long before she and Matt met. Perhaps when Matt was well, she would approach the topic of fostering a child or maybe even adoption. She moved her hand from the ornaments and turned toward the register instead, grabbing a pen and jotting a message in the card.

She tried to shake off the melancholy settling in as she walked the corridors back to Matt's room. Not quite able to master a convincing cheery mood yet, she paused by the nurse's station to check Matt's stats.

"We're down to hourly draws," said his nurse, a fortyish woman named Carla. "We need five more, and then the doctor will run the numbers and design Matt's chemo protocol to drop him near zero immunity."

"How many days before he'll be ready to receive the stem cells?" asked Mikaela.

"You know I don't know that." She patted Mikaela's hand. "I can guess, same as you, cancer nurse, but if I were to guess,"—

Carla humorously shifted her mouth left and right—"I'd say . . . hmmm . . . three days or so, if we keep him healthy." She burned a warning into Mikaela. "You've got to be extra aware of your own health now that his immune system is dropping. Be hyper-vigilant and grab a gown and mask if you feel so much as a tickle in your throat. We've got to protect him."

Mikaela pumped hand sanitizer into her hands. "Got it. And thanks for the update."

She steeled herself to enter the room and face Matt's needs. To her surprise, his mood was cheerful, and she was met with a bright smile. "I've missed you."

"You just want to sniff me for food residue."

"Busted!"

Her heart chugged on as she dangled her bag.

"A doggie bag?" His weary voice was nearly breathless. "Is that dietary contraband?"

Mikaela slowly moved the bag across his face, tempting him while a devilish smile teased further. "Guess."

"You Devil."

"Guess," she said in a singsong voice.

"Temptress." Matt closed his eyes as rapt anticipation caused his eyebrows to narrow and a smile to dance upon his lips. "A cheesesteak sub and a praline malt from the Cooper's Deli near Gino's florist shop."

Mikaela's bottom lip puffed out in a pout as she offered Matt the bag. He extracted the card and tore open the envelope. "Give the contents a whiff," Mikaela said.

Matt reached in and pulled out the flat strawberry-scented car freshener, held it near his nose, and drew in a long satisfying breath. "Nice. This really was going to be my second guess."

"Sure, it was."

Matt shifted his face around in comical thought as Carla had a few minutes earlier. "It was on my list . . . around the 7912 slot." He raised his arms to Mikaela, and she happily filled them, lying beside him on the bed.

The phone buzzed with a message from Matt's parents. Mikaela read the text and turned to Matt. "How are you holding up? Your parents would like to visit."

"I'm okay," he replied with convincing confidence. "Ask them to come in an hour or so, okay?"

"You've got it." She sent the reply and felt her optimism rise on his smile. "Five more hourly blood draws, and they'll have enough info to set your protocol. You could be ready to have your transplant in three days."

"That's great. Kate and Daniel came by. Kate and I had a good chat."

"You've been worried about her."

"Not so much anymore. I think we connected today."

Mikaela looked into his eyes and saw a return of the peace that had been absent since she returned from Ireland. "I'm so happy for you both."

"Me too." He stroked the hair back from her face. "She told me about my family. They had it hard, Mikaela. In every way. My father was a real piece of work, but my mother was a good woman. Kate told me she grieved for me every day."

Mikaela saw a sheen brighten Matt's eyes and heard a tremor in his voice. She wondered if this unspoken question had been the cause of the private agony Matt had been battling since Kate's arrival and perhaps all his life. She didn't know what to say, so she took Matt's hands and gave them a squeeze as he continued.

"She talked about Hugh, how hard it is for her to look at me and not see him. But we're finally talking about him, and I think it's going to be easier for her. I know it's been good for me."

"I hope she stays for a while. You have a lot of ground to make up."

He nodded thoughtfully. "Daniel invited her to volunteer in the art department. He's assigning her the task of helping rebuild the image of a cretin Daniel is representing."

"Oohhh . . . so they'll be collaborating at work too?" Mikaela clapped her hands together. "It sounds like things are getting cozy."

Matt gave Mikaela a dubious glance. "Daniel's smitten with Kate, but I'm not sure she's looking for more than companionship."

"Uh oh. And you're in the middle. This could get messy for all of you."

Matt took her hands again. "I'm not borrowing trouble yet. I have more good news. Daniel's rogue of a client is desperately in need of redemption. He's looking to make a huge donation to a worthy cause."

Mikaela held her breath as the skin on her arms prickled. "Like the mobile clinics?"

"Yes. Daniel thinks his client's board of directors will jump on the idea. He's presenting it this afternoon. He'll know soon, but it looks very promising."

Mikaela laid her head on Matt's chest and hugged him. "Thank you so much for suggesting it to Daniel. I know you think I'm getting in over my head, but I love you even more than before because you believed in me and trusted my instincts. It means the world to me."

Matt kissed the top of her head. "I'm sorry for how I reacted. How could I not believe in you? I'm proud of you for seeing others' needs and offering solutions instead of just sympathy." He tugged at her chin with his finger until she lifted her head to face him. "I want you to explore all your possibilities. Maybe some you haven't considered before."

He smiled sheepishly, and Mikaela caught the shy, schoolboy dip of his head. She couldn't help but smile. "What?" she teased back. "What is it?"

Matt closed his eyes and blushed, laughing aloud.

The joy of the moment lightened her own heart. "Just say it, you crazy Irishman. Just tell me."

Matt opened his eyes and pushed his bed's controls until he was in a full sitting position. "Come here," he whispered to Mikaela in a husky, love-filled voice. She carefully moved beside him, noticing how his eyes never left hers. Gone was the light-heartedness of the earlier moment, as her heart responded to the heady mix of nervous want shining through Matt's fatigue and pain. Mikaela shivered at the graveled resonance of his voice as he asked. "Do you love me, Mrs. Grayken?"

"With all my heart, Mr. Grayken."

She could feel his breath on her face as he scanned her reaction to every word. "Then I have a proposal for you. Just a proposal. No pressure. Just an option I'd like you to consider."

Mikaela held her breath and watched Matt's eyes begin to glisten.

"Would you be interested in having a child with me?"

She felt much as she had on the ride when she was young, when the stopping Ferris Wheel jerked her back and then jolted her forward as it loaded the next car and began rotating again. Mikaela tilted her head slightly to be sure she'd heard Matt correctly. "Our child?"

She watched Matt's eyes move across her face, studying each brushstroke of her confusion as if she were a work of art. He had reason to be concerned about her reaction, if she understood him correctly. "Are you saying—"

He nodded and took her hands. "When I was sixteen. The doctors suggested we bank my sperm in case the leukemia returned."

"Is this the contingency plan? I don't understand." She straightened and pulled her hands away. "Why didn't you share this with me before?"

His skin tone blanched. "You're angry."

"I'm . . . I'm . . . I don't know what I am." Powerful converging emotions spilled over one another like two mighty rivers, pulling her under. Her hand moved to her mouth, and she bit her knuckle as she stood and paced away from his bedside.

Matt leaned forward, reaching for her. "I'm sorry. I never should have brought it up. I worried I was asking too much of you."

"I'm not angry about the possibility of a child. I'm upset because I closed the door on that possibility. I grieved and accepted it, and then I moved on, and all you had to do was talk to me."

Matt's mouth dropped open in a speechless panic. He sputtered until he was finally able to say, "I'm . . . sorry. The possibility of having a child didn't exist in our original marriage contract. We weren't supposed to fall in love, remember?"

"But we did. Months ago."

"Yes, we did." He leaned back and sighed. "But by then, we were fighting to keep me alive. I hoped we'd have a future but I was living day to day. I didn't want to look ahead."

Mikaela's eyes began to burn. "What changed?"

She heard the swish of the door as the tech arrived for the next blood draw. She slipped into the bathroom to process the possibilities opening to her. A child. There could be a child! She remembered with agonizing clarity the night she and Matt finally became husband and wife in every sense. How he had been afraid to surrender to the want they both felt because the chemo meds had left him toxic, making him a risk to any child that could be conceived. As a cancer nurse, Mikaela understood, and when there had been no mention of Matt's having banked his sperm, she grieved alone and silenced the dream of a family with him, to spare him further feelings of inadequacy. And then this announcement? She wanted to shake him, to yell at him, to tell him how much hurt his silence caused her. She wanted to vent all that anger and frustration, and yet what she wanted most was to lie in his arms and talk about this dream of a family.

She dabbed at her eyes and waited for a swish signaling the tech's departure. When she exited the bathroom, she remained detached and reserved.

"Please, forgive me," Matt asked with his hand outstretched. "Come sit with me. I don't want to discuss this most intimate human experience from opposing courts."

She returned, not to his bed, but to her chair, keeping her emotions in check. "You said you didn't want to look ahead, and then something changed. What was it?"

Matt took her hands and rolled his lips before speaking. "It was actually two events. The first occurred when you were off in Ireland, looking for Kate. My parents were making plans to move me to New York to see some specialist at NYU, and all I could think about was that if they moved me, I might never see you again. That I might not live long enough for you to find me or get to me, and if that happened, everything we were and what we had would be little more than a dream. I would be gone, and you would eventually move on, as I would want you to do, finding a new love and a happy life. But I felt like vapor. It terrified me."

Mikaela felt her heart clutch. Cold rushed over her as she felt Matt's fear. "I do not want to have this conversation, because I refuse to accept your death as our reality, but I will because you need to know that you're wrong. We don't just evaporate when we die. We are woven into the fabric of all the people who love us. We are changed by one another. You, Matthew Grayken, are woven into me." She placed his hand over her heart, and hers over his. Mikaela's throat grew tight. "Secondly, there's not a place your parents could have taken you on this good green earth that I wouldn't have found you."

Matt ran a loose tendril of her hair through his fingers and nodded. "I know that, deep down, but in quiet moments, I can't stop myself from going to dark places. I thought it would get better when you came home, but it hasn't. I don't know if you've felt it, but I've been struggling within myself lately."

Mikaela could barely swallow past the lump his honest words caused. She spread her hands on his thin, bony chest and looked into his eyes. "I've felt it. Your unsettledness and lack of peace."

"It's not about you. It's Kate. For the first time, my birth family is real to me, and I can't explain it, but I struggle over the thought of her being my donor. Her arrival has stirred up so many feelings I never considered."

"Guilt? Indebtedness?"

His eyes widened. "How did you know?"

This was an area in which Mikaela's work in the cancer center proved a blessing. "These feelings aren't uncommon in transplant patients, Matt. Lots of recipients struggle with feelings of guilt or indebtedness, especially if the donation came because of a death. Kate is giving you a great gift, and the best part is that she offered this gift to you before we asked. You said you felt better since your talk. Don't you still feel that way?"

He laid his hands over hers and squeezed them. "I feel much better about the donor part."

"Then what's still haunting you? What you've learned about your family?"

"It's hard to explain. I've been thinking about the importance of genes versus experience. One set of parents pushed me away. The other held on too tight. My parents' failings lessened my confidence that I could do any better."

He winced and drew three slow, deep breaths. Mikaela waited until the wave of nausea abated and he was able to continue.

"Kate said something that helped me sort things out. She told me my mother loved me. That she never wanted to give me up, but she did what she thought would give all her children the best chance of a good life. Just hearing that, knowing I was loved, filled a hole, an empty space in my self-worth."

Mikaela wanted to wrap him in her arms and protect him from any future hurt, but she refrained, blinking back tears as she waited for him to continue.

"I realized I've avoided the idea of children because I saw them as an added burden to you and the life we could have, but something else Kate said hit me like a lightning strike. She said my mother grieved because she missed the opportunity to get to know me and see the promise I might have brought to our family. A child is an opportunity . . . for joy and love. A tiny baby brings the promise of a previously unimagined future. Does that make sense?"

Matt's wonder over the revelation warmed Mikaela's heart. "Remember me? The wife with seven brothers?"

"Once again, I'm only learning what you've already known. Thanks for being patient with me on this topic and so many others. In any case, yea or nay, this has to be your call. Give it some thought. I just wanted to give you the option."

"I don't need to think about it, Matt."

"It's a big decision, Mikaela."

"I carried the dream of a child from the day I met you, and then I tucked that dream away." Her eyes began to shine. "I want our child." She stretched her neck to reach his waiting mouth. His weak arms wrapped around her, and she slid into the bed beside him, suddenly alight with the need to feel his body alongside hers, their unified closeness consummating their decision. "I'm going to be a mother," she whispered so quietly she didn't think Matt could hear.

"Things could still go wrong."

Mikaela refused to have her hope dimmed. "It will happen. We're going to be parents." She felt Matt twisting strands of her hair. "What do we do next?" she asked.

"I called my family doctor and asked that question. We choose a fertility specialist down here and arrange to have the sample transferred when you're ready."

An idea struck her. "Do you think this hospital has a fertility clinic?"

"Maybe. It would be easy to find out, but there's no rush. We have a rough road ahead these next few weeks."

Mikaela sat up to pose her rebuttal. "It could take weeks before I get an appointment, weeks more before they feel I'm ready for the procedure, and months before I get pregnant. We should at least check, don't you think?"

Matt's mouth spread into a mile-wide smile as he drew her face to his. "I love you, Mrs. Grayken," he whispered before kissing her again and urging her back down. Techs came and went over the next few hours, fighting today's battle, but Matt and Mikaela paid them little notice as they lay side by side in a hospital bed, pondering future dreams.

CHAPTER FOUR

Matt awoke the next morning and found Mikaela curled up in her sleeping chair, intently scrolling on her phone. Her long dark hair hung in loose chaos around her shoulders, having been set free from the band that corralled it during the night. Even dressed in floral scrub bottoms and a sloppy tee, she was beautiful. Just the sight of her anchored him, mind and soul. He wished he could capture and hold that very image of her in his mind forever.

He caught his own reflection in the wall mirror and had to look away. His hair was so thin now, more of it absent than present, and his face was thin to the point of looking gaunt. He was grateful for the photo Daniel took of him and Mikaela at their courthouse wedding, when he still sported a full head of hair and his torso was muscled and broad. It sat on the windowsill as a reminder to him and the staff of who their patient really was and hoped to be again. He wondered who Mikaela saw when she looked at him. The man he was or the patient she saw before her? Regardless, she treated him as if he was every bit that audacious stranger who asked her to marry him the first day they met.

She looked over at him and beamed a smile. "You're awake!" She literally bounced up from her chair and onto his bed. He faked injury and groaned, and she issued a teasing smack followed by a good morning kiss. "Guess what? There is a fertility clinic here, and because of yesterday's snow, they have a cancellation. They can see me today at ten!"

The remaining fog of sleep was quickly dismissed as Matt pulled the threads of the conversation together. "Today?" He spread his arms out, drawing attention to his situation. "I . . . hoped . . ." He slumped in resignation. "I wish I could be there with you."

Mikaela's head tilted to the side. "I know, but it could be weeks before your immune system is strong enough to handle the germ level of a walk through a hospital. I told the doctor about our situation, and she's willing to let me teleconference you in. What do you think?"

His heart wanted to slow the process down until he was fully well, but knowing that might never happen, he chose to enjoy every bit of the adventure in any way possible. "Let's do it."

Matt braced for the sonic-boom-level squeal he expected Mikaela to unleash. Instead, she framed his face in her hands and kissed him through her hopeful smile. "Thank you. I love you."

The door opened, and jovial Dr. Marcosky peeked in, offered a "whoops!" and headed back out until Matt yelled, "Come in. It's okay. Come in!"

"Well . . . I was going to say good morning to you, but clearly it already is!" He chuckled and blushed. "Matt, I've looked over your labs and set a course of chemo to bring your immune system down to where we need it to be. The nurses will start a regular IV drip this morning, and we'll draw blood a few more times during the day to make sure we don't exceed the desired level."

"Okay. You're the doc. How long before I get the stem cells?"

"Well . . . how about tomorrow?"

"Tomorrow?" The doctor's question surprised Matt. His head shot left to gauge Mikaela's response, and he found her as shocked and delighted as he was.

"Kate will have made enough stem cells by then?" Mikaela asked.

"We haven't been waiting on her to get ready. We've been waiting on Matt. Kate's been preparing for five days. Didn't you two know that?"

"No," replied Matt. "I thought she just began."

Dr. Marcosky shook his head. "She called here from Ireland to see if our protocol was the same as the one she expected to undergo over there. It was very similar, so she had appointments lined up before her plane touched down. She's a very determined lady."

Matt laughed through trembling lips and toyed with the edge of the blanket as the enormity of Kate's generosity overwhelmed him.

Dr. Marcosky made his way to Matt in three steps and patted his leg. "I feel very good about this transplant. There's a lot of love in this team."

With a final nod to Mikaela, he left the room, and a nurse entered with a new bag of chemo drugs. Mikaela chatted with the nurse about medical details that flew over Matt's head. His thoughts were on Kate and her dedication to his cause. More of their previous conversation returned to him, and a new concern picked at his peace.

The arrangement made it possible for Mother to keep a roof over the rest of our heads during very lean years. In some respects, I suppose I should be thanking you. . .

Matt couldn't help but wonder if Kate's help was about love or guilt or what she perceived as her own indebtedness. He needed to know, and he needed to know before the transplant.

After the nurse checked Matt's vitals, she completed the setup of the IV and looked at both Mikaela and him. "From here on out, we have to be vigilant about germs and sickness because, Matt, your body's immune system won't have any ability to fight. Mikaela, any concerns, coughs, throat tickles?"

Mikaela swallowed and shook her head. "Nope. I'm feeling great."

"I know you know all this, but I had to ask. I'm going to park a 'sterile cart' outside the door. No one sick can enter, but well guests will need to put on a gown, gloves, and a mask before entering."

"Got it."

The close of the door was a welcome sound, giving Matt privacy and quiet to process all that was swirling in his head.

"What a day of miracles. Aren't you excited?" asked Mikaela, whose face now showed confusion.

"About your doctor's appointment or about the transplant being moved up?"

"Both, but the transplant news is phenomenal. Why are you so glum?"

"Another of those inner struggles. Kate had never met me, and yet she flew across the ocean at her own expense to donate her stem cells to a man who's just a DNA strand above a stranger to her. Why do you think she did that?"

"I have a few ideas, but tell me yours first."

"Do you suppose this is her way of making up for what happened to me?"

"You think she's been motivated by guilt?" Mikaela cocked her head to the side. "Give me three words that describe Kate."

Matt regretted verbalizing his crazy insecurities. He thought about Kate and knew what he saw in her. "Strong-willed, brave, loyal."

"I think you've summed her up well. That strong-willed, brave, loyal woman was ready to fight your twin, Hugh's, cancer, but she never got the chance to even suit up for that battle because an enemy she was powerless against stole him from her —a random, senseless motorcycle accident. And then she heard she had a chance to save a brother lost to her, a brother she'd missed and thought about for thirteen years. In some ways, I think she probably needs this as badly as you do."

Matt bit his lower lip and thought about Mikaela's words. He wanted a bond of kinship to develop between himself and Kate.

"It's going to be wonderful Matt. You're each a gift to the other. Don't overthink this. Just accept her gift. Be grateful for her love and love her back."

He nodded and closed his eyes to let it all settle in, and then his phone rang. Daniel's enthusiastic voice boomed through. "The board ate your suggestion up!"

Matt cringed at the news. He longed to return to the previous night, when he and Mikaela were alone with their dreams. Reality was setting in, a reality filled with fertility appointments, post-transplant isolation, and Mikaela's whopping new plans. Matt feared the combination of responsibilities would overwhelm them.

He swallowed his concerns. "It's Mikaela's project. Do you want to talk to her?" A glance at Mikaela showed her standing with her fists tucked under her chin, all but illuminated with excitement.

"I've gotta run to another meeting, but tell her I'd like to come by this afternoon and brainstorm this out, you know, get a general idea of what level of financial commitment it's going to require. Between you and me, I hope it hits this guy hard. He's a total jerk."

Matt had barely ended the call before Mikaela began pressing him for details. "What did Daniel say? Does his client want to help?"

"His board does, and that's what matters."

Mikaela squealed and did a jiggle dance that made Matt think of a wilting gelatin mold. He turned his head to the window, bringing Mikaela's revelry to an abrupt halt. Without a word from him, she moved to his side and brought her face within inches of his.

"This is a happy day, Matt. How can we have so many prayers answered and not want to give something back?"

"This mobile clinic project could be all consuming."

"We won't let it be. Look what you've already accomplished from this bed! You got the project funded. That's huge! We'll have fun laying the groundwork during your isolation period. Once you're well and I'm expecting, we'll reevaluate how involved we want to remain. Okay?"

She gave him *that* smile, the one that dismissed his clouds and cajoled the sun into shining. "Okay."

"I promise that getting you well and having our baby are the two most important things to me."

"More than painting the kitchen?"

"Definitely more than the vegetable boxes, but painting the kitchen? Hmmm... That gray has got to go."

His brow remained creased, signaling that he still had reservations.

"I promise you, Matt, nothing comes before us. Whenever love is on the line, I'm always going to choose us."

"Me too."

THEY HAD BECOME SO ACCUSTOMED to lab techs and blood draws that Mikaela barely noticed when the next tech came in. She checked the clock and felt excitement zip through her. "It's time," she said, pausing to change out of her tee and into a sweater. She bent down to get a final kiss from Matt. "Is your phone charged?"

"Fully."

She searched his bedside table and said, "Maybe you should plug it in just in case. And do you have a good signal? What if I can't reach you?"

Matt took her hands. "My phone is charged. My signal is strong. My heart is pumping, and there are no hurricanes or tornadoes in sight. You can do this." He smiled up at her. "You can do this for both of us."

With a quick nod of her head and a return for a final, final kiss, she waved and left the room to make a stop by the nurses' station to let them know she'd be away for an hour. She wasn't shy about working the "peer card." Making sure the staff knew she was a trained cancer nurse had afforded her certain privileges and courtesies. They kept her apprised of details regular family members wouldn't have understood, and she was given access to the beverage fridge and closets full of items that would make Matt more comfortable.

She tugged on her sweater to check her appearance and felt

a tickle in her nose, probably from a loose yarn fiber she thought. She sneezed as she left the nurses station on route for the elevator. A short ride later, she was on the second floor, standing outside the elegantly decorated fertility clinic. She missed Matt instantly and video-called him.

"Look at this place, Matt! My heart is racing."

"Now settle that heart down, or they'll think you're in A-fib."

Mikaela laughed. "I love you Mr. Grayken. You're good for me."

"Let's convince that doctor we're ready to have a baby."

Mikaela checked in and had a short wait before being led back to Dr. Chapman's office for her consult. The doctor ran a hand through her gray-peppered, close-cropped hair while Mikaela angled the phone just right so Matt could see and be seen. Once they made their introductions, Dr. Chapman took a deep breath and leaned forward. Her over-forty eyes appeared to grow more tired as they moved from Mikaela to Matt and back.

Mikaela sensed the doctor's apprehension, and she jumped in to state her case. "Thank you for giving me your canceled appointment. We're anxious to get started. I'm a nurse, so I already understand how long the process can take."

"Yes, yes. My nurse filled me in on your background and on your husband's medical situation. I must say that while most of my patients have some sort of medical condition preventing them from conceiving naturally, I've never had a couple come in the middle of a fight like you two are currently facing. You're already under a tremendous amount of stress. Are you sure you want to add to that right now? If you asked ten fertility specialists to take you on as a patient, a few would likely agree, but I think most would advise you to throw everything you've got into getting your husband well before taking on another medical fight. That's also my advice to you both. Come back in six months, at which time it would be my pleasure to help you."

Mikaela couldn't see Matt's response, but she felt their opportunity closing. She scrambled to know what to say, how to define their fight in a way that was honest and hopeful and yet urgent. Before she could assemble her thoughts, Matt spoke up.

"Some people would look at me and say I'm dying. Others just see a fight ahead. In either case, whether I die or conquer this cancer, the hope of having a child may be the only parental experience I'll ever have. The dream of having a baby with Mikaela adds to my fight. It doesn't compete with it. Can you understand that?"

The doctor nodded in silence. When she spoke, her voice was gentle but weighted by concern. "I can, but we're talking about a child, Mr. and Mrs. Grayken. A life, requiring and deserving a lifetime commitment. A baby is more than a motivational tool or prize. You can't decide to have a child on a whim."

Mikaela knew that in her excitement over the immediate appointment, she had blurted out too much information to the scheduling nurse, including her thrill over getting an appointment so quickly after the decision to conceive was made. She pressed her point anew. "Dr. Chapman, how many naturally conceived children come into being without so much as a 'whim?' I come from a family of eight children. I never imagined a childless life until I fell in love with Matt, but if there is a chance to have Matt *and* a child, I want that chance."

Matt's voice broke in. "We are not people who run from responsibility. The easy thing for me to do would be to surrender and die, but I don't. I fight. For love. First it was for Mikaela. Then it was for us together. Now, it would be for the hope of a family. And as for Mikaela, if she ran from responsibility, would she be here, sporting a sick husband she carries around via a video feed?"

Dr. Chapman placed an elbow on her desk and pressed a finger over her mouth. "I suppose not."

Mikaela thought she sensed a softening in the doctor's position. She scooted to the front of her chair to make a last plea. "The opportunity to have a child is new, but I've always desired to be a mother. My enthusiasm isn't a whim. It's joy. Pure joy over a dream that can be realized . . . with your help."

The doctor's chin slipped into her hand. She eyed Matt on the phone and then returned her gaze to Mikaela. "I need you two to fully see what you're up against."

Mikaela held her breath as the lines creasing the space between doctor's eyes diminished. "All right you two. Here's the Intrauterine Insemination method."

She discussed the process, from first examination and lab tests, to the medications Mikaela might have to endure to get her body ready, and on to the transfer of Matt's specimen. "Assuming Matt's sample and your body are both healthy, I think we can forego the use of fertility drugs during the first few IUI cycles. These drugs increase the potential for multiple births. Or were you hoping to have multiples?"

Mikaela switched the perspective on the phone and looked at Matt. "How do you feel about that, Mr. Grayken?"

Matt rubbed his balding head and winced. "I think one at a time is good."

Dr. Chapman chuckled. "In this case, I'm inclined to agree." She explained the importance of charting ovulation and basal temperature. At the end, the doctor asked if they had any questions. To Mikaela's surprise, Matt asked for a few minutes in private. When Dr. Chapman left the room, Mikaela switched the camera so he could see her.

"What do you think?" Matt asked. "Are you absolutely certain about this? The IUI protocol sounds as daunting as chemo."

"We've done that. Are you saying you think you're tougher than me?"

"Never."

"All right then. We did chemo, Matt. We can do this too."

"So . . . you put a cold rag on my neck when I throw up, and I'll put one on yours?"

"Sounds terribly romantic."

"That's how we roll. I love you, Mrs. Grayken."

Mikaela opened the door and found the doctor in the corridor. "How do we begin?"

A half-hour later, Mikaela was armed with an appointment for her first gynecological exam with Dr. Chapman and with a folder about IUI, ultrasound tests, fertility drugs, and ovulation monitors. This technical process wasn't how she'd imagined having a child, but it offered her the chance of having a child with Matt, and that made it beautiful and miraculous.

She was floating as she stepped into the elevator and called Matt, anxious to see his expression as they discussed not just their hope but their plan. "How are you feeling about this? Are you excited?"

"I almost can't wrap my head around it. Yesterday it was just an idea, and now . . . it's really happening."

Mikaela sensed a sadness in Matt. She worried as the busy elevator stopped at each floor. "I hear something in your voice. Something's not right. Talk to me."

"Don't panic. It's . . . just that I'm on sterile protocol now."

"But not with me."

She heard his pause, and then she remembered the sneeze. "Oh, no. Not today! Not now! I'm not s—" She started to argue and then stopped. First of all, it would do no good to tell the nurses she wasn't sick, and secondly she should be thanking these nurses for their vigilance. It was the price she'd have to pay to keep Matt well.

"Daniel came to speak to you. He's in the family lounge on six."

"Oh, Matt. I just want us to have some time to process all this."

"We'll do what we always do—the best we can. Take whatever time you need. I'll just wait for you here, at my regular table." said Matt.

When the elevator doors opened on the sixth floor, Mikaela saw redheaded Daniel leaning against the wall. He met her in three steps, sweeping her into a hug.

"Matt told me you were at an appointment. Everything okay with you?"

She sidestepped the topic. "I don't know how to thank you for choosing this project for your client. We're going to do a lot of good for local communities."

"It's a win/win for me too, Mikaela. Come with me. Since Matt's room is on sterile protocol, I grabbed a corner of the family lounge, so you can talk and I can take . . ." Daniel's comment ended abruptly, and his voice lowered into a growl.

Mikaela followed his gaze back to the man exiting the elevator. The vibe given off by his dark, unruly hair matched that of his stubbled chin, black thigh-grabbing jeans, and chest-tight black tee peeking beneath a camel-colored sports coat. Designer shades were pushed into his hairline, and gold and diamonds swamped the ring finger of his right hand. He carried himself as if accustomed to attention, flashing his straight white teeth Mikaela's way as if she was lost at sea and he was the lighthouse. She noticed Daniel's red-flushed face and felt him physically move between her and the man. She had a good idea who this was. Life with Matt had taught her to recognize the details in expensive clothes and accessories. From the retina-burning polish of his Italian leather boots to the sparkle of his diamond-studded gold Rolex, Mikaela knew this man had money. Loads of it. This was Bennett Sadler, and Daniel had clearly not invited him.

Daniel barreled up to the thirtyish man, paying no mind to the fact that the hulking Adonis was at least three inches taller than him. "What are you doing here?"

The man didn't flinch. "You don't think for a minute that I'm going to leave my future in the hands of a board comprised of out-of-touch Neanderthals, do you? The board can recommend a course of action, but I'm the acting president of P&S Med Tech, and I have the final say on all large investments."

Daniel grew angrier by the minute. "How did you find me?"

Bennett sneered. "It didn't take a genius to pay an Uber driver double to follow you from the office. Once you walked into the hospital, all I had to do was check in at the front desk and ask for the room of the man whose name was listed on the files you handed out at the board meeting." He turned to Mikaela and bowed ever so slightly. "Young, beautiful, feisty, and smart, with a dying husband. You're perfect."

Every muscle in Mikaela tensed for a fight. She shot around Daniel and faced the man directly. "Excuse me? Who do you think you are?"

"Your benefactor," said Bennett as he walked around Mikaela, sizing her up as if she were a prize heifer. "The public will eat you two up, and with Daniel broadcasting my role as your patron, my indiscretions will be forgotten in a year, and I'll be as noble as Father Christmas."

Daniel stood chest to chest with the man, then backed off

when a group of hospital visitors came around the corner. Instead, he took Mikaela's arm and led her away. Bennett followed, calling out, "Hats off to you, Daniel. You know your stuff. Thank you for putting this plan together. You couldn't have found a couple with a higher favorability rating if you hired a focus group or went to central casting."

Daniel spun around. "Consider our agreement canceled from the minute you made the incalculable mistake of following me here. You're not just foolish, you're loathsome. I'd axe my career before I'd allow you to exploit people I love."

Daniel headed away again with Mikaela in tow, but her anger and sorrow merged as she saw the mobile clinic project slipping away.

Bennett continued to call out to them down the hall. "All right, all right. Perhaps I crossed a line, but let's face it, we're all here because we need each other."

Mikaela heard a shift in his voice from cocky to contrite. The subtle change gave her hope that the deal could be saved, and when she turned around to test her instincts, she noticed the shift in his stance from squared shoulders to slightly rounded. The steely glint in his eye was now clouded, leaving him far less formidable, and almost sympathetic. While Bennett's words were for Daniel, his focus was clearly on Mikaela, almost pleading for her to hear him out.

"Put yourself in my shoes. You've tied me to a cause and to its sponsors for a year of my life. Didn't I deserve the chance to meet my new partners? Mrs. Grayken needs my money. You need to prevent my company's multimillion-dollar account from leaving your firm, and I need some redemption. Let's say it straight. We're all using each other."

Daniel's jaw bulged in anger. He released Mikaela and said, "Go to the nearest nurses' station and call for security."

"Do you really want that?" asked Bennett. "Being thrown out of a hospital is the least of my worries, but do you want that kind of PR for you or for Mrs. Grayken. Just talk to me. That's all I'm asking."

Mikaela strode up to the man and looked him squarely in the eye. "Let me correct a few gross misunderstandings, Mr. Sadler. First of all, let's clarify your relationship to me and my husband. We're not your property, your investment, or your friends. Got it? Secondly, this arrangement has nothing to do with us. It's about serving the needs of the poor and the uninsured in our community. Neither my husband nor I *need* your money. We are capable of funding the project ourselves if need be, but we hope the project will become more sustainable with a broader committee and funding. You weren't our *last* hope. You were the *first* to be *offered* the opportunity, and that's what this is . . . your opportunity, not ours. So, if you can internalize those new understandings, we can talk. But not now. Not today. Set up a proper meeting with Daniel, and I'll be there at my convenience, because my first priority is in room 635, where I'm headed now."

She turned to Daniel. "Can you set this up for another day?"

Daniel nodded with pride glowing in his eyes. "You bet."

Mikaela turned back to Bennett Sadler. "And bring your checkbook, Mr. Sadler. The cost of the project just went up. I think we'll aim for two mobile units, not just one."

She walked away without another look back. The impact of the confrontation didn't hit her until she passed through the door to Matt's wing, when her knees began to shake and her rapid heart rate left her dry-mouthed and giddy. After grabbing a drink from the water fountain, she looked down the hall and saw the cart that held the gowns and gloves and masks that would define her contact with Matt for the foreseeable future. Unexpected problems were clouding a day that should have ranked among the best of their lives. Determined not to allow the joy of the day to be dimmed, Mikaela got an idea.

She pulled her phone from her purse and quickly searched for a particular song. When it was queued up, she stopped by the nurses' station and gave them advanced warning about what she was planning to do. They laughed in support and gathered behind her as she approached the glass partition that separated Matt's room from the hall.

Matt's gaze was already fixed on that spot, as if he had been waiting for her to appear. His face lit up upon seeing her, and then dimmed despite his efforts to disguise his disappointment over the protocol. "There's my girl," he said to Mikaela through the slightly ajar door.

The longing in his voice pushed away whatever residual anger or hurt Bennett Sadler had inflicted upon Mikaela. His next question cut her.

Matt looked past her to the nurses and asked, "Can we just hold off on the masks long enough for one last kiss?"

Mikaela knew the answer, but she let the staff deliver the sad news while she pouted from afar. Matt waved for her to come, but she said, "I believe I promised you a floorshow."

His head titled sideways, and then, with widened eyes, he answered, "That's right. I believe you did."

"And I always pay my debts."

Mikaela clicked on the preselected song and the "The Stripper" opened in a low volume with its famous trombone slide. She handed the phone to another nurse and picked up a plastic-wrapped gown from the box, dangling it from two fingers with a flirty glance Matt's way. Gripping the cellophane package with two hands, she tore the package open with an abrupt rip while simultaneously shimmying her body in her hubby's direction. Various wriggles and pouty glances continued while she slowly opened the yellow gown and slid her arms into the sleeves. A few seductive shoulder rolls ensued as the gown's ties were tied.

At this point, drawn by the music and the nurses' cheers and laughter, staff began to gather with cell phones at the ready to record the scene. "Way to rock sterile protocol, Mikaela!" hooted one nurse with her camera in record mode.

Mikaela tackled the latex gloves next. Each slipped from the box with a series of slow tugs timed to the beat of the song. When both were out, Mikaela swung them before her like pom-poms, and Matt roared until his eyes began to tear. She wiggled down and then up as she slithered one hand and then the other into the gloves, adding a little snap to the wrist as each slipped into place. With palms out, she slid her open hands across her eyes harem-girl style while winking at Matt.

The mask was the last and most depressing addition to the ensemble. No kisses for a while or shared smiles or the other nuances of emotion, but without further delay, she pulled a mask from the box by its string and twirled it over her head a few times before slapping it across her shoulder with a few more awkward shimmies for emphasis. She could only imagine how ridiculously uncoordinated she must look. Her modest, aged mother certainly didn't pass any stripper moves on to her only daughter, and her brothers taught her man-slamming moves, not man-snaring ones. But Matt's pleasure superseded her own embarrassment, as her final act of the dance was about to begin. Using two fingers on each hand, she held the mask before her face by its elastic ear loops. Only her eyes showed above the fabric as she swayed snakelike in a dance that would have made Scheherazade laugh. When the two ear pieces finally slipped into place, she rolled her arms forward with dramatic flair and bowed.

The nurses clapped and laughed, but Mikaela's one concern was Matt. When she looked up from her finale, his arms were stretched her way. She gave her growing audience a final bow and shut the door before running into Matt's arms. "I'm so sorry about all this."

"Don't be sad," he whispered into her hair. "These precautions are just for a little while."

"But I don't even think I'm sick. I just sneezed."

"It's okay," he repeated. "We're good at hard things."

She looked up at him, hoping her eyes conveyed the love she felt for this man. "Yes, we are. Just imagine. We could have a baby by this time next year."

"Then we'll do whatever we must to make that happen. Just lie here beside me and tell me everything you're feeling. I want to hear it all."

Mikaela made no mention of the loathsome Bennett Sadler or the details of the rescheduled meeting. That reality was for another day. This day was for dreams.

CHAPTER FIVE

The massive expectations resting upon Matt's stem-cell transplant left him too anxious to sleep soundly the night before the procedure. He wrestled with worry until one and awoke with the same burdens at five. The happiness of everyone he loved hinged on the procedure's success—his parents, Kate, Mikaela, a child he hoped they'd conceive and meet, and of course, his own. Like a blessed cat, he prayed with all the faith in him that his life be spared one more time. He was only twenty-nine. He still had so many dreams to fulfill.

His mouth was dry and sticky. He longed to feel normal again. To have strength and stamina. To feel confident on his two legs again. To have hair and a complexion that didn't already look dead. He wished to have bright eyes that reflected happiness instead of fatigue. But he would bear the scars of the disease —the weakness and its youth-stealing debilitation—simply for more time.

He looked at Mikaela resting in her lounge chair, regretting the months he had rigidly clung to the terms of their marriage contract—friendship only and end-of-life care. No admissions of love. No romantic contact until, like a breached dam, their staved love and emotion and want burst past the rules and they finally became not merely married, but man and wife. But it had come so late, too far into the cancer's march, leaving them so little time. A few tender nights that changed his view on life and death and what he'd sacrifice for love.

He wondered if he'd ever sleep with her by his side, untethered to machines. Or would he ever make love to her again? He found it hard to press the bitterness back. He endured the fight out of love for Mikaela, but there were moments when his dark thoughts stole past his hope, whispering his greatest fear, that the woman he'd come to love so wholly, so desperately, might one day tire of his ugliness and demanding care when there was so little romantic return on her investment of love. In those terrifying milliseconds, fear told him he'd have been better off clinging to the safety of their original agreement, their sterile, friends-only alliance of companionship, than to experience the agony of her departure and the loss of all he had known with her. Losing Mikaela, would be a slower, deeper, soul-consuming death greater than any cancer could inflict.

But then the memories of their quirky love and snappy humor centered him again. The magic of their few impassioned nights, knotted fiercely to one another, dispelled the darkness and its lies. Mikaela knew his cancer fight was his sacrifice for love. She had said so in words and with her tear-filled looks and tender administrations to his needs. She loved him more for paying that price for them, and in return, he would sacrifice anything, everything, for more time, even one more day, with Mikaela.

The sun had not yet risen, but the room was dimly lit by the lights on the monitors binding him to his bed. The glow of lingering moonlight illuminated the curves of Mikaela's face. He smiled at the dark, messy tousles forming a chaotic halo around her head. He loved her hair. It was so much like her—playful, busy, unpretentious, apt to follow its heart, unconcerned with the opinions of others. Did she know how much he loved her wild hair?

He pulled his computer from the bedside table and began writing a love note to Mikaela. The first line read, "Do you know . . . ?"

MIKAELA BRUSHED HIS CHEEK, bringing Matt awake. Her bright eyes, the only portion of her face visible, smiled down at him. "Good morning, sleepyhead," she whispered from behind her mask. "You're the last one to the party." Matt slipped a hand through the bedrail and took hold of hers. Mikaela pointed to the right side of the bed where his parents stood.

Matt blinked and squinted until he was able to focus on his masked and smiling parents. He slipped his other hand through the bedrail to take his mother's, offering his father a smile. "What time is it?"

"A little before eight," answered Donovan Grayken. "We just arrived. We wanted to give you two some space, but we couldn't miss the big day."

Mikaela saw the wince that accompanied Matt's smile. She could imagine the myriad emotions surrounding this day. His already weak body would be put through the wringer when it reacted to the introduction of Kate's stem cells.

"Dr. Marcosky popped in. It shouldn't be long now." Mikaela placed a hand on his shoulder, feeling unequipped to offer anything meaningful that hadn't already been said.

Donovan filled the empty space with talk of football scores and news headlines, but Matt simply nodded his assent and held fast to Mikaela.

Morning assessments were completed, and then the precious bag filled with Kate's stem cells was hung from his IV pole and connected through the central line in his neck.

Dr. Marcosky arrived like a spring breeze, his big voice cheery and hopeful. "What shall we call today? New Year's Day? Or your second birthday? Most patients mark it somehow."

"What's the date?" asked Matt.

"December 28th," replied his mother.

"December 28th. The date alone will be magical enough."

"Well said," Dr. Marcosky replied. He winked at the nurse who opened the valve to allow the stem-cell-rich blood to flow into Matt.

The process itself lacked drama. Matt asked Mikaela to turn on the news. She knew he found the TV an annoyance most days, but today it proved to be a precious distraction, a strategy to occupy anxious eyes that otherwise drifted to monitors or worse, to him. He closed his eyes and fell asleep or into what posed as sleep.

The Graykens went to the cafeteria for breakfast and returned with hot cocoa for Mikaela. Before the IV drip finished, Matt's fever was already on the rise, and chills set in. The nurses were at the ready with another IV to lessen the side effects. He complained of a headache, and Mikaela applied cool compresses to his head and neck for comfort until the nausea set in. He threw up twice, and heaved twice more, and then he fell asleep.

"I wish we knew how to help," cried his mother.

"The nurses are doing all that can be done. You've been up so long. Why don't you go back to the house to rest? I'll call you if anything changes. Take my car."

They agreed and left. For three days, they came and went, tag-teaming with Daniel and Kate, encouraging Matt through more chest-rattling coughing and bouts of nausea. Matt's red cell counts plummeted, and concerns were voiced about pneumonia and folding lungs as they feared his were collapsing. Mikaela stayed and battled with him, soothing his fevers with cool cloths, layering on blankets for the chills, encouraging him to use the spirometer to strengthen his lungs. The Donovans appeared as ashen as their son during the worst of Matt's symptoms, and then, on December 31, Matt turned a corner. His breathing cleared, and the nausea abated. He sat up and ate a small meal and welcomed Mikaela's offer to bathe him and redress him in a clean gown.

His parents were nearly giddy with relief. Barely a moment passed without one or both of them touching his hands or shoulder or face. Matt pressed them to head home early before inebriated New Year's Eve revelers overran the train platform in D.C. and, worse, in New York City. They finally left, and Mikaela and Matt settled in for their first New Year's Eve together.

"How shall we celebrate?" asked Mikaela as she sat in her chair, holding Matt's hand.

Matt's voice was graveled and raspy from the coughing as he said, "Sleep is good."

She queued up the first episode of the space saga Matt and her brothers so loved." Only for you, Mr. Grayken. Only for you."

Matt dozed in and out while Mikaela watched the first four films in an intergalactic marathon. As midnight drew near, she turned the TV on to catch the ball dropping in New York City, putting that experience on her list for next New Year's Eve.

Matt's phone blew up eight times in rapid succession.

Mikaela laughed, having a pretty good idea of the source of the fourteen messages on her own phone. They were Happy New Year's messages of love and support from her brothers and their families scattered across the globe. She took a moment to quickly reply through the text group they set up.

The eight messages on Matt's phone had her laughing so hard Matt awoke. "What is it?" he asked with a start.

Mikaela placed a hand over her mouth to stifle her laughter and apologized as she turned the phone around to reveal the repeatedly sent image caught on the screen. There, standing before Matt and Mikaela's Georgetown brownstone, were Nelson, Gunther, Jacob, Russell, Porter, Miguel, and Daniel, all seven members of Matt's infamous DVP gang, clad in nothing but black top hats and a banner that read, "Get Well Soon, Matt," to cover their nether regions.

A smile teased at the corners of Matt's mouth, spreading until his eyes crinkled and tears squeezed out of the corners. When his laughter died down, he said, "Those are some scary Baby New Years."

"Oh, it gets better," said Mikaela. "It's a video."

She hit play, and the motley band of seven friends sang a well-rehearsed barber shop version of "Auld Lang Syne," complete with harmonies. At the end, they dropped the banner, revealing their diapered bottoms.

Matt wiped his eyes and laughed more while Mikaela turned the camera on him to tape his response. "Well done, guys! Well done. That was smashing!"

They signed off and settled in for the night, hoping the positive turn in Matt's health and mood were signs that the road ahead was bright.

The first day of the new year was alight with sunshine that added to the brightness of the attitude in Matt's room. The day began with Mikaela's cheery, "Happy New Year," shared in an exuberant whisper as she leaned over her sleeping husband. He couldn't muster the energy to straighten out his cockeyed good-morning smile, which he was quite sure matched the crooked tilt of his eyebrow as he forced his eyes open into fluttering slits. He swallowed and felt a tiny sting in his throat.

"Sore throat?" asked Mikaela with worry in her voice.

"A little. Not bad." He felt as limp as wilted lettuce, but he wasn't nauseated, and his temperature was normal. All in all, he counted it a good day.

She placed her hand to his forehead and checked his arms and chest for a rash. Seeing none, she studied the monitor to read his stats. "No fever, but we need to keep an eye on that sore throat. It's probably nothing, but we want to watch for any sign of GvHD, Graft Versus Host disease."

"Rejection?"

"More like intolerance. It's treatable, but we want to catch it early because it can be very unpleasant."

"Imagine that," he said with a smirk.

Hovering an inch above Matt's mouth, Mikaela said, "I have a few New Year's presents for you." She pressed her masked lips to his dry, cracked ones, barely making contact.

"I miss your real lips."

"I hope we'll get to remedy that soon. They've taken my temperature for three days. No elevated temp, no coughing, no runny nose or headaches. I could be cleared as healthy soon."

"Are you sure you're feeling okay? You seem unusually lethargic."

"It's your fault."

"Mine? Don't you mean yours? I warned you that you can't start watching those movies and then just stop cold turkey after episode four."

"Wait a minute, buster. You were asleep. How did you know when I quit?"

"I wasn't asleep. I was watching them in my mind."

"In your mind, huh?"

"Yes," he reiterated. "When you've seen them as many times as I have, you can picture every scene, even with your eyes closed."

"Did you start episode five?"

"I'm embarrassed to confess that I bought them for my phone when you fell asleep since I couldn't get out of bed to change the DVD. I ran out of steam in the middle of episode seven. But wait. This isn't about me. What did you think? You loved them, right???"

"They were . . . entertaining."

"What? Entertaining? A street performer making balloon animals is entertaining. These are masterpieces!"

Mikaela was enjoying his pain too much. "They could have used a little more romance."

Matt closed his eyes and groaned.

"And I had a hard time telling the good guys and the bad guys apart in the battle scenes. The stars kept getting in the way. And I think they could have found another plot line besides just shooting each other all the time. It got redundant."

"So, what you're saying is that these classic movies had too many *stars* and too much *war*?"

"And—"

Matt placed his index fingers in his ears and began saying, "Lalalalalala . . ." When Mikaela's critique was silenced into laughter, he jutted one hand forward and said, "You're officially excused from ever watching them again. I can't listen to you besmirch the films that form the basis of the DVP poker ritual. I-I-I just can't."

"Agreed. In return, I offer you a free pass on all things Jane Austen."

Matt offered her a cockeyed wink. "I actually enjoy Jane Austen's work."

Before she could explore that confession, Daniel popped in with Kate on his arm, each of them dressed in masks and gowns. Matt saw complete expectation on Daniel's face as he awaited a review of the DVP group's New Year's Eve performance, but once again, Kate seemed wary and nervous about seeing him.

"I wouldn't have expected to see you so early after the night you had," said Matt, shooting a glance at his sister. "Kate, did you see how Daniel rang in the new year?"

"Aye." Kate rolled her eyes, and for a moment, the wariness left her face. "I have to say, after meeting your group of prep school friends, playing the part of the Baby New Year wasn't much of a stretch for any one of them."

Daniel winced and said, "Ouch! You loved it. Admit it."

Matt laughed along until a coughing spell hit him. He noticed caution return to Kate's eyes, and he rushed to assure her. "My throat is a little dry. It's nothing to be worried about."

She nodded and turned to Mikaela. "Let's leave these men to their folly." She turned back to Daniel, "And I use the term 'men' loosely. Mikaela, shall we?"

She and Mikaela moved to the seating area across the room and chatted while Daniel sat with Matt.

"Nice video last night. Who was behind the camera, Kate?"

"Yep. How'd you like those harmonies?"

"Very nice. Gunther did a good job holding the baritone line without me. He did me proud."

"We've come a long way since prep school chorale."

"It seems your performance may have been a bit too much for Kate."

Daniel stole a glance her way. "Nah. Kate's a trooper. She's just worried about you."

"She looks at me as if I might evaporate before her very eyes."

"She just found you. It's to be expected that the chance of losing you would upset her. But she doesn't know the Matt Grayken I know."

"That I'm secretly a superhero?"

"No. That you're obviously married to one. You're invincible with her by your side."

"True."

Daniel leaned in. "Did she tell you how she cowed Bennett Sadler the other day?"

It was the first Matt had heard of any meeting between Mikaela and Bennett. "Fill me in."

Daniel gritted his teeth and growled under his breath. "The jerk followed me here to the hospital on Thursday, the day I told you I wanted to meet with Mikaela to discuss the mobile clinics. He came right up on the next elevator and approached Mikaela as if he were her new boss. I was ready to deck the guy, but Mikaela put him in his place and Bennett folded like a dinner napkin. It was great."

Matt stole a glance Mikaela's way, wondering why she hadn't mentioned the confrontation. He slumped deeper into his bed. "She's pretty formidable when she needs to be. Good thing, since I'm not a very intimidating protector these days."

"Matt—"

"I'm glad you were there," he interjected quickly. He was not in the mood to hear Daniel make excuses for him. "Maybe we should get a different investor for the project."

Daniel tensed and sat forward. "You'll have a hard time finding one with pockets as deep and willing to be picked as

Bennett's. After meeting Mikaela, Bennett seemed ready to grant her anything. Which is why I think we need to move while he's in a generous mood. Do you think I could steal Mikaela for an hour tomorrow to outline the financials of this agreement?"

"Will Bennett Sadler be there?"

"Yes, but so will I. You be assured I won't allow him to rattle her."

Matt knew Mikaela would be livid if she heard Daniel and Matt's plans to protect her based on their nineteenth-century sensibilities. She would drop them both like stones while reminding them that she was the girl who was raised with seven brothers/soldiers who taught their baby sister self-defense. Still . . .

"It's Mikaela's decision. She's been by my side every minute for days. She could use a break."

Daniel placed a hand on Matt's shoulders. "Thanks, buddy. I can't wait to get these contracts approved and pass Bennett Sadler along to marketing. I'll keep the meeting short. I promise." Daniel called across the room to Mikaela. "Matt says I can borrow you for a short meeting tomorrow. Are you ready to present the project's budget requirements to our investor?"

Mikaela's brow furrowed as she stood. "I can't leave Matt right now."

Matt would have loved to allow her answer to stand with a "Sorry, Daniel," but he told himself he was a better man than that. A better husband than that. "Go. I'll be fine for a few hours. I have more chaperones here than a Victorian debutante."

As she moved to his side, he saw the wrestle going on within her and knew he needed to set her mind at ease. "I'm doing so well today. You know the nurses or I will call you if anything changes. Go. Let's get this ball rolling. It will do us some good to focus on something besides med schedules and vitals."

She bit her thumbnail before finally saying. "Okay. A short meeting. And set it somewhere I can come dressed in scrubs or sweats. It's all I have with me."

"Great. Shall we say ten? Brennan's café is a block down the street from the hospital. I see nurses and doctors in there all the time dressed in scrubs. Meet us for brunch."

She looked at Matt, and he gave her his most convincing I-agree-with-this-plan smile.

"Okay. Sounds good."

CHAPTER SIX

Mikaela started January 2nd by rereading the prospectus Dr. Gorman emailed. She wanted to be fully prepared for this meeting about the mobile clinics. The costs were based on the absolute necessities required to provide screening for basic medical care. Dr. Gorman had gathered a long list of generous physicians, nurses, and dentists, some retired, some in current practice, willing to donate a day a month to staff these clinics. Therefore, the greatest cost was, of course, the motorized coach fitted to house the medical equipment and a few exam cubicles, but the costs quickly mounted as basic medical and diagnostic equipment and furniture were added to the list. And then there were all the small first-aid supplies needed for redressing wounds, not to mention the administrative needs like laptops, file boxes, chairs and tables.

Dr. Gorman provided a second list. This contained the supplies they wished they could acquire to triage and treat patients or diagnose them and send them for ongoing care. Equipment like portable X-ray machines, doppler units, and portable EKG machines. And in a perfect world, a mobile dental clinic because so many health problems began because of dental issues or medical issues of the mouth.

Dr. Gorman had also added a link for a company that designed, customized, and equipped, beautiful mobile clinics. Mikaela clicked the link and was awed by the medical access and care that exorbitant amounts of money could buy. Clearly, the communities needing such mobile service were the very ones least able to afford it.

She ogled the vehicles on the website, playing with numbers and lists until she heard Matt's bed rustle.

"Good morning," she said. "How's the throat today?"

Matt swallowed and winced. "A little worse, but not terrible. My mouth is sticky." He reached for his Styrofoam cup of water. "This is all normal, right?"

Mikaela hid her worry. "Probably. I didn't see patients this soon after their transplant. Let me get a nurse." She turned for the door, but Matt caught her hand.

"She'll be in soon enough. Then it'll be like NASCAR in here, with nurses swooping in and out all day long."

"They're taking very good care of you."

"I know, and I'm very grateful. When will we know if this transplant worked? What's that called?"

"Engraftment, and it's when the new stem cells you received begin producing healthy new blood cells. It usually takes between ten and fifteen days."

"Today is day five."

"You're doing great. Do you have any other questions?"

"No. I just want to talk about something besides illness. Let's have a dose of that bright future you promised me." He pulled her down to sit on the edge of the bed. "Are you still feeling good about bringing a baby into all this?"

"Yes." She bent over and pressed her forehead to his. "Are you?"

His hand slid up behind her neck, and he gave it a weak squeeze. "When I can't sleep, I dream of what it'll be like. You, me, and a little person toddling between us."

Mikaela sat up and smiled in wonder at how closely his dreams resembled hers. "Me too. What do you see? A boy or a girl."

"It honestly doesn't matter to me. I can't choose, when either would be a miracle."

"My first appointment is on the twenty-third."

"In exactly three weeks. I could be home by then."

"That's a little fast, but I do like the way you think."

Matt grew quiet as he threaded his fingers through Mikaela's. "Daniel told me you had a little confrontation with Bennett Sadler the other day. Why didn't you mention it?"

"Because I had just come from meeting with Dr. Chapman, and then you told me about the sterile protocol, and all I wanted was to be with you and think about a happy future."

"Daniel said you put him in his place. Good girl. I'm proud of you. But feel free to walk away from his money if he becomes more trouble than he's worth. I'd find you new investors."

She cupped her hands over his. "I know you would. You're my white knight."

"Please make sure gigolo billionaire Bennett Sadler knows that."

"And you make sure to text me if anything changes while I'm gone."

"Will do."

"I'm going to need something more binding. I think this calls for a pinkie swear."

Mikaela held her pinkie out, and Matt linked his in hers and shook.

"You won't run off with Sadler, and I won't buy a ticket to the morgue."

Mikaela rolled her eyes and headed for the door.

"How's Matt?" asked Daniel as he and Bennett Sadler rose from their corner table to welcome Mikaela. She scanned the room and felt somewhat comforted that most of the customers were casually dressed, but Daniel and Bennett looked as if they'd just stepped out from a board meeting.

Bennett moved behind her, pulled out her chair, and helped scoot her back in close before matter-of-factly taking his seat and replacing his napkin in his lap. Mikaela wondered if the man was giving her a first-class snow job, or whether he'd actually been a gentleman at one time.

"He's,"—she decided against saying anything less than positive about Matt in front of the man whose first instinct was to use Matt's cancer as a marketing ploy—"doing great, thanks. But I don't have a lot of time today. Shall I just dig in?"

Mikaela barely took a breath as she explained the need and benefits of bringing mobile clinics into poorer neighborhoods. She circled the ten areas of greatest need on a map. Each sat outside the D.C. metro area. "Dr. Gorman says he could easily double that list. Each community has a doctor shortage. Accessing health care means taxing bus rides by sick people who spread their illness further. Then they face long waits in clinics or ERs for issues more expeditiously handled with a quick office visit. It's no wonder some people don't even try to seek care. We could relieve so much strain on the system."

As she spoke, Bennett kept his dark eyes fixed on her, drinking in every word. She saw a change come over his face, a softness filled with sympathy and sadness. She didn't understand it, but she believed the project had touched him on a personal level. "Could you serve all these areas with two mobile clinics?" he asked.

Mikaela drew in a deep breath and blew it out with a sigh. "Well, we could reach each area twice a month. We don't yet know how many people we could see in a day and how many we'd have to turn away because of time."

"And people would have to hope they get sick on or near the date the clinic is in their area."

"Yes. It's not perfect, but it's a start."

"And staffing?"

She explained Dr. Gorman's success in getting doctors and nurses to voluntarily staff the units. Then she slid the paper with the cost analysis across the table. Daniel shot her a wink and mouthed the words, "Good job" to her.

Mikaela sipped her fruit smoothie, and waited as Bennett Sadler spent several quiet minutes looking over the proposal. He pulled out his phone's calculator app and worked some numbers. After a few minutes, he wrote another number on Mikaela's cost analysis and slid it back to her.

"This, Mrs. Grayken, is the amount I'm prepared to offer you for this project."

Mikaela felt a chill zip through. Her face prickled, and every hair on her arms and neck stood on end as she gazed upon a number that far exceeded her expectations.

"But I also have another proposal for you. My mother was a doctor who did volunteer work in Central America. She took me with her several times, so I saw what she did to maximize her reach. She used churches as clinics."

"Really?" said Mikaela, who saw new possibilities opening up.

"Each of them was outfitted with basic equipment—tables, chairs, movable walls, and exam tables. The doctors were able to hold clinics weekly, and the mobile clinics, which were outfitted with the diagnostic equipment, came around monthly, but each unit could service many more communities because the primary care was being handled locally."

"Weekly care?" Daniel repeated. "Imagine that, Mikaela."

Bennett continued. "The mobile clinics would provide screenings, mammography, dental exams—those sorts of things."

Mikaela was beyond impressed. She looked at her cost sheet and did some quick math. "But each church clinic would also come at a cost—"

"Less than a third mobile unit," said Bennett, "which I'd be willing to fund if you prefer to stay with your original model of mobile clinics only. But I think that figure I gave you would fund over forty weekly community clinics. Of course, we'd have to have more physician and nurse volunteers and a central place depot from which we could resupply them."

Mikaela posed the next statement carefully. "You said your mother *was* a doctor."

Bennett's chin dropped to his chest. He nodded and returned his attention to Mikaela. "She passed away when I was young. She was also a pilot. We were coming home from one of her medical trips when our private plane went down in a forested area over Costa Rica. The crash wasn't terrible, but a tree limb came in through the windshield and killed her instantly."

"I'm so sorry. How old were you?"

"About eight."

Mikaela muffled a gasp. "I'm sorry. What did you do?"

"Our plane was found quickly, and my father flew down to get me. The business became his life, and I was groomed to take it over when he died, although I've gotten off to a rather rocky start."

Mikaela heard her phone buzz in her purse. She was shocked when she pulled it out and realized how long they'd been talking. "I need to get back to Matt."

Daniel jumped from his seat. "I'll drive you."

"No. I can walk. It's only two blocks." She looked at Bennett. "Thank you for your generous offer and your ideas. I'll take them back to Dr. Gorman and we'll be in touch, if that's all right."

"Perfectly all right." Bennett reached for her hand and held it a moment too long for Mikaela's comfort. "And please give my best to your husband," he added, holding her in his eyes.

She broke away and slipped through the door, glad to put distance between herself and the complex Mr. Bennett Sadler.

MATT'S TEXT had been vague. "Still here, but you might want to get back."

Mikaela rushed down the corridor to the transplant wing and peered in Matt's room while grabbing her gown and mask. A vacuum pump had been rolled in with a handheld wand Mikaela recognized from the chemo unit. It helped patients clear the mucous and saliva from their mouths when they couldn't swallow.

Matt was lying back against the mattress with his eyes closed and the wand in his hand. A nurse stood by his side adjusting two new bags that now hung from his IV pole along with the bags containing his immunosuppressant drugs.

"What's happening?" asked Mikaela. "Is it GvHD?"

"We don't have confirmation on that, but it looks like it. I came in here a while ago, and he was pretty miserable. He has sores in his mouth and throat. We're just trying to make him comfortable with a little morphine drip for the pain and some antibiotics to stave off an infection. He's not able to talk comfortably. He'll be asleep in a few minutes."

Mikaela sat on the edge of his bed and ran her fingers through his sweaty hair. He had clearly been struggling, and she had been away. "I'm sorry I wasn't here."

Matt opened his eyes and waved his wand at her. He suctioned his mouth and muttered, "Don't. Not your fault."

"I do have some good news for you," said the nurse. "Dr. Marcosky deemed you healthy, Mikaela. You're cleared to take off your mask."

Mikaela wanted to cry at the irony. She was well, and Matt was sick. Maybe very sick. Matt slept most of the day, eating nothing but liquid nutrition. Mikaela endured the lonely hours by alternately furthering the plans on the mobile clinic project and scrolling Internet pictures of baby nurseries and compiling a list of wants.

Matt was much better by the morning. His throat was still inflamed, and sores were visible inside his mouth, but having the ability to control his pain through the morphine pump did wonders for his mood. As they'd promised, the DVP group set up poker in Daniel's apartment and sent the live feed to Matt that evening. Kate sat in his seat and held his hand to the camera, but Matt called his own plays to Kate through an earpiece she wore. The diversion lessened the futility of the past few bedridden weeks.

On January fourth, eight days post-transplant, an occupational therapist and physical therapist arrived to help get Matt strong. As weak as he was, barely able to bear his weight after so many bedridden days, his morale was nevertheless boosted by the progress of dressing himself and showering from a chair. Mikaela cheered each step as he used a walker to take short strolls around the suite. Each day, the number of steps increased, until Matt was pronounced able to leave the bed unassisted.

Daily infusions and blood testing continued, and on January eighth, day twelve, Dr. Marcosky came into the room. "I have the results of your most recent blood test."

As well as Matt was doing, those words still left room for bad news, and Mikaela felt her breathing hitch. In a voice filled with practiced optimism, she smiled at Matt, as if expecting great news, and asked, "What does it show?"

The doctor handed Mikaela the report and extended his hand to Matt. "We have engraftment."

"Yes!" shouted Matt while Mikaela pressed the report to her chest and danced in a circle. She grabbed Dr. Marcosky and hugged him, catching him completely off guard.

Matt's next question was the one Mikaela dared not ask. "When can I go home?"

The doctor's mouth slid to the right as he looked at Matt. "You have reason to celebrate, but we still need to be cautious. Your immune system is weak, and your blood counts are climbing but still very low, which means the risks of infection, anemia, and bleeding are elevated. I generally like to keep my patients in the hospital until their numbers are a little higher."

Matt cajoled the doctor with his puppy eyes. "Doctor, I believe I hear a 'but' coming."

The doctor eventually succumbed to Matt's charm offensive. "The protocol requires the continuation of daily infusions and blood draws. Additionally, you must continue the precautions we've outlined . . . but you're very fortunate that your wife is a trained cancer nurse, and you do live very close to the hospital, so it would be possible for you to return daily and get here quickly if anything went wrong."

Mikaela clung to every word.

"Taking all that into consideration . . . if all continues to go well, I'll release you to your home in three days."

Mikaela rushed over to Matt and caught him in an embrace. Tears filled his eyes, and Mikaela couldn't hold back her own.

"I'm going home, Mrs. Grayken. Imagine that. I'm really going home."

THE GOOD NEWS spread quickly throughout the extended family. The Graykens, who had returned to New York, now braved the falling snow and took the train down to stock the cupboards and prepare food, while Kate and Daniel cleaned the house to make it ready and safe for Matt's return. On Friday, January 11th, Mikaela drove her husband home.

The yard was a flurry of activity as the DVP guys shoveled walks and cleaned the gutters so the melting snow could drain. Mikaela crooked her arm and helped Matt to the back door that led to the kitchen. His father waited there to help him up the steps. As soon as the door opened, Matt could smell the enticing aroma of his favorite dish—his mother's bangers and mash. He had never felt more loved.

The Christmas tree that had bolstered his will to fight cancer one more time, still stood aglow in the corner of the living room with all her ornaments shining. Matt took Mikaela's hand and walked to it, fingering the tree and car ornaments the couple exchanged at their hospital chapel wedding a few weeks earlier. He found it hard to swallow past the lump growing in his throat as he asked, "Can I tell you a secret?"

Mikaela bit her trembling upper lip as if she already knew what he was about to say.

"I didn't really think . . . I mean I hoped, but I wasn't sure I'd ever make it back here."

Mikaela wrapped her arms around his shoulders and pressed her face into his collar.

"Mrs. Grayken, please don't ever let me take this gift for granted, no matter how long it lasts. Promise me."

Her head moved silently against his neck.

He pulled away and wrapped his hands behind her head. "We've cried enough these past months. I want to celebrate today."

He called out to Siri, his Internet assistant, asking her to play an Irish jig. In a moment, accordions, flutes, and Irish drums filled every inch of the Graykens' brownstone with happy tunes that led to laughter. Donovan grabbed Mikaela's hand and set her off dancing around the floor. Before Daniel could find Kate, Catherine took hold of him, inviting him for a similar spin.

Still weak and easily fatigued, Matt clapped and whistled until he noticed how Kate hung back from the celebration, keeping herself busy in the kitchen when everyone else was in the living room catching up. Matt checked on her and found her rolling dough on the counter.

"Are you making a pie?"

"A beef pastie," she answered with barely even a glance Matt's way. "For tomorrow night. I made them all the time for—"

She caught herself, and Matt slowly moved to her, opening his arms. "For Hugh? It's okay to talk about him, Kate. I want you to tell me all about him. And I want you to talk about yourself." He looked around the room and said, "You gave me back my life. I'd like to finally hug my sister."

Kate began to shudder. When Matt was mere inches away,

her arms finally opened to receive his embrace. "I didn't want to love you if there was any chance—"

"I know. I know."

"And don't you ever thank me again for giving me back my own brother, agreed?"

"Agreed."

They stood there, crying and laughing, bridging time and claiming new beginnings. Matt saw a suitcase sitting near the door. "What's that?" he asked.

Kate wiped her eyes and laid a hand on her brother's shoulder. "You and Mikaela have been extremely kind to open your house to me as if it were my own, but you need your privacy now."

"We want you here. I want you close by, so we can get to know one another."

"I'm not going far. I have two places in mind."

"Are you and Daniel—"

"No." She was emphatic in her reply. "I admit he's good for a lark, and I enjoy having a younger man's attention, but he's a bit of a dandy whose life has been charmed. I'm six years his senior, and I don't have time to raise a child to be the father of my own."

"I think you underestimate him, Kate. He's a good man. When things looked darkest for me and I needed someone to be there for Mikaela, Daniel's the one I asked. And he's quite taken with you."

"I'll give it a good think, Matt. For now, I plan to take your parents' offer to set me up in a little place for a few months in exchange for me painting an Irish landscape on a wall of their home in New York. I'll be just around the corner."

Matt wondered if loyal Daniel was about to get his heart broken.

Eyes were moist at the dinner table as Donovan offered a

January prayer of Thanksgiving and Catherine Grayken told each person at the table how much she loved them.

Matt and Mikaela watched the last taillight pull away down their street. Mikaela quickly closed the door and wrapped herself up in Matt's arms. "We can't risk you getting a cold. Let's sit by the fire and warm you up."

Matt's minimal brogue had grown thicker since spending time with Kate. In a husky Irish lilt, he said, "That's not how I want to get warm."

"Matt . . ." Mikaela cautioned.

He combed her hair through his fingers. "I know what the doctor said. I'm still an outpatient with a port in his neck. No lifting or strenuous physical activity." He gave her a silly eye roll. "But I at least want to feel my wife beside me again. Really feel you there. Your softness. Your warmth. I want to get tangled up in this wild mop of yours and kiss that lovely neck whenever I choose. You are the medicine I most need, Mrs. Grayken." He lifted her hair and felt her sigh in expectation of the coming kiss. He whispered in her ear, "Would a nurse deny a man the life-affirming treatment he requires?"

Her eyes half closed, and a smile curled the corner of her lip. She slowly unbuttoned his shirt to his chest and placed a kiss in the deep hollow there. A soft moan issued from Matt as Mikaela took his hand and pulled him toward the den they'd converted into a first-floor bedroom to keep things easy for Matt.

"Cuddling only," she warned with a wag of her finger.

"Sounds perfect. Take me home, Mrs. Grayken. Take me home."

CHAPTER SEVEN

Mikaela didn't realize how bone tired and soul weary she'd been until the next morning when, without machines beeping and nurses entering, she slept uninterrupted until seven. Matt was wrapped in the comforter and sleeping soundly when she finally arose and padded past him and to the kitchen. She turned the calendar page to January seventeenth and was about to start breakfast when Matt called to her, begging her to come back and keep him warm.

"Give me a second to get you a fresh glass of water and round up some food."

"I don't need food. All I need is you."

"Not true." The teasing sound of his voice was like joyful music to her ears. "Remember that Dr. Marcosky put me in charge of taking care of you, so prepare to eat."

She grabbed two protein drinks and a bottle of cold water and headed back to bed. Matt extended his arm, signaling for her to rest her head there. As she snuggled close, he rubbed his hand on her belly, laying her hands over his.

"When is your first scheduled appointment with Dr. Chapman?"

"In a few weeks. On the twenty-third."

"Do you think I'd be able to go with you?"

She softened the answer by laying her hand along his cheek. "I'm sorry, buddy. I don't think Dr. Marcosky will clear you by then. Your immune system will still be too weak." She watched the wonder in his eyes dim.

"Then tell me everything again. I want to be a full partner in this."

Mikaela rolled onto her side to face Matt. She decided against arguing the point that he was already fully involved. All that mattered was that he felt removed and distant, and words alone couldn't change that.

"We've talked about our options—IUI, IVF. What else would you like to know?"

"I guess I want to know where the donor dad fits into this? How can I help?"

"You could remind me to take my temperature first thing every morning, before I get out of bed. I chart the numbers on a phone app to figure out when I'm ovulating. Other than that, and taking some fertility meds, I'm just like you, waiting."

He drew circles on her tummy, offering no further questions or response.

"Hey, Baby Daddy," Mikaela teased, hoping to pull Matt from his contemplative mood. "Twenty minutes, and then you need to get up. We're due at the infusion center by nine. We'll whisk you in through their sterile portal. You'll feel like a president, or a rock star."

"Got it."

"Your folks are arriving this afternoon to watch the Giants

game. If you're up to it, I could use your help going over the equipment bids on the clinic project before they arrive."

Mikaela noticed a change in mood as Matt rolled onto his back and focused on the ceiling. "Where do things stand now?"

"Dr. Gorman likes the idea of outfitting the churches as weekly clinic stations."

"Bennett Sadler's idea?"

"Yes. It's a good one. A more compassionate arrangement that provides weekly access to health care to even more communities. We're in strange territory. The committee expected it would be a year or two before we raised enough money to fund one partially equipped mobile unit to start, but Bennett is willing to fund two fully equipped mobile diagnostic units and provide enough funding to outfit each church clinic. Now we're scrambling to catch up. Dr. Gorman and some colleagues have been meeting with a New York company that customizes these mobile units. You just check off the boxes of what you want, and they put it in."

"For a pretty price."

"Which Mr. Sadler already knew and agreed to pay. He said his plan was adapted from a model his mother used. In Central America."

"Sounds like your opinion of Mr. Sadler is changing."

"Let's say I was . . . surprised by his interest in the project and his ideas for improving it."

Matt turned to look at Mikaela. "Such inconsistencies from a man who gouged dying heart patients a few months ago."

The reminder of Bennett Sadler's reason for getting involved in the project sobered Mikaela. "I haven't forgotten that. I just think there's got to be more to it. He's a puzzle. I'm just grateful for his donation."

Matt returned to staring at the ceiling. "So what's next?"

Mikaela laid her hand on Matt's chest. "After you help me run the numbers today"—he rolled close until no space separated them—"I'll prepare the final equipment bids and present them to the committee on Wednesday. If they're approved—and I think they will be—we'll place our order for the mobile units and have a model on site for the big announcement."

"The press conference?"

"Yes. On Monday, the twenty-first, at the D.C. branch of the Providence Cancer Treatment Center."

"Who's presenting? You and Dr. Gorman?"

"Yes. And Daniel."

"And Bennett Sadler?"

"Of course." Mikaela leaned on her elbow to look at Matt. His expression took her back to October's Irish Embassy Ball, when a flirtatious young boor accosted Mikaela within sight of her weakened husband. Matt's inability to protect her left him embarrassed and demoralized. Likewise, Matt neither liked nor trusted Bennett Sadler, or his tabloid-driven reputation. His initial rudeness to Mikaela sealed his fate where Matt was concerned. But Mikaela didn't want to spend their first day home together discussing Bennett Sadler.

"You don't have to worry about Bennett. He's been a perfect gentleman since that first day, Matt, I promise. And even if he weren't, I can handle myself. I don't let people bully me." She jumped off the bed and pulled a comic Ninja warrior move involving a cross kick that nearly terminated a table lamp. "See?" she asked with a laugh as she steadied the wobbling appliance. "Bennett Sadler is no match for a Grayken."

Her husband made a valiant effort at remaining stoic, but Mikaela struck the Warrior Pose from yoga and held it while pasting an ominous sneer on her face, and little by little, her husband's mood softened and his tight lips relaxed into a smile.

"Okay. Let's get past this treatment, and then we'll take a look at your numbers."

She leaned across the bed and stretched to place a kiss on his nose. "Thank you, my brilliant, business-savvy hubby. You'd rather crunch numbers than paint the kitchen, right?"

"One hundred percent."

Matt's infusion treatments went uneventfully for the next week with daily blood draws and more labs. The cell counts slowly increased, and the trend, though slow, was positive, but Mikaela was most encouraged by the changes she saw in Matt. His appetite increased, and his endurance improved until he began video-conferencing with the Great Expectations board about current projects.

As expected, the committee unanimously approved the mobile clinic plan, and Mikaela placed orders for over two million dollars' worth of vehicles, equipment, and furnishings. Her hands shook as she stood beside Bennett Sadler and Dr. Gorman to sign the orders for two fully fitted million-dollar units.

She nearly floated into the house that evening, finding Matt equally animated about his own day's work. "It's official! I just bought two mobile clinics!" She reconsidered the comment. "I spent the committee's money to buy two mobile clinics. And we finally decided on a logo for the project and the buses—The Metro Mercy Project. What do you think?"

Matt pulled a piece of paper from his tableside printer and hugged Mikaela. "Congratulations! I'm so proud of you. I probably haven't told you that often enough." Pride shone from his eyes. "You did it. You really did it."

Mikaela fell into his weak arms and relished the improved strength of his squeeze. "Not me alone. It was you who took the cause to Daniel. Without you, Bennett Sadler never would have known about me or this project. You're my hero."

She felt his arms relax, and he pulled back, his face twisting sheepishly. "No. Bennett Sadler's your hero. He made your dream possible. I'm happy for you." He folded the paper he had previously seemed so excited about. "This calls for a celebration. I've arranged for one of those food-Uber's to bring us dinner."

"Food-Ubers?"

"Yeah. You know. Those drivers who pick up carryout orders from restaurants that don't deliver. I ordered Chicken Marsala from Belini's. I called them as soon as you texted that you were on your way home. It should be here soon."

"I could have stopped."

"I wanted to surprise you. It's your day. I wanted to do something to make it special."

"What else have you planned? I saw the paper you were so excited about. What is it?"

Matt shrugged and handed her the sheet. "I had a conference call with the Great Expectations board today. I presented your other whopper to them."

The rush of activity started by Bennett Sadler's donation had all but obscured her other idea. "The program to grant people's wishes?"

"People's meaningful *requests*."

"Yes, yes, yes! What did they say? What are they planning to do with it?" Mikaela led him to the armchair and guided him to sit while she propped herself on the arm.

"As expected, they loved it. They discussed how to find worthy recipients and how to administer the fulfillment. They asked how involved we wanted to be. I told them I'd speak to you and get back to them."

Mikaela saw the expectation in his eyes. "I don't suppose we can . . ." She stopped when her eyes focused on the port in his neck, reminding her of how far they still had to go with Matt's health. "What do you think we should do?"

Matt took her hands and looked into her eyes. "How do you see your role with the clinic project going forward?"

"I'd love to be hands-on for a while . . . at least until it's running smoothly."

"Then do it. I can shepherd the new program along for the first year, and at the end, we'll evaluate. How's that sound?"

Mikaela slipped backward, into Matt's lap, where he cradled her. "Thank you. If I get pregnant, we'll also reevaluate, but if it doesn't work out . . . if we can't have a child, having this to pour ourselves into will help."

***

MATT'S IMPROVEMENT was so encouraging that Dr. Marcosky changed the lab schedule to blood draws every other day. Buoyed by his progress, he and Mikaela set their sights on two dates circled on the calendar—Monday, January twenty-first, the day of the press conference for the Metro Mercy Project, and January twenty-third, the day Mikaela would meet with Dr. Chapman for her first medical appointment and the first step toward having a child.

Kate drove Matt to his infusion on Monday so Mikaela and Daniel could leave early for the press conference. When the Kate and Matt returned back to his house, he asked Kate, "Would you like to stay for lunch?"

"Oh, Matt . . . I'm sorry. I'd love to, but I'm expected at the press conference today too. Mikaela asked me to paint the logo on the sides of the buses. I need to see the model vehicle so I know what my canvas looks like. How about a rain check?"

"Sure . . . sure." He was the only one not in the clinic's inner circle, and he felt like the last kid picked for volleyball.

Once Kate had him settled in, he made a sandwich and turned on the local news report at noon to catch the story about Mikaela's big day. The audience was peppered with civic leaders and politicos, but his eyes locked on Mikaela, who looked as beautiful and proud as he'd ever seen her. She, Daniel, Dr. Gorman, and a striking taller man stood in front of the sample mobile clinic which was wrapped in a giant red bow. Matt scooted closer to the screen to identify the tall, broad-shouldered man standing by Mikaela. The caption underneath the report identified him as Bennett Sadler, but this clean-cut, suited man bore little resemblance to the scruffy-chic playboy scandalized on the front pages of the business section of the *Times*. If Daniel had orchestrated this Professor Higginsesque transformation, he was a miracle worker, but the longer Matt watched the screen, the more cause he had for believing there was yet another source of the change.

Dr. Gorman put the giant ribbon-cutting scissors into Mikaela's hands, and the next hands on the cutters were Sadler's, as he reached around Mikaela, basically caging her within his arms. Matt passed that odd moment off as awkward and watched on as the news story covered the group conducting tours of the sample clinic. Wherever Mikaela stood, Bennett Sadler was close at hand. When she moved to a group of children, Sadler suddenly had an interest in children as well, and when she pulled back from the camera to give the spotlight to Dr. Gorman, Bennett likewise became camera shy. For Mikaela, the day was all about the project. For Sadler, the day appeared to be all about Matt's wife.

He set the sandwich down, no longer feeling hungry. As the afternoon wore on, his head began to ache. He wasn't surprised.

He was as tight and high-strung as a cello string, and stress headaches hit him frequently. He tried to muster the welcome home Mikaela deserved after her big day, but as soon as she walked into the house, her hand extended to his forehead to check his temperature.

"I'm fine," Matt argued. "I just have a headache." He held his tongue as to the cause. "Come sit down and tell me about your day."

"If you're sure," said Mikaela.

"Completely."

"Oh, Matt." She swooned, her hands coming together prayerlike. "It was so amazing! There's incredible excitement and support for this project. We're going to change a lot of lives."

He hoped the changes the project was bringing to his and Mikaela's lives would be good ones. Instead of saying something thoughtless along those lines, he sucked up his feelings of pity and focused on Mikaela's win.

She had planned for the next day to be a quiet one at home with Matt, but the excitement generated from the previous day's press conference kept the phone ringing and the emails piling up. Matt threw a couple of omelets together for brunch. Mikaela silently thanked him as she rolled her eyes at the incessant barrage of incoming calls. Matt felt his headache intensify until working from the computer was too unpleasant to continue. He turned on the TV, which served as a backdrop of white noise while Mikaela made dinner and took another call. He felt his frustration increase and his mood plummet, further aggravating his headache. By the time dinner was actually served, he had little appetite and went right to bed.

Sleep came easily enough, but Matt felt a pain in his abdomen in the middle of the night, and when he tried to urinate, he moaned, bringing Mikaela to him at a run. His legs went limp from the pain that shot into his groin. Mikaela's face went ashen when she looked in the toilet and saw the dark color of his urine. Her reaction sent fear shooting through Matt.

"What's happening?" Matt asked.

"It might be a small infection."

"Or?"

"It might be GvHD. In either case, we need to get you to the ER," she said calmly as she dressed, placed his mask over his nose and mouth to filter airborne germs, and helped get him to the car.

"Graft vs. Host Disease? Does that mean the transplant is failing?"

"No, no, no." Her rapid, high-pitched delivery made her words sound more worried than reassuring. "They can intervene. Whatever this is, it's treatable."

Matt heard as much fear in her voice as he felt.

A transplant fellow met them in the ER and had labs drawn and run in short order. The diagnosis was a urinary tract infection caused by the common BK virus. While easily remedied in most people, it posed a dormant threat to someone in Matt's fragile state, serving as another reminder that Matt wasn't "most" people, and he knew he might never be a normal person again. Adding to his dilemma, the immunosuppressants the doctors would use to combat the infection were the very drugs Matt was already on. The doctor explained that he couldn't increase those meds further or risk upsetting the delicate balance that allowed Matt's body to tolerate Kate's foreign stem cells. He was in a wait-and-see pattern, and, as feared, he was admitted back into the hospital.

He slept most of the next day and awoke to find Mikaela sleeping in the chair by his side with her Bible lying open across her legs. The day's date was written in big green letters on a white board hung on the wall across from his bed—Wednesday, January twenty-fourth. His heart sank. He couldn't allow his health to take anything else from Mikaela.

He reached an IV-bound hand to her and woke his sleeping wife. She abruptly leaned forward, her eyes darting to the monitor to check his numbers.

"This is no big deal, Mikaela. I'm just hanging out so they can keep an eye on my numbers. No matter what, promise me you'll make it to your appointment with Dr. Chapman."

"I'm not leaving you."

"I'm not in danger. I'm being babysat. Promise me you'll go."

He couldn't muster the clarity or the energy to argue the point further. The cycle of hope and despair, home again/hospitalized again, improvement and loss, frustrated him. He wondered if his life would ever level out or if he would yoyo back and forth from his bed at home to a hospital bed for the rest of his life. It all seemed pointless, futile, and overwhelming, so he surrendered to the malaise and fell asleep.

He searched the room when he awoke and found Mikaela still sitting in her chair, her head bowed. He didn't know if she was crying or praying, and then he looked at the clock. It was five twenty-three, well after her appointment.

He called out to her. She paused for a moment and leaned toward him. She had not been crying, though she had reason to. She had been praying. For him.

"You missed your appointment, didn't you?"

"It doesn't matter. It's just a delay. Not an end."

Her courage broke his pride again and humbled him.

"I'm sorry. I'm so sorry." He turned his head and closed his eyes, offering his own prayer, asking God for strength and courage and enough fight to get through this round.

"How'm I doing?" he asked.

"First, how are you feeling?" she countered.

He debated answering with a joke or replying truthfully. From the look on Mikaela's face, she wanted truthful information she could work with. "On a scale of one to ten where one is let's go dancing and ten is call the hearse? I'm a solid six."

Mikaela's lips pressed tightly. "Okay. Let's work together to get you down to a five by bedtime. Okay, Mr. Grayken?"

He offered her a weak little salute.

"Tell me exactly what you're feeling. Every detail."

Facts. She wants facts, not bravado. "The pain is still there. Sharp and low."

"I'm sorry. That's the bladder infection, but the good news is that the infection is still only in the bladder. It hasn't affected the kidneys."

"And the not-so-good news?"

"Viruses are a tough fight for an immunosuppressed person. Dr. Marcosky feels confident that the situation will resolve itself with a little help. He wants to flush the infection out using an IV, but that could elevate your blood pressure, which would be hard on your liver, so they're going to monitor you closely."

IVs were set up to flush the infection away, and others were hung to provide pain relief. Sometime in the middle of the night, Mikaela placed her hands on either side of his face and called his name to get his attention.

"Matt. Matt. You've got to drink. You need fluid, but the IVs are causing your blood pressure to elevate. Drinking is the solution."

He wasn't thirsty, but he trusted Mikaela completely, so he drank on her command, every fifteen minutes throughout the night, as if she were the drinking equivalent of a rowing captain, cheering him on every sip of the way. He knew she had to be exhausted. He'd slept on and off during the day, but Mikaela was awake when his eyes opened. And awake when he drifted off again.

When Matt awoke about seven, he found her sitting in her chair, leaning forward with her folded arms resting on Matt's bed, serving as her pillow. She was sound asleep.

Dr. Marcosky entered the room and smiled admiringly at Matt's sleeping wife. "The nurses said she refused to sleep until your blood pressure came down to normal."

Matt remembered. "She kept waking me to drink at least a few ounces several times each hour. When I last checked the clock, it was almost three."

"You married a good one."

"Far better than I deserve."

"How are you feeling?"

"Maybe a little better. I still have cramps in my gut."

"I'd like you to remain in the hospital, hydrating one more night so we can continue flushing the infection and monitor that blood pressure a little longer."

In the rush to get to the ER the other night, they had left Matt's phone at home. Mikaela silenced hers once they arrived, but it now began buzzing, waking her.

She blindly slapped and reached for the buzzing phone until her hand finally landed on the device. Squinting, she read the number. "It's Daniel," she said, thrusting the phone Matt's way. She checked the monitor and nodded, and, apparently satisfied with the numbers, she looked at her patient. "Are you okay?" she asked zombielike. When Matt assured her he was, she grabbed her blanket and curled up in the chair, falling back to sleep.

After a brief conversation to assure Daniel, and therefore the entire DVP group, that despite radio silence, he was actually okay, Matt ended the call. Nurses, techs, the dietician, and a young man pushing a library cart passed through the room until both Matt and Mikaela abandoned all hope for further sleep.

Matt's blood pressure remained steady through lunch, but the fatigue that plagued both him and Mikaela made conversation a chore, so they watched a movie until Daniel and Kate came by to check on Matt and to bring Mikaela some clean clothes. After a few minutes spent catching up on Matt's health, the conversation drifted to the clinic project they all shared. All, that is, except for Matt, who felt somewhat like the new kid who hadn't yet earned the right to the club's secret handshake.

Kate carried a valise from which she withdrew her design for the clinic vehicles. After showing the drawings to Mikaela, she turned them for Matt to see. The words *Metro Mercy Project* framed a rainbow-colored heart made from hands. It was simple in design, but easily recognizable, an iconic image people would quickly identify.

"It's really wonderful, Kate." He barely had enough breath to complete the sentence.

"Do you really like it?" she asked, bringing it closer for Matt to examine.

The bright colors made it inviting and warm, but Kate's gift shone through in the small nuances, such as the elaborate lettering, the details in the hands that reflected every race, gender, and age, and the joy the overall design reflected.

"I do. I truly do." He was delighted by how happy his praise made her.

"Bennett is going to love it," added Daniel.

"So . . . you two are on a first name basis now?" Matt took another deep breath to deliver the rest of his message. "I thought you couldn't stand the guy."

Daniel shrugged. "He was a jerk, don't get me wrong, but I

think this project has changed him. He's actually a nice guy. *The Sun* is running an interview with him next Sunday."

"Whoa," said Mikaela. "That could be painful."

"If he answers honestly," Matt tossed out with a side of snark.

"He told them they can ask anything," said Daniel. "I think he wants people to see that he's changed."

Kate glanced Matt's way, and the two made brief eye contact. Matt flushed red at the thought that she caught his jealous scowl.

"Daniel, could you be a love and fetch me a sandwich or something before I faint? I didn't eat breakfast and I'm feeling a bit lightheaded. And Mikaela, take advantage of my baby-brother-sitting service here and feel free to take a shower. I'll just sit here with Matthew for a while and do my best to keep him out of trouble."

Mikaela's hands folded under her chin. "It might be a long one."

"I'm up for it. Take your time."

When Daniel and Mikaela were beyond earshot, Kate looked at Matt and said, "So I take it you don't like Bennett Sadler."

"Let's discuss your artwork."

"You're changing the topic. So I'm right."

Matt pulled his blanket up under his chin and took three slow breaths before offering any rebuttal. "Never met the man. I just object to the way he treats Mikaela. Calling her all the time. Sending her emails day and night. She's not his personal assistant."

"That sounds like the Fitzpatrick coming out in you. We're a hot-blooded lot."

"I like the sound of that . . . knowing you see some of you in me."

"It's not a part to be crowing over." Kate's expression offered him a comical scolding.

"So this is what big sisters do? Admonish and instruct?" His eyes closed as he smiled at her. "If so, I approve."

"Are you all right, Brother? It's as if just talking to me is wearing you out."

"Mikaela and I got very little sleep last night."

"Seems like more than that." She stood and took his hand. "Maybe I should get a nurse."

"I'm just tired." Matt opened his eyes and tried to assure her. "Carry on with your sisterly advice. You were pleading Mr. Sadler's case."

"Ah yes. Bennett Sadler. Does Mikaela also feel he's smothering her?"

"No. She's grateful to him for making this project a reality."

"Then I think all you need is a good dose of gettin' well. Everything's harder and more aggravating when we're tired or sick. Give yourself a few more weeks to get better. Then meet the charming man for yourself. You'll probably come to like him."

Matt changed the subject and sent Kate off on a travelogue of Galway, Ireland, until Daniel and Mikaela returned. He heard bits and pieces of the conversation as the group chatted for another hour, but his focus was on the upset occurring in his stomach. Their voices became a random buzz. Tired. He felt so tired. And warm. A hot-blooded Fitzpatrick. The reference made him happy.

He barely acknowledged Daniel and Kate's exit. The nausea continued. He was thirsty, but he could barely raise his limp arm far enough to reach his cup. His oxygen alarm sounded, and

Mikaela stood and checked the position of the finger scanner, but the alarm continued. Next, she checked the monitor as a nurse arrived.

Matt heard concern in Mikaela's voice as she said, "His oxygen level is down."

The nurse checked his finger scanner, touched his head, and then began asking questions he was too tired to answer.

"Matt? How are you feeling, Matt?" She scanned his forehead, checked his IVs, and then his port. "The shift is changing. I'm going to call Dr. Marcosky."

So many hands and voices. Another cramp hit him in his gut, and he vomited before anyone could grab a basin. He cringed and moaned and felt another cramp hit him. His body felt completely out of control. His chest felt heavy, each breath requiring more effort than he had energy to supply. He looked for his wife as the sense of urgency in the room increased. Then he felt her hand take his.

"I'll be right behind you, Matt. I'll be right there."

And then her hand slipped away as the nurses pushed him from the room and down the hall.

CHAPTER EIGHT

Mikaela wrapped her arms around her midsection and rocked as she watched Matt being connected to oxygen and heart monitors in the ICU. Labs were ordered to determine the cause of his rapid distress.

She had missed the changes. How did she miss them?

Her heart clutched at the terror in Matt's eyes, bringing painful bits of conversation from their first date back to her.

You're good for me. You have a kindness about you that gives me peace. When I die, I'd like to be in my own home, feeling those things. Not fearful in some sterile room. That's just not how I want to go.

Not fearful in some sterile room like this ICU.

She covered her mouth with her hand to muffle her shuddering breaths. Every promise she'd made to him about honoring his wishes had been obliterated when they crossed the line, breaking the contract, moving from friendship to love. He had foreseen the consequences. The pain.

"I am not asking for a full marriage, nor am I looking to fall

in love. I want to avoid that, as much to protect me as to protect you."

"*I don't understand.*"

"*I don't want to grieve for anyone else as I pass, nor do I want to leave someone else grieving for me.*"

As soon as the nurses completed their work, Mikaela moved to Matt's side and sank into a chair.

"I'm sorry, sweetheart. I'm so sorry."

"What? What's happening?" he asked from behind his oxygen mask.

"They're not sure. They're running labs now. We'll know soon."

His face twisted in pain. Mikaela took his hand and squeezed. She felt powerless and inept, babbling on to fill the frightening silence with her voice as guilt pounded her.

More bags were hung from the pole and pain meds were pushed through his port, allowing Matt to sleep. A transplant resident arrived with the lab results and a cart of supplies. The good news was that the infection was in Matt's port and not a reaction from the transplant. The bad news was that the port needed to be removed, even though the BK virus was tenaciously hanging on.

Mikaela stayed in his room whenever possible. Matt's parents caught the next train out of Grand Central Station and arrived to provide additional support. The three tag-teamed to keep Matt company. When Mikaela wasn't in his room, she was in the hospital chapel, the place of their wedding some thirty days before, pounding the doors of heaven for understanding and help.

She found the chapel empty during one of her pilgrimages there. The silence, the echo of her shoes on the wood, amplified her aloneness. She knelt and placed her folded hands on the back of the pew in front of her. Her heavy head pressed upon them as she cried out all the fear and hurt within her.

"Why did You bring Kate here and give us hope and let us dream of a baby and then allow Matt to become so sick? I don't understand," she cried out to the walls. Her head fell back down again. "I don't understand. Please. Please, help me understand."

She argued on with God in silence, ashamed for questioning His love, after all the times He had answered her prayers, and yet so certain of His love that she believed she could ask her questions. A placard listed the names of donors who had paid for the chapel. A verse from the Book of James was written below the names: "But be doers of the word, not hearers only."

The verse spoke to her personally. *Haven't we been doers? Haven't we tried to do good to others? Why give us Kate? Why give us hope? Why let us dream of a child and then let Matt become so sick?*

She repeated the questions again and again, distilling them down to the critical points. Kate. Hope. Baby. Matt. Kate. Hope. Baby. Matt.

She began to see each point as a stepping stone to the next. Kate's arrival gave Matt hope. Matt's hope gave him the courage to dream of having a child with Mikaela. Whatever happened, whether Matt got better or not, there would be a child. Mikaela could have a child. Even if Matt died, Mikaela would not be alone. That was the gift Matt wanted for her. Was that the gift God had intended? Was it never about Matt surviving?

She wasn't ready to accept that. She wanted more. She wanted it all. Her husband *and* a child.

She bowed her head and petitioned heaven again. When she looked up, she saw another placard near a painting of Christ and a woman at a well. The scripture came from Romans 8:28: "And we know that all things work together for good to them that love God . . ."

She read it again. *All things? For good? Not just the happy and positive things? What about the hard things? The sad things? The things that break you?*

Mikaela knew miracles were tricky. The road to them was often long and rough. Most weren't bestowed instantly, like granted fairy wishes. They often came at a high personal cost, a sacrifice of faith. And sometimes, even after down-on-your-knees-pleading, the answer was still a loving but painful no. In those circumstances, the real miracle was the ability to remain faithful and find gratitude in a shattered heart.

Her mind was an exhausted swirl of emotions as she left the chapel to return to the ICU. As she exited the chapel into the hospital's main lobby, she heard someone call her name. Bennett Sadler stood there, dressed like a dandy in a pricey suit and holding a large sack from a local restaurant. His expression looked both excited and wary.

Their first hospital encounter, when he brutishly hijacked her a few weeks ago, returned to Mikaela with stinging clarity. She was in no mood for anyone's intrusion into her private pain, especially this man's. She spun on Bennett. "What are you doing here?"

He backed up a step and held out the bag. "Daniel mentioned you wouldn't be in any committee meetings this week because Matt was back in the hospital. He slipped and also said your in-laws were down to visit. I wanted to help somehow, and I thought . . . food. You still need to eat. It's enough for four people . . . if Matt is up to . . ."

Mikaela kept her hands by her sides, making no effort to receive the offered gift. A teenaged girl wearing a green volunteer's apron approached.

"I wasn't going to come up. I promise. I actually just tipped this very nice young lady to deliver it to the nurses' station." He turned to the girl. "Didn't I, Marla?"

The wide-eyed girl nodded and reached for the bag.

Mikaela noted a slight quiver in Bennett's hand as he suspended the bag between her and the girl in an awkward standoff. Mikaela finally reached for the bag and offered a tightly smiled thank you to the volunteer. "I'll take it." As Marla withdrew, Mikaela glanced quickly at Bennett and offered a terse, "Thank you."

He slipped his hands in and out of his pants' pockets before folding his arms in front. "No thanks needed. I'm in your debt."

Mikaela considered the comment against the fat check he had recently written. She didn't want a debate. With a tip of her chin she said, "Thank you," again and turned to go.

"I know you don't like me. I deserve that, but please know that I'm at your disposal if I can do anything to help."

She turned back around, making no effort to disguise her skepticism. "Why? Why are you so interested in us?"

Bennett's feet shuffled, and he looked at the tiled floor as if expecting to find the needed answer there. "Because . . . I . . . admire you. Both of you. I hope to become the kind of people you are."

The muscles of Mikaela's face turned to dough, slowly deflating as her eyes began to burn. She tried to speak, but the lump in her throat blocked all sound.

"I don't profess to know you or to understand your relationship, but what I do see is loyalty and love. It extends beyond your marriage to others . . . Daniel, Kate, Dr. Gorman." Bennett smiled and leaned closer. "You do know that Dr. Gorman loves you a lot more than most doctors love colleagues, don't you?"

Mikaela smiled and nodded while trapping an escaping tear.

"He says I'm the daughter that he and the wife he never married never had."

Bennett arched his neck back and laughed. "That makes sense."

Mikaela noted how his laughter and his joke had lightened her heavy heart. She contrasted his efforts at friendship with her treatment of the man. "I apologize if I've been rude to you."

He shook his head. "No . . . no. You've always been gracious and honest."

"And for the record, I don't dislike you. I don't understand you and your choices. But that's none of my business. You offered your help, and I accepted it. You've honored your part of the agreement, and for that I'm grateful."

He grimaced and dipped his head. "See? Always gracious."

"What do you want from me, Bennett? I'm kind of an empty well right now."

"I don't want anything from you, least of all your gratitude. You're doing me the favor." He rubbed his mouth in thought. "I take that back. I would like something from you—your respect."

"Why? I'm no one important."

"You're respected by so many, therefore, your opinion of me matters. I really do want to change or, rather, change back to who I once was. I've made foolish choices, but I hope mistakes don't have to define us forever. I'll know soon enough, I suppose. You've probably heard that I'm being interviewed." His hand swept across an invisible marquee in the sky. "*Bad Boy Billionaire. The Good, the Bad, and the Ugly.*" He chuckled sadly.

"I'll be sure to pick up a copy of *The Sun* that day."

"Sure. But when you have a minute, I'd like to explain my choices to you personally. I won't excuse them, but I'd like you to hear the whole truth . . . from me."

She felt the weight of his expectations press down upon her

already burdened shoulders. "Bennett . . . I . . . I really need to go now."

"Of course."

She lifted the bag. "Thank you for the food. It was very thoughtful."

"Happy to do it. Goodbye, Mikaela."

Before she could respond, Bennett Sadler was five long paces away and hurrying for the door. She didn't know what he wanted from her, but it didn't matter. Everything that mattered to her was still waiting in the ICU.

Three days crawled by. The broad-spectrum antibiotic brought Matt's fever down. His blood pressure stabilized, but the bladder cramping, the pain, and the shortness of breath continued. Even so, the progress was enough to warrant a return to a normal room.

The nurses supplied him with a nasal canula during the day so he could have oxygen support and still converse, but positive conversational topics became difficult to find. Any talk of projects or work seemed to cause Matt stress, and he moved into sobered silence when the topic centered on anything in the future. Stories from the past grew thin after two days, and so the television became the default entertainment.

On the afternoon of the fourth day of his hospitalization, Matt awoke from a nap and said he was hungry in a strong clear voice. Mikaela cheered the news. The scanty meal was eaten, and it stayed down. Encouraged by that development, the shift's nurse, a man named Jesse, asked Matt if he would like to get out of bed and take a short walk. Matt agreed happily. Jesse strapped a gait belt around Matt's waist to provide additional support when he walked. After sitting at the side of the bed to check for dizziness, he stood, leaning on a walker while Jesse and another nurse each held on to one of the straps of the belt. After a steady stationary minute, they allowed him to walk around the room with their support. That small effort exhausted Matt, but the positive change in his attitude was evident. After an hour's rest, he called the nurse and asked to try again. This time, he took a short stroll up and down the hall with nurses by his sides and Mikaela, cheering from behind. He returned to bed slightly winded and chilled, and wearing an ear-to-ear smile.

"That's a good sign, right?"

Mikaela clapped her hands. "A very good sign. You're shaking. Are you tired or cold?"

"A little of each," he said, rubbing his arms. He also opened and closed his hands a few times, noting the tightness in his fingers. "And I feel a little puffy."

Mikaela checked the monitor, and his temp was normal. "I'll mention the puffiness to the nurses. And I think it's time to pull out the knitted cap to keep you warm. What do you say?"

Matt rubbed his head. "That hat was an admission that I'm almost bald." Sorrow tugged at the corners of his eyes and mouth. "I really didn't want to lose my hair."

Mikaela sat on the edge of his bed and held his hand. "I know, buddy. I would have been crying weeks ago, at the first sign of my scalp peeking through. You've been a champ, and I'm so proud of you, but I definitely think you need the hat for health reasons."

He raised the mirror on his overbed table and stared into it, fingering the few remaining patches of hair. "I look ridiculous. Scraggly hair, barely any eyebrows. Who am I trying to kid?"

Mikaela braced for another wave of depression.

Matt closed the mirror and pushed the table away. "I stood on my own. I walked around the hall. I'm channeling my inner Dwayne Johnson. I think it's time to go shiny."

Mikaela's heart cheered the decision and was cheered by his humor. "Are you sure?"

"Not completely, so we'd better go with my spontaneous decision. And act fast before I lose the action-hero courage."

"Got it!"

Mikaela headed to the nurses' station and inquired about a shaver. Within a few minutes, one was found and sent up. Mikaela plugged it in and turned it on, assuming a Statue of Liberty-like pose. "Speak now or forever—"

"Do it."

Within minutes, the shaver was off, and Matt and Mikaela observed his new look. She sat on the edge of the bed and rubbed some lotion on his pale head. "You were blessed with a good, round noggin. I have to say, you look rather sexy, Mr. Grayken."

"Thank you, ma'am. Thank you very much."

Matt was back in the fight again. Was she? The question startled her. She excused herself from the room on the pretense of returning the shaver, but she took a detour to the empty family lounge, closed the door, and sat. She thought about their dream of a baby, a dream that had been delayed because she missed her appointment with Dr. Chapman. Had she made a new appointment? No. Because she was reacting to everything happening to Matt.

They had fallen into a pattern of being reactive instead of proactive. When they had a hard blow, they went down, with nothing to inspire the next rally. She bowed her head and prayed silently for help, for strength, for answers. Then she thought back to the verse she'd seen in the chapel a few days earlier—"Be ye doers of the word." *Be a doer. . .* She looked at the calendar. Friday, February first. Day forty-two post-transplant. Eight days past her gynecological appointment when a day or two could mean a month's delay because of ovulations cycles. Mikaela was now on a mission.

She hurried back to Matt's room, picked up her phone, and dialed Dr. Chapman's office. Before the receptionist answered, Mikaela was determined to get on next week's schedule. After introducing herself, she briefly explained about her missed appointment and asked for a spot the following week. When she was told that was impossible because they were booked over a month out, Mikaela pressed on.

"Do you have a cancellation list? Great. Put me on that. And I'd like to speak with Dr. Chapman herself, please. I'll hold."

When the receptionist explained that it could be Monday before the doctor even returned her call, Mikaela asked, "What time does Dr. Chapman leave the office?" When the nurse stammered that it could be four or five or later depending on how the day went, Mikaela replied, "I'll stay on hold until midnight if that's what it takes to speak to Dr. Chapman today."

The receptionist disconnected the call. Mikaela called back.

Matt opened his eyes and sat up in the bed. "What are you doing?" he asked with his face twisted in what appeared to be doubt of her sanity.

"Trying to have our baby. Shhh." She pressed her finger to her lips to focus on the call.

"Hello. Yes, this is Mrs. Grayken again. Is Dr. Chapman available now?" She tried not to flinch at the anger level rolling from the phone. In response to her thorough chastening, she remained calm and repeated her willingness to be placed on hold, at which the woman groaned and called for the office manager.

A few moments later, a new voice came on the phone. "Ma'am, is this an emergency?"

"It is to us."

"Then I suggest you head to the ER."

"Let me explain," Mikaela said with increased urgency. "I'm not crazy or an anarchist, and I don't want to be a nuisance, but I need to get rescheduled next week. It's not a matter of life and death, but it's a matter of peace and hope, two highly undervalued principles, which you have the power to restore to me and my very sick husband. Can you help us?"

There was no immediate reply, but Mikaela could hear the woman breathing, and she also heard the click of computer keys, signaling either a willingness to help or an effort to delete Mikaela completely from the system. After a few tense moments, the woman returned to the conversation.

"Mrs. Grayken, Dr. Chapman has a conference on the morning of the eleventh. She should return to the office around one, but we've left her schedule open until one thirty in case of traffic. If you're here at one, and I mean not a minute later, we'll find a way to squeeze you in."

"Thank you! Thank you!" She ended the call, stood, and did a little happy dance. More importantly, she saw Matt lean forward.

"What did she say?"

"The eleventh! It's not as soon as I'd hoped, but it's within the next cycle. It means we might be able to start in April instead of May!"

A smile graced his lips. "I thought you'd lost it. Completely lost it."

"I'm tired of reacting. I'm going to be a Grayken warrior. How about you?"

He held a puffy hand up. "Come with our A Game every day?"

"Yes. Just like we promised." She halted. "Oh, no. You're retaining fluid."

He flexed his hand. "Get a nurse in here, but don't panic. We'll deal with it. Don't forget that we're Team Grayken. We can do hard things."

"Because we're not alone in this, Matt. We just need to remember all the times and all the ways our prayers have been answered, like that call just then. We got bumped up four weeks sooner than I expected!"

"Because you were a crazy lady."

"What if it's because I prayed, and He inspired me to press our case?"

Matt didn't answer but he laid his hand against her cheek, and she covered it with her own.

"The other day, when I was in the chapel, I realized that most of the challenges we saw as roadblocks were actually stepping stones. I think God is leading us, but when our circumstances get hard, we don't understand, so we feel like we're being punished or tested, and we end up fighting Him. Let's lean in to Him. Let's trust Him and see where He wants us to go."

"I am praying, Mikaela. The best I know how."

"Let's combine our efforts." Mikaela cupped both of Matt's hands within hers, prayerlike, and felt a tingle radiate up her spine.

Matt noticed it too. "Praying together . . . It's very . . ."

"It's soul to soul. Maybe it's as much about Him helping us reach each other as it is about us reaching Him."

"I like that. I think we need it."

"Me too."

Over the next seven days, Matt and Mikaela started and ended each day by praying together. The effort buoyed him to work harder to walk a little each day and participate in physical therapy despite the discomfort of the fluid retention. Progress was slow and minor, but the water weight steadily decreased.

On what they hoped was his last day in the hospital, Dr. Marcosky ordered an endoscopy to take tissue samples to be biopsied. He suspected that Graft versus Host Disease might be the cause of Matt's setbacks. He assured Matt that the presence of the disease itself would not be alarming as long as the numbers were within a certain range. With that caution, Matt prepared to go home.

Over half of Mikaela's weekly video chats with her family had been missed since the transplant, their contact being reduced to group chats, individual calls, and photos sent across the globe. On the day of Matt's release, she sent a quick video of him posing for the camera with his bald head and scrawny but IV-free arms. Then she called chauffeurs Daniel and Kate when the release papers were signed.

Mikaela held fast to Matt's hand on the short ride home, noting a curious eye exchange going on between Daniel and Matt via the rearview mirror. When they pulled into the garage and walked into the house, the reason became clear. A large "Welcome Home, Matt" banner had been strung along the back of the house, earning a look of surprise from Matt and a swoon from Mikaela.

"I guess that was my welcome-home gift. But look! There's one for you too."

Mikaela followed his finger point to the backyard fence which was lined with tiered planter boxes, filled with soil and ready for spring seedlings. Mikaela's hand flew to her mouth over the surprise, and then she saw more gifts: two large cold frames for starting seeds.

She turned to Matt in shock and saw that he was impressed but not surprised. "You did this? I mean you made this happen?"

"Some people who love us asked what they could do to help.

I sent them a copy of my honey-do list." He spread his arms. "This is the result."

"But who? The DVP guys?"

Matt grimaced and pointed to the house. "Let's get inside. I need to sit."

Mikaela helped him get into the house and found another surprise awaiting her. The kitchen had been painted in the buttery yellow she'd chosen, and the delicate lace curtains she'd found on a website now adorned her kitchen windows. She wrapped her arms around Matt and kissed him. "Thank you for doing this. I love it."

"Don't tell me. Tell the workers."

Again, Mikaela followed Matt's pointing finger, this time to the staircase where not one, but three of her military brothers were standing, waiting to yell "Surprise!"

Mikaela shook with excitement and started to cry as she rushed toward Thomas, James, and Abe. "How is this possible? When did you get in?"

"We've been texting with Matt," said Thomas. "It was easy for me since I'm stateside now."

James caught Mikaela up in a long hug. "As soon as Matt told us his go-home date, Abe and I started applying for leave."

Abe leaned close and whispered in her ear, "We've been praying for you both, Mickie."

"Thank you. I love you all so much." She wiped at her eyes and grabbed Matt's hand. "Matt, these handsome soldiers with whom you've been texting and video-chatting are some of my wonderful, crazy brothers—Thomas, James, and Abe."

The room was filled with loud chatter as Daniel and Kate, who were also involved in the surprise, joined the homecoming. Kate set out food she'd already prepared, and Daniel carried the couple's things in from the car.

The group settled around the kitchen table as Mikaela surveyed the newly painted kitchen. "I just love this color. It reminds me of—"

"—home," chimed Thomas, James, and Abe.

"We thought about that the whole time we were painting. We even sent a picture of the finished room to the rest of the Compton clan," said Abe. "I think we made George cry."

Thomas chimed in. "He and John would much rather be here than in theater, but their COs just didn't think painting your kitchen ranked as a family emergency. Frank couldn't leave Amy this close to her due date, and Dwight couldn't get leave."

"I understand," said Mikaela. "I love them just for thinking about coming."

"Speaking of home . . ." Thomas pulled a crumpled envelope from his pocket. "Kristen gathered seeds from the marigolds that lined Mom and Dad's sidewalk. She's been planting from them ever since, and last fall, she saved these for you. Now you have starter seeds for spring."

"A piece of home," Mikaela muttered as she blinked back tears. "Thank you so much, Thomas. Tell Kristen this was the greatest gift she could have sent."

Abe sat back and studied his baby sister. "You look good, Mickie. Marriage agrees with you."

Mikaela glanced at Matt. "I got a good one."

"Yes, you did," agreed James. "He's been staying in touch with us. He felt you could use some love from your big brothers." James sent her a wink.

Her eyes welled with happy tears. "I can't tell you how much this means to me . . . to us. I need to call Nancy and Sarah and thank them for letting me have you. How long can you stay?"

"We're only here for three more days, Mickie."

"Three *more*?"

"We've already been here for two days building the boxes and frames. We barely finished the painting an hour ago, so don't lean against a wall." Abe laughed and slung an arm across his sister's shoulders.

The next two days sped by. Matt spent some portion of each one in the hospital for infusions and tests, but the remainder of the time was filled with raucous stories, more handyman work, and many games of poker. On their last night together, Matt threw out a suggestion that nearly floored Mikaela. "Why don't we all try to be together for Thanksgiving this year? Do you think everyone could make it?"

"We're so scattered," said Thomas.

"And the expense of moving our families on military pay?" Abe winced.

"It would be our treat. Mine and Mikaela's."

"No, no, no," said James. "That's too much. It would cost a fortune."

Matt grew animated. "Guys, this is what I do for a living. I make special moments happen for people. Let me make one for our family. All our family," he repeated, as he looked at Kate and Daniel.

"I'm game," said Abe. "I think the rest of the clan would be too, if they can get away. When was the last time we were all together?"

"Probably at Dad's funeral," said James.

"We'll poll the family and have them start making plans," said Thomas. "Thanks for the offer, you two. Matt, it makes me doubly glad George didn't take you out last trip."

Matt chuckled at the joke, and Mikaela moved beside him to whisper, "Thank you for doing this."

Sunday, the tenth of February, was a special day for Mikaela, as she and her brothers attended church together for the first time in several years. Thomas held one of her hands, and James took the other as they prayed and sang together, strengthening her for whatever fight lay ahead.

Mikaela drove her brothers, one by one, to the airport or to Andrews Air Force Base for flights back to their places of deployment. When she arrived home, the house was quiet, and empty except for Matt, who was sleeping on the sofa, lying on his side with his back pressed tight into the upholstery. She grabbed a quilt, tucked it around her tired hubby and slipped into the sliver of space that remained. Matt's arm instinctively wrapped over her, cradling her in place.

"Do you know what tomorrow is?" she asked.

"You bet I do," he whispered in her ear. "It's Monday Night Football."

She gave him a gentle punch. "It's my appointment with Dr. Chapman."

"I know. One o'clock, not a minute late." Matt kissed her head. "I was just kidding."

"You're a horrible tease."

"I'll try to improve before the baby arrives."

"Mmm. . ." cooed Mikaela. "I like the sound of that."

"The part about me trying to change or the part about the baby arriving."

"Both. It's a twofer, Mr. Grayken. You can't take either part back now."

"Not a chance, Mrs. Grayken. Anything for you."

Mikaela reached for Matt's hand which seemed more swollen than it had been earlier. "How are you feeling?"

"Glad to be home."

She sat up and laid a hand on his forehead. Relief flooded over her when she found no sign of fever. "I'm glad to have you home too, but how are you feeling?"

He shrugged. "A little tired."

"And? Your voice sounds raspy."

"My throat's a little sore and I have a cramp in my stomach."

"Anything else?"

"It's your turn to say the prayer."

Mikaela prayed with Matt, and then laid back down and prayed silently about what his biopsies would reveal.

CHAPTER NINE

The morning dawned with a bright beam of sunshine blazing through the opening between the curtains. Matt hadn't slept well, and the taunting sun easily lured him to a window for a glimpse of the morning's beauty. His throat was still sore, and his stomach ached, but the sun's warmth bathed his face in light and heat. He checked his phone for the temperature. A high of forty-four was expected. Matt longed to slide into some sweats and go for a run. He killed the thought immediately. It was ridiculous on so many levels. He barely had the stamina to reach the bathroom and return.

Joggers were already out running, some sipping lattes, some in twosomes with their dogs or partners. Cars filled with well-dressed people took their place in the traffic that led to D.C. and the surrounding suburbs, where deals would be made, laws would be crafted, and empires would be built. Life was happening in those cars, and it was jogging down those streets. He grabbed his arms and noted how thin and loose they now were. Bald head, bony arms, distended belly from whatever was happening in there. He wasn't sure what to call his situation. It wasn't living. Not really. Yes, he would get on his computer and conference in with the people from work, but he wouldn't feel the energy they felt or enjoy the sense of satisfaction they'd leave with at the end of the day. He wasn't essential anymore. He was an addendum.

Except to Mikaela.

He gazed at her as she slept. She was beautiful, even asleep, without adornment of any kind. She still made him feel as if he was everything, even though he feared to touch her as a husband should and take the chance of raising emotions in her or himself that he couldn't satisfy. So they cuddled like best friends and dreamed of better days.

Better days . . .

He checked his phone's calendar, February eleventh. He remembered Mikaela's appointment. Today was her big day. The first appointment and the beginning of their parenthood journey. He wanted to make this special for her, but how?

He left the bedroom and moved into the living room to rummage through the drawers and cupboards for some ideas. He remembered the day his round of chemo treatments ended last fall. It was before he and Mikaela crossed the line from friendship to love. Even then, when he was certain he was an emptying hourglass, when she was technically just his nurse and companion, she arranged little surprises to make every day meaningful. On that day, she arranged things so Matt opened the bedroom door in the morning and walked straight into a bouquet of five helium balloons. He remembered marveling over how she'd pulled that surprise off. She explained that she'd purchased a little helium tank at the party store.

What else did she say?

"Everything is better with balloons."

He needed balloons.

He checked the few places downstairs where a little helium tank could be stored—the hall closet, the garage, the study-turned-bedroom closet, and it was nowhere to be found. Exhausted and breathless, Matt looked at the enemy staircase and knew it stood between him and that blasted tank. Grabbing the banister, he leaned over to rest, and tackled the first step, then another and onward until he reached the top, nearly collapsing on the floor. After a few minutes' rest, he stood and searched the actual master bedroom he had given to Mikaela after their courthouse wedding. It was the first time he'd been upstairs since that night, when he showed Mikaela to her room, a floor apart from where he slept.

He sat on the bed and studied the décor. The master was spacious and sunny, with an elegance that elicited a feeling of welcome and romance. The contractor he hired to transform the space for Mikaela's use followed his instructions to perfection. The soft gray paint with yellow trim was sophisticated and yet welcoming, unlike the modified study where they now slept.

He walked to the en suite bathroom Mikaela still used because she loved the Jacuzzi tub and the jetted shower. The space smelled like her—musky cologne and lotions, and citrus shampoos. Three candles in glass holders sat on the edge of the tub. He imagined her there, long and lean and beautiful, soaking out her stress and worry alone.

A cologne bottle sat on an open shelf. He picked it up, closed his eyes, and breathed Mikaela in, and for a moment, he was himself, a man in love, with a beautiful wife. Each waft of the earthy scent filled him, replacing weak muscles with imagined vitality. Replacing fatigue with hope and want. And then he caught a glimpse of himself in the mirror, shattering the moment and returning him to reality. He set the bottle down and surrendered to another wave of regret and self-castigation for time he squandered. For allowing his pride and fear to keep Mikaela and him apart when his body was strong and he was handsome, or at least more handsome than the man he'd become.

His thoughts returned to Mikaela and to the task at hand. He closed the en suite's door and forced his heavy feet and legs toward the closet, where he found the box containing the helium tank. It was barely more than five pounds and eighteen inches square, but to Matt, who was already wondering how he was going to get himself back down the stairs, the added burden of the tank seemed almost insurmountable.

He considered abandoning the idea altogether and settling for making Mikaela a cup of hot cocoa instead, but he was tired of substitutions and almosts. He wanted to give Mikaela a moment. A lump of frustration grew in his throat. After all that had been lost to him, all he might never do or see or be, he wanted this stupid, meager victory, and he wanted it deeply, desperately. He felt hot tears on his face as he lifted his eyes to the ceiling and beyond and cried.

"Please, God. Please," was all he said to heaven, and then he got an idea. He wriggled the box beyond the closet door and pushed it with his foot until he reached the stairs. Fully spent, he slid his back down the post until he was seated on the top step, and then cradling the box in his arms, he slid down each step on his bottom until he reached the floor. Too tired to stand, he pulled five balloons and five lengths of ribbon from the box and filled the balloons as he sat on the step. Enthusiasm fueled him back to his feet as he searched for and found the perfect location to tether the balloons for maximum surprise. Pleased with his victory, he closed his eyes and said, "Thank you."

The sweetness and satisfaction of that victory spurred him on beyond the nausea and the cramp in his belly. He revisited the hot chocolate idea and made Mikaela a cup, and for added pizzazz, he stirred it with a leftover candy cane, sloshing some on the counter. As his puffy shaking hands pulled a paper towel from the roll, he envisioned a banner where each towel square hosted a single letter. Thirty paper towels never looked lovelier as Matt ran a strip of packing tape across the entire twenty-foot-long message, which he strung across the living room wall. The effort left him sweat soaked and shaky, so he fell onto a stool to observe what an hour of work and a serious amount of perspiration had created.

His phone dinged, signaling an email. With a groan and a grunt, he left the comfort of the stool to grab it from the counter, dreading the effort the moment he saw the tagline—"Your lab results are available in your Patient Portal."

If the news was good, it could wait, but considering the crummy way he felt, Matt saw little cause for optimism, and bad news could definitely wait. The only thing over which he had any control at this point was making this moment special for Mikaela.

His labors were soon rewarded. She awoke and called for Matt. When he didn't answer, she threw open the door and called his name again, responding with an excited gasp as the balloon bouquet caught her eye.

In a voice filled with wonder and delight, she called out, "You did this? For me?"

Her response filled him with so much pleasure that no effort was required to grin like a kid with his first crush. "You once told me that everything is better with balloons . . . so . . . Voila!" Next, he pointed to the banner that read, "Happy Step One, Momma Grayken!"

Mikaela started to slide into his lap and then glanced at the port still protruding from Matt's neck. She paused and slipped to her knees in front of Matt's chair instead, laying her head in his lap. "Thank you," she said, adding, "I love you so much."

Matt folded over her and whispered, "This is a big day. It deserved to be marked."

"It's just an appointment . . . but it's a beginning."

"Beginnings are important."

Mikaela sat up and wrapped her arms around Matt, looking at him eye to eye. She smiled with forced optimism. "Your biopsy results could come in today. How did you sleep? You were up early."

Matt didn't tell her he'd had a rough night. "I couldn't resist seeing that sunrise today. It was beautiful. And I had to put my plan into action."

"I loved your plan. How about some breakfast? Could you eat a little something? Some eggs maybe?"

Matt swallowed to test the soreness of his throat and determined that eggs were about all the texture he could handle, while the thought of eggs actually added to the unsettledness of his stomach. He conversed more than ate, strategically moving the eggs around his plate to camouflage how little was actually disappearing. All he wanted was to have this one morning be about life and hope, devoid of concerns about him or cancer. He wanted it to be about Mikaela.

After breakfast, he showered while Mikaela cleaned the kitchen, and when she went upstairs to bathe, he found an innumerable assortment of tasks and Internet searches to help him avoid the Patient Portal.

Around noon, she emerged, dressed in her favorite outfit—a billowing broomstick skirt and a crocheted sweater with lace, her face aglow with expectation.

"You look radiant," said Matt, barely able to pull his eyes from her to grab his phone. "Let me take your picture." The fact that she offered no protest was assurance that marking this day was as monumentally important to her as it was to him.

She walked to him and wrapped her arms around his neck. "I'll wheel you to your infusion and then I'll head to my appointment. I'll call you during the consult."

He questioned whether he had heard her correctly. "What? Wait. I was planning on coming to your consult. I'll already be in the hospital."

"In a germ-controlled area. I don't think Dr. Marcosky wants you out and about in such a potentially germ-filled public place like the physician's building."

He felt the door closing on him again. "I could wear a mask. At least let me run it past the transplant team."

"All right. We'll ask the nurses in the infusion suite."

Matt bit his knuckle and stared out the window on the ride to the hospital, preparing his argument for the transplant staff, but it was as Mikaela said. A big no.

Mikaela knelt by his wheelchair and laid a hand on his shoulder. "I know you're disappointed, but we're so close now, Matt. You're doing so well. Let's be patient a little longer. Today is just my physical exam. We have lots of time to get you well before there are baby heartbeats and sonograms to share."

The rightness of Mikaela's counsel didn't lessen its sting, but Matt nodded his understanding.

"I'll conference you in for the consultation."

"I'll be waiting."

She kissed him soft and long. "I love you. Mr. Grayken."

"You too. With all my heart, Mrs. Grayken."

As soon as she walked away, Matt rolled up to the nurse's desk and asked for the results of the biopsies. She told him Dr. Marcosky would be in to explain, and Matt braced for the news. The results were a mixed bag. The bad news was, he had

GvHD. Stage one in some areas and stage two in his stomach. It explained so many of his symptoms. The good news was, Dr. Marcosky didn't seem too concerned. He helped Matt focus on the positives. GvHD meant the transplanted stem cells were fully grafted, and he believed Matt's puny, inadequate immune system could get things in balance without another hospitalization. That news cheered him, despite the incessant discomfort in his gut.

Dr. Marcosky asked about other symptoms. Encouraged by the doctor's previous optimism, Matt checked off a short list of his most annoying concerns.

"My left arm is still swollen."

"I see the swelling in your hand." Dr. Marcosky had him remove his shirt. "I think we need to get an ultrasound of that arm."

"What's the worst case scenario?" Matt had come to expect that the option with this label was generally the one that applied to him. Fortunately, the fix was fairly simple. In addition to his daily infusion, two injections of blood thinner were added to his daily regimen. The infusions drained him physically, while living in a constant state of weakness and isolation from life drained him emotionally and spiritually. He thought of Mikaela and the significance of her appointment. With a quick silent prayer of gratitude, he rallied for Mikaela and vowed to be her brave warrior.

MIKAELA SLIPPED up the street from the hospital and grabbed two dozen donuts for Dr. Chapman's staff to ease any residual frustration they held for her over the way she barged into the day's appointment schedule. The raised-eyebrow stares the receptionist gave her softened at the first whiff of Krispy Kreme.

As promised, the wait was brief. Within minutes of arriving, Mikaela was taken to an examination room to prepare for the doctor's arrival. Moments later, the doctor knocked on the door. After the examination, Mikaela was sent to Dr. Chapman's office for the consultation. As promised, she conferenced Matt in.

"I'd like to plan for IUI or intrauterine insemination first, assuming all the tests prove that Mikaela is healthy and we have no indication that she has any fertility issues." She handed Mikaela a folder filled with lab slips, a list of supplies, and information on tracking ovulation and basal body temps. "It's the simplest plan, and it doesn't increase the chance of multiples the way in vitro does." She went over each page and then asked, "Any questions?"

Mikaela dropped about a baker's dozen in quick succession, and when they were all answered, Dr. Chapman handed her a folder filled with a prescription for vitamins, a lab slip for an ultrasound exam, the name of the doctor's preferred ovulation monitor, and a link to an app to chart Mikaela's basal body temperature. Having done that, she left her office to give the couple time to process what lay head.

Just holding the folder made it all seem real, that her dreams of a child were more than wishes and maybes. They were possible and probable. She kissed Matt's image on the phone. "This is it. The real beginning!"

"Now our homework begins," said Matt.

"Isn't it exciting?"

"The best news imaginable. And it's a dream we can actually work toward."

"We should celebrate tonight. What if we pick up some crab cakes for dinner?"

His eyes wriggled with interest, and then he shook his head. "Tempting . . . but don't bother. That's out of our way."

"I'll go anywhere for you or your crab cakes, Mr. Grayken."

A single chuckle escaped, and then his mouth twisted with emotion. "You've already proven that, Mrs. Grayken. Dozens of times."

Mikaela wiped at the moistness welling in her eyes. She felt an urgent need to get to him, right away, and she told him, "I'm coming for you. Are you ready?"

"I'm all signed out."

"Good, because all I want is to be home right now . . . with you."

On the ride home, she asked, "Did you get the biopsy reports?"

"I did."

"And?"

"I'm a blue-ribbon winner, with Graft vs. Host in my gut, and a blood clot in my armpit."

The news didn't shock Mikaela, but she hurt for Matt, nonetheless. "Let's stop by the pharmacy. I need a few items, and I want to pick up some things to help you. We've got this, okay?"

"Whatever you say."

She held on to her OB/GYN papers as if they were a talisman as she walked through the aisles of the store collecting the needed items. A healthy husband and a healthy baby. She wanted both.

MIKAELA PERSISTED in her hopeful nagging until Matt downed

thirty grams of peach-flavored protein. Then they spent an hour discussing her appointment and the regimen of charts and numbers they needed to keep.

"Where *is* the chart?" asked Matt.

"It's an app on my phone. We just plug the numbers in."

"I thought it would be a real chart we can see."

Mikaela brushed the comment aside as she pureed fruit and poured it into ice cube trays to make nourishing, throat-soothing popsicles for Matt. Noting the dark circles under his eyes, she sent him to the living room to warm himself by the fire while she cleaned the kitchen. Once done, she found him hunched over his laptop typing into the search bar.

"What are you doing?"

"Nothing," he said, but his wide-eyed false innocence and the urgency with which he closed the lid screamed that he was guilty of some nefarious activity. Mikaela enjoyed the game and played along, gently pushing the culprit back against the sofa so she could lie down and place her head in his lap. "Good," said Mikaela as she asked their electronic home assistant to play an album from their playlist. "Then you won't mind if I use you as my pillow."

"Not at all," Matt replied. "I welcome it."

"We start charting everything tomorrow. Are you ready, coach?"

Matt pulled a pen from his pocket. "Locked and loaded."

"Excellent, except all you need is a finger capable of typing on my phone."

Matt set his pen on the end table and raised his digit as proof that it was at the ready. For the next little while, Matt traced his typing finger along Mikaela's jawline as they stared into the fire and listened to soft jazz. At some point, Mikaela felt the hypnotic motion stop, replaced by ragged snoring and a rumbling she could hear through his belly. She sat up and gently awoke Matt to give him his evening meds and help him into bed. She soon regretted wakening him at all. Matt struggled to fall back asleep between the nausea that sent him to the bathroom again and again, and the cramping that left him in pain. Exhaustion finally overtook him in the darkness of the early morning hours. By then Mikaela was wide awake and panicked about how her inability to sleep would affect her basal body temp in the morning. She rolled over and saw the grimace etched into Matt's gaunt face as the thought returned to her.

Be thou a doer . . .

Their first Valentine's Day was only a few days away. Between the clinic work and Matt's care and her appointment, she hadn't planned a thing.

Be thou a doer . . .

She slipped out of bed and saw the lighted Christmas tree, a bit more rumpled, but still lit with full Christmas regalia because Matt wasn't ready to have it taken down just yet. She considered how attached he had become to the tree. He was even more attached to what it and its ornaments symbolized—hope, memories, relationships, and the value of every minute of every day. The thought of a baby did that for her, but the dream of a child was still too abstract for Matt. He needed something tangible, something measurable to mark the passing days from weakness back to health.

She walked to the kitchen to get a drink and found the envelope of marigold seeds. Inspired by that find, she hurried to the computer to do some online shopping and found Matt's pen lying there, inspiring another idea that launched a few online searches. The plans she conjured pleased her so much she clapped her hands and giggled with delight.

"What are you doing out of bed in the middle of the night?"

a voice behind her called. When she turned, she found Matt standing in the bedroom doorway in pajamas that looked two sizes too big.

"Plotting and scheming."

"Won't all this midnight scurrying about throw off your temperature and ovulation calculations?"

"You're right. I'm done." She closed the laptop. "Did I wake you?"

"That would imply that I had actually been asleep." He headed for the fridge to refill his water bottle, clearing his throat three times during the trip. Each gurgle became louder than the previous one, and when he drank a sip of water, he grimaced during the swallow. Mikaela knew his throat was raw.

"How are you feeling?"

He answered the question with a fake smile. "Great. Just great." Then he padded back to the bedroom and closed the door, leaving Mikaela wondering what had just happened. Getting to sleep was her current priority, so she chalked Matt's sarcasm up to utter frustration and headed to bed as well.

Both of their alarms sounded at seven a.m., awaking them with a start. Matt was a little foggy, but Mikaela was clear on their assignment. Before speaking or rising from her spot, she handed Matt her phone and placed the new digital thermometer under her tongue. Once it beeped, she read the number and repeated it out loud to Matt, who entered it in the app.

Once done, she kissed Matt and said, "Day one."

"Day one," replied Matt with a yawn and a pained smile. Mikaela moved in for a kiss, but Matt stopped her to ask, "What about that ovulation meter test?"

"I don't start checking until day nine of my cycle. Today is only day four."

"So many numbers." Matt yawned and groaned again in

pain. He brushed her concern away, offered her his cheek, and lay down for another twenty minutes.

Rousing Matt proved more daunting than normal that day. When he finally left the bed, he moved to the window seat and sat with his arms wrapped across his stomach and his head pressed against the glass. Mikaela finally realized he was staring at the people walking along their busy Georgetown street.

"Your infusion is in an hour, Matt, and you still haven't eaten or dressed."

"I'm not hungry."

She expected that. "How about a protein drink?"

"I just drank some water."

"Then why don't you take your shower and see if you feel better after that?"

He reached a swollen hand up, childlike, and pressed it against the frosty glass.

"Matt?"

He pulled his hand back and bent his chilled fingers, as if experiencing the sensation and numbness of cold for the first time.

"Sweetheart?" She moved slowly to him, concern and angst brimming in her heart. She slowly lowered herself to the seat beside him and asked, "What are you doing?"

"Just . . . feeling." Then without further explanation, he rose and went into the bathroom.

When they arrived at the transplant center of the hospital, Mikaela went to the nurse's station and requested a moment with Dr. Marcosky, who discreetly led her away to an office while the nurses began Matt's infusion.

The doctor closed the door. "Your request sounded urgent."

"I'm worried about Matt. He's fine one minute and then

withdrawn and unusually quiet the next. He spent part of the morning *feeling* the cold window. It's not . . ."

"Normal? What part of this is normal, Mikaela? He's depressed. Understandably so. Nothing about his life feels or looks as it did. Everything he knew has been stripped away and he's in an alien body that hurts and feels sick and exhausted."

"I'm still here. At least he's home. We're making progress."

"Mikaela," said Dr. Marcosky as he tipped his head to look at her over the rim of his glasses. "Yes, you're both home together again. But in the way married people should be together?"

She felt a wave of heat spread over her at the veiled reference to their celibate life.

"I don't mean to discount his progress, or the blessings of being out of the hospital and back in a house, but Matt is grieving, and he's trying to do it without seeming faithless or ungrateful or cowardly in front of you."

The sting of the doctor's words caused her eyes to tear. "I love him. He can tell me anything."

Dr. Marcosky gently touched her arm. "I don't think he can right now."

Her lips were trembling as she asked, "Then can't you find someone he can talk to?"

"I've tried. Many times. I can't make him go, but I will ask again, all right?"

DR. MARCOSKY PAUSED at the side of Matt's treatment bed, causing Matt to brace for bad news. "One of our counselors popped in and encouraged you to meet with her. She said you politely refused the offer. Would you like to tell me why?"

The doctor's question felt like a knife cutting away at the

tattered cords holding his resolve together. Part of him longed to throw open the windows barring him from the real world and scream until his ragged breath was exhausted, but he also feared what destruction might befall his psyche if he surrendered and gave voice to his grief. And then the ingratitude hit him, along with the sister emotions of shame and guilt that he, a man sought by cancer and, by all rights, destined for death, was still in the fight because of the miraculous tenacity of God and three women—first his mother, then Mikaela, and then Kate.

Dual voices tugged at him. One reminded him daily that things could be worse. Pain and nausea, while unpleasant, were still evidences of life and therefore hope. The other mocked the depletion of his manhood and fed the grief that overtook him each time he looked in the mirror and saw the bald, shriveled being he had become. That voice fueled his anger over the unfairness of cancer for genetically stalking his family line, awakening his most wrenching fear—that Mikaela would one day simply wear down and walk out from the strain of his needs. Despite all her love and patience and medical training and her valiant efforts to hear his silent, unspoken cries, she didn't understand what was happening to the core of him. Not really. Perhaps it was impossible for anyone outside such a medical battle to understand the fight, not only to improve, but to simply hang on for another sickly day without surrendering ground to the fatigue and futility.

He knew he needed to talk to someone. Someone who would not be shocked by his despair nor diminished by their inability to "fix" it. He had found a resource that intrigued him, but he hadn't pursued it, perhaps because he was afraid to fully face what cancer had done to him, or perhaps to prevent Mikaela from recognizing it. So instead, he watered down his emotions, doling a weakened tea of truth to the good doctor, one that might satisfy his concerns without releasing the full flood of Matt's emotions.

"I'm sad, and depressed sometimes, but I don't want to be that man all the time, so I pull it together. I'm doing all right."

Dr. Marcosky leaned closer until his gaze drilled into Matt. "Psychology isn't my forte, but even with my limited clinical psych experience, I'd say anyone in your situation would benefit from talking to someone professionally. I'd like you to reconsider finding an outlet. If not a one-on-one counseling session, how about a support group? Some of my patients have found great support anonymously online."

MIKAELA HEADED FOR THE LADIES' room and cried after talking to Dr. Marcosky. Matt was hurting in ways she could not imagine or fix or even discuss with him. Dr. Marcosky said depression was not uncommon in such a trying medical period, but he was clearly worried about Matt too.

She entered his infusion suite near the end of Matt's treatment. Her eyes were still puffy, but she'd done her best to conceal their redness.

"All done?" she asked in as cheery a voice as she could muster.

"Yeah," Matt replied as he gathered the devices that entertained him during the treatment.

"Did Dr. Marcosky have anything new to say?"

He held his puffy arm up. "Two shots of blood thinner every day for the clot, and steroids for the GvHD."

"I'm sorry."

Matt looked up at her for the first time. "You've been crying."

"It's my hormones."

"Mikaela?"

She heard the return of concern and caring to his voice. "I'm worried about you. I keep wanting you to be happy, but I'm adding to your pain and isolation, aren't I?"

"It's not you."

"It's okay, Matt. I want you to feel you can talk to someone. I know I can't fully empathize with all you're going through, but how about a therapist or an AML support group?"

His head cocked sideways. "You'd be okay with that?"

"Did you think I wouldn't be?"

He looked away. "I don't know what I think anymore."

Mikaela felt her throat tighten. "All I want is for you to have what you need. I'll always be there if you want to share anything with me, but I love you, Matt, and what's best for you is what I want you to do."

"Thank you." He felt his throat tighten so he picked up his protective mask and slid it over his nose and mouth. Mikaela didn't press the point further as she wheeled him out the door and to the car for home.

Matt slept most of the day, and when he awoke, Mikaela felt she saw a renewed spark in his eyes. She crawled into bed beside him and clasped her hand in his.

"Just for the record, Mr. Grayken, I'm expecting a package tomorrow, so keep your grubby, swollen little hands off, okay?"

"Ditto, Mrs. Grayken."

"Oh . . . I see." She snuggled into his shoulder and teased him to keep the mood light.

Matt crossed one arm over his forehead and stared at the ceiling. "And about this morning. Thank you."

"Are you going to do it? See a therapist, I mean?"

"I don't know yet, but I found an online support group a few days ago."

"Like a chat room?" Mikaela mumbled into his shoulder.

"You're upset."

"No . . ." She knew she didn't sound very convincing, even to herself. "I just need time to adjust to the idea that you need something I can't provide. You always said I was everything you needed. I thought so too until today, but I accept your need to share candid, honest feelings with people who understand this uniquely terrible experience."

Matt brought their clasped hands to his lips and placed a kiss on her wrist. "Thank you, but you're still not comfortable with this, are you?"

"Just promise me you won't run off with an AML chat room girl, okay?"

He pressed his lips into her brow. "Not a chance, Mrs. Grayken. Not a chance."

February thirteenth began with phone alarms, a temperature check, a blood thinner shot, and pills. When Matt and Mikaela returned from Matt's infusion treatment, two boxes were waiting on their back stoop. They each scooped up their respective boxes and hid them away in the house.

On Valentine's Day morning, alarms sounded, and Matt and Mikaela began their new routine, except this time, when Mikaela announced her temperature reading, she didn't hand Matt her phone. Instead, she took his hand and led him to the bathroom and pointed to the wall behind the door.

"Real charts!" exclaimed Matt as he walked over to touch and study each. "One to track your ovulation chart and one for temperature."

"Something visual, to make this process feel more real for you." She wrapped her arms around Matt's neck and kissed him.

"I'm sorry I didn't understand what you were trying to tell me before. I want you to see that I *am* listening. Happy Valentine's Day."

Matt tightened his embrace. "Thank you . . . for these."

Mikaela pulled back. "I get that you need to talk to someone who understands. Just don't count me out completely on that front. Please." Her eyes welled, and Matt drew her close.

"I promise."

They held each other for several seconds and took a moment to transfer their previous data to the chart. Matt smiled. "Maybe it sounds strange that something this small means so much to me, but it does, and it means even more that you understand."

"So now you have two morning jobs."

"Two?"

She smiled and nodded as she pulled him toward the door and on to the kitchen. "Uh huh. You're in charge of the charts, and I have another surprise." She left Matt on the barstool by the counter and opened the door to the garage to grab her now-opened box. After setting it on the counter, she reached in and came out with two pairs of gardening gloves, a mask for Matt, a bag of soil, some plastic trays, peat pots, and various seeds.

"We're going to grow a garden?" asked Matt.

"More than that." She pointed to a planting chart on the fridge door. "We're going to plant seeds and watch them sprout, and then we're going to nurture the little plants along until they can go into the cold frame. We're going to count each seedling, chart its growth, and watch the miracle of life unfold around us every day." Mikaela held her breath, hoping the symbolism wasn't lost on Matt.

"Surrounding us with life . . . I like that."

She held up the envelope of marigold seeds. "Remember these seeds from the flowers that lined my parent's walkway? I want to plant them in these peat pots and start them in these plastic trays. We'll set them along the windowsills, and when the weather warms up a bit, I'd like to plant them along our sidewalk too."

"You're bringing a little of the outside I can't yet reach, inside to me." His lips quivered.

Mikaela touched his cheek. "If you keep trying to talk to me, I'll keep listening. I promise."

"I like that we're passing something along that was a part of your family."

She threaded her arms between his and hugged him close. Hope soared in her as she felt his arms tighten around her with strength he hadn't had the day before. She pulled back and looked at his arm, which was less swollen today. "Are you feeling better?"

Matt's brow wrinkled in thought. "I think so . . . at least a little. I guess the extra meds are kicking in."

Mikaela snuggled back against him. "I'll take that as a win."

"Me too. And I have a little Valentine's Day surprise for you. It's just something small." He took her hand and led her to the living room, where the Christmas tree stood lit and decorated in dozens of red and pink hearts.

Mikaela turned to him. "Oh, Matt. When did you do this? You must have worked all night packing up the old ornaments and hanging these."

"A few hours. It's okay. I love this tree and what it stands for. I want to decorate it for every season." He led her to the tree, where two small ornaments hung, small booties instead of hearts. "I know I don't always seem 'up' and happy, but I am completely excited about the prospect of a child with you, Mikaela. No matter how glum or dark or grumpy I sometimes seem, hold on to that, okay?"

CHAPTER TEN

Even Valentine's Day couldn't halt the daily routine of infusions and shots. Just before they left for the hospital, the stress increased when Mikaela received a call from Dr. Gorman asking her to fill in for him at a meeting in two hours.

Panic hit her as she looked at Matt. "Under any other circumstances, I'd be happy to, Dr. Gorman, but they're adjusting a lot of Matt's meds right now, and I want to be there for him."

Matt overheard the conversation. "It's okay, Mikaela. I'll be all right."

She mouthed the words, "But it's Valentine's Day."

"I'll be attached to an IV pole. It's okay."

She made a pouty frown and relented. "I can make it, Dr. Gorman. Where's the meeting and what's it about? I don't remember planning anything for today."

"I'll text the details to you. It's at Prospect's Rockville office. And you don't remember this meeting because I agreed to chair it at the last minute. The pastors whose churches are hosting the walk-in clinics had a meeting of their own last week, and they want us to get the clinics operating as soon as possible, regardless of when the mobile clinics are ready. I was afraid we'd start losing their support if we delayed, and I didn't want to bother you with everything you had going on, so I agreed to meet with them to organize the delivery of the supplies. They each also need a practice run for setup and takedown. Once the dates were set, I planned to pass them on to you to coordinate volunteers."

"Got it."

"Thank you, Mikaela. You're saving me. You generated the equipment lists, and the vendors sent the delivery schedules to you, so you should have all the data you need for today."

After the call ended, she thought of several questions she wished she had asked, but Matt's appointment was looming, so she grabbed her laptop and they left to begin their day. Once Matt was settled, she headed for Rockville, making snail's progress through the crowded city traffic. She whipped into the one open parking space in the garage, counting it a blessing that one was available. She parked and raced upstairs to the conference room, passing an older African-American woman and three Hispanic-looking children. When she entered the room, twelve clergymen and one casually dressed Hispanic woman were already seated.

Mikaela quickly apologized for her lateness and for Dr. Gorman's absence and got the meeting started. A gray-haired, African-American clergyman named Reverend Coolidge asked to speak on behalf of his colleagues and for the people in their communities who would be served by the clinics. As he prepared to read a typed statement, the conference room door opened, and Bennett Sadler rushed in.

"Good morning, everyone." He set his eyes on Mikaela.

"Good morning, Mrs. Grayken. I hope you'll forgive my lateness. I've been circling the garage for fifteen minutes, trying to find a parking space."

Mikaela didn't know Bennett Sadler was also planning to attend, but she greeted him and caught him up to speed. "Welcome, Mr. Sadler. We appreciate the personal interest you continue to take in this initiative. Reverend Coolidge was just about to share a statement with us." She returned her attentions to the pastor. "The floor is yours, Reverend Coolidge."

The reverend's statement detailed painful statistics about lives lost and lives altered because of a lack of accessible health care. He then stressed the importance of moving forward without delay on opening the walk-in clinics. To prove his point, he introduced Alaina Valerio, the young woman seated beside him, and asked her to share her story.

Alaina's nervous shaking transferred to her hands, rattling her handwritten note and making reading her message all the more difficult. Reverend Coolidge touched her arm and smiled at her, encouraging her to set the paper aside and tell her story from her heart.

She swallowed and released a long slow breath before beginning. "I have three children, a boy five, a girl three, and a baby boy. My son David fell down the old concrete stairs and tore a deep gash in his knee. I cleaned it and bandaged it as best I could. I didn't have any antibiotics and traveling to the city clinic with three kids takes two bus transfers and money we don't have, so I waited and kept cleaning it, but the leg got redder and redder until David was in tears from the pain. It took the last of our cash to get everyone across town to the clinic so he could be seen. By the time it was his turn, the doctors said the infection had reached the bone, and they sent my little boy to the hospital.

He was there on IV's for five days, and all because I couldn't reach a doctor to tend to his cut knee."

Reverend Coolidge leaned toward her and said, "I could have brought you a dozen Alainas from my own block. We need those clinics now. Every day that passes is another story, some even worse than this."

Mikaela's heart rent for this pretty young woman, whose eyes seemed old for her years. She wished she could take the entire family home with her. That wouldn't help any of the other families with similar stories. But the clinics could.

Mikaela thanked Alaina, who rose and left the room. Mikaela assumed the three children being tended in the hallway were likely Alaina's little ones.

After acknowledging the need to expedite the startups, Mikaela set the wheels in motion to get the first wave of clinics opened within two weeks. She passed out lists of equipment and supplies for each church's clinic and scheduled deliveries from the central storage facility to each hosting church. Then she created a schedule to practice setting up the clinics according to the physicians' recommendations, asking each clergyman to arrange teams to handle the physical labor required and to get the word out to their communities.

The meeting ended, but the attendees lingered, as if they each felt what Mikaela was experiencing, a flood of joy and purpose she personally needed to refill her draining well.

Bennett Sadler lingered behind, serving as the official thanker-in-chief as each person exited the room. Mikaela was packed and making her own exit when Bennett leaned against the doorjamb and said, "You're amazing."

She stopped and eyed the door, making sure she could exit without interference. "I chaired a meeting. There's nothing very amazing about that. Now if you'll excuse me, I'm needed elsewhere."

He moved a foot to the left, completely freeing the door. "I think you missed the dynamic shift that happened in this room in the last hour. Thirteen people came in here, expecting to have a fight on their hands to get those clinics opened quickly, and you not only listened to them and sympathized with them, you laid out a plan that's frankly going to kill you in order to make it happen, and then you also gave them assignments that empowered them to make these clinics a success. That, Mrs. Grayken, is far more than simply chairing a meeting."

Mikaela was still focused on the part about how she was likely going to die. She set her valise down and pulled out her laptop. "What did I promise them?"

"To singlehandedly be present at twelve clinic setups in the next two weeks."

Her breathing hitched as Matt's schedule, the clinic schedule, doctor's appointments and lab tests all collided. "I-I-I didn't . . . I don't remember . . . I created the schedule to run the practice setups, but I didn't mean I'd be at every one. Did I say that?"

"That's definitely what they thought when they left that meeting."

She dropped onto the end of the conference table. "I can't possibly be at every one." She checked her watch and knew Matt would be finished his treatment before she could get there. "I need to go. I-I-I'll figure this out later."

"Mind if I walk with you to the garage? Maybe we can brainstorm this on the way."

Mikaela was deaf to everything but the sound of the blood pounding in her head over the stress she felt.

"What if you and I run a practice setup for some volunteers?

Teach them first, and then assign each of them to one or two clinics?"

Mikaela caught the end of Bennett's suggestion, and relief immediately settled over her. "Where will we get the volunteers?"

"I'm sure I can convince a few company employees to step up for a good cause."

That suggestion gave Mikaela an idea. "And I'm sure some of Great Expectation's employees will help as well."

She stopped her scurrying and breathed for a moment. "Thank you, Bennett. You're a lifesaver."

"Glad to help, Mrs. Grayken."

"Please call me, Mikaela, Bennett."

He extended his hand. "Friends?"

She took it and gave it a hearty shake. "Friends."

Bennett looked at the first row of parked cars, where a black Range Rover sported a flat tire. "Some poor guy is going to need a friend today. Look at that. They rolled right over a broken beer bottle."

Mikaela gasped and then slumped, realizing that she found the empty parking space every other driver purposely avoided. "I'm that poor guy. That's my car."

"Oh, dear. I'll call the auto club."

"How long will that take?" she asked in a panic. "I need to pick Matt up at the hospital. He's having a treatment today."

"We can leave the car's location and info with the auto club, and I can give you a ride to the hospital. You can either have them tow your car home, or I can drive you back here to get it later this evening."

As generous as his offers were, the last thing Matt needed was to have her spend the bulk of her day with Bennett Sadler. She pulled her AAA card from her wallet and called them, giving them all the details about the car, it's location, and where she needed it to end up. The service would cost a tidy sum, but right now, budget issues were not her first priority.

Bennett stood by, watching from afar until she completed her arrangements. "You're a very stubborn and independent woman, Mikaela. Will you at least accept a ride from me?"

"Thank you, but I've also called for an Uber. I don't want to tie up any more of your day."

"You still don't trust me, do you?"

She hedged before answering. "It's not about you. It's about me and my husband and a little thing called a vow." She watched a crease form between Bennett's eyes as he looked at her, as if he were looking into her. "I know it sounds old school, Bennett, but my parents were old school, and I'm a product of their lovely old school values. Appearances matter to me."

He blinked and chuckled. "No explanation needed. I was simply trying to be a gentleman, but I appreciate your loyalty *and* your old school values."

"Thank you."

"Would I be a gentleman or a cad if I offered to stay here until your Uber arrives?"

"You'd be a gentleman and a friend."

He offered a slight bow and leaned against her disabled vehicle. "Did you get a chance to read the interview I gave to the Sunday paper?"

She hadn't even thought about the article since the last time he mentioned it, but she offered a grimace and manufactured a believable sigh. "We've had so much going on."

He brushed her apology aside. "I understand. I'm not asking out of vanity. I'd just like you to get your reservations about me out of the way. Since you didn't read the article and we've got

162

some time to kill, I'm at your disposal to answer any and all questions you'd care to ask."

There was one seemingly inexcusable decision she wished he'd explain. "Okay. Why did you jack up the price on that heart medication right after you became CEO?"

"The million-dollar question. I'll give you the public answer I gave to the paper, and then I'll give you the private answer. The public answer is that I took some bad advice about balancing the research and development costs of that medication. I was too proud to listen to my board, and out of pride, I made a terrible mistake."

"And the private answer?"

"It's much longer."

Mikaela looked at her phone's Uber App. "My driver is three minutes out."

"Oh, a race. Let's see if I can summarize. My parents had a real love story. They met in college and were going to help the world. My father, through his research, and Mom, through patient care. When my mother died, my father didn't cope well. P&S became his new wife. He threw everything into it, and he enlisted me in the cause, whether I wanted his life or not. I enjoyed numbers, not science, and my father labeled me a slacker who didn't apply himself."

"I'm sorry."

"We often become what people tell us we are, so I proved my father right. I could have mastered the science, but for reasons only my therapist understands, I didn't want to comply. I did master the business classes, but I also enjoyed my irresponsible lifestyle, and I graduated with grades just good enough to carry me on to a master's program where I could delay entry into the real world for a few more years."

"And then you went to work for your father's company."

"Yes. From the proverbial ground up. My father knew his health was failing so he handed me the reins under his guidance, but I hired a CFO who graduated summa cum laude in everything but ethics. He didn't understand what my father had tried to drill into me, that a pharmaceutical company must spread its profits and losses over all its products. It's the only way to bring a new drug into the marketplace without doing what I did, gouging the very people it was created to help."

"And this CFO is the one who convinced you to raise the price exponentially?"

"He said Research and Development had other promising drugs that had been abandoned because my father felt the cost of the trials would bankrupt the company."

"Was that true?"

He shrugged and shook his head. "It's true that other promising drugs had been tabled, but those that were completely abandoned had been dropped because during our delay to run the trials, other companies beat us to the market. I didn't want that to happen with the new samples."

"Why didn't you discuss your concerns with your father?"

"If he disagreed with my plan, would I back down and follow his direction? I wanted to be the hero who pulled the company's profits up and funded the breakthroughs P&S was poised to deliver. I thought the ends justified the means. That I could make him proud."

Mikaela bit her lip to prevent herself from saying something that would add to the man's pain.

"Instead, I almost destroyed the company, and I hurt a lot of innocent people. My father had a stroke and died a few weeks after I announced the price hike. I caused it."

"You can't know that."

"I remember how he looked at me . . . with searing disappointment. He'll never know the lengths I've gone to, making amends to all the people I harmed and to redeem the company and the family name. Hurting him and having him pass on thinking I was a disappointment are my most painful regrets."

The Uber matching the description on Mikaela's phone pulled into the garage with the tow truck close behind. Mikaela turned to Bennett and laid her hand on his arm. "I'm sure he does know what you've done to redeem yourself and the company, Bennett, and I'm sure he's very proud of you today."

"I hope so. Can you manage from here?"

"Yes. But thank you for asking. And I accept your offer to train volunteers on the clinic setups."

The light returned to his eyes. "Very good. I'll start lining up volunteers as soon as I get back to my office. And where should we hold the training?"

"Reverend Coolidge offered his church. It's in Upper Marlboro. I'll confirm with him and text you the information."

"It sounds like a plan. I'll look forward to hearing from you, Mikaela."

MATT WAS STILL BEATING himself up over Mikaela's phone call. She explained she'd be late because of the debacle with the flat tire. Once again, when she needed him, he was completely useless.

He did feel better than he had in a few days, and spurred on by his inability to be Mikaela's hero, he decided he could at least walk a few extra steps and work toward being available the next time a need arose.

The hospital's infusion center had a small lobby. Twenty-seven shuffling steps took him from one side to the other. Matt knew he could do better than this old-man shuffle, so he played a game, increasing the length of his strides with each pass, lowering the number of steps needed to cross the room each time. Twenty-five, twenty-four, and then he stretched his leg out so far that his weakened calf protested with a cramp. He laughed it off, enjoying a familiar, non-critical pain he'd experienced before after failing to properly stretch before a run. When the cramp subsided, he picked up the pace and went for a twenty-four-step path, then a twenty-three. That length of his steps and the speed of his pace caused his heart rate to increase and his breathing to become labored, but he pushed on for three more laps. As he headed for the wall, the cramp in his leg returned and down he went, smacking his head on the wall.

He was more embarrassed than hurt, but panic ensued as the small gash in his head bled out uncontrollably. Two nurses ran over with a wheelchair.

"It's the blood thinners. You're not in any danger. Let's get you back in a treatment room and bandage that wound."

Matt looked like a brain surgery patient by the time Mikaela arrived. He tried to head off any unnecessary alarm by saying, "I'm all right," but Mikaela still raced to him, rattling off her own assurances.

"Dr. Marcosky says everything is fine. They just need to cut back on the blood thinners."

"I know," he said feeling more like a child than a man once again.

"I had the towing company bring the car here. It's out in the parking lot."

Matt turned the radio on in the car to head off conversation. Back at home, he said he was tired and headed into the bedroom, where he curled up in a ball. Mikaela came in and lay down beside him, the curve of her body matching his. She wrapped her arms around him, and he leaned into her warmth. Then she asked questions about his fall, the maternal worry apparent in her voice. She either didn't hear him or she didn't believe him when he explained that for thirty minutes, he had almost felt like himself. Rather than argue the point, he forced his body to slip into a steady breathing pattern Mikaela assumed was sleep.

When she left the room, he pulled out his phone and typed in the web address of the AML online support group. A conversation was underway between veterans of AML and a newly diagnosed patient still reeling from her recent diagnosis. He felt their compassion and understanding, particularly that of a young woman named Lily, who was out of remission and back in the fight.

Matt put the day's experience into words and asked, "Did you ever worry that your spouse would never again see you as a healthy adult?"

Comment after comment rolled up. Some were personal tales from far enough in the person's past that they could laugh about the circumstances. Some were fresh and tender, like Matt's. The newer experiences gave him comfort. The older ones gave him perspective.

Lily asked him to introduce himself to the group. Part of him wanted to bond with these fellow warriors, people who knew the horrors and frequent hopelessness of the fight they were each engaged in, and then he remembered Mikaela's warm arm across his back, and the efforts she had gone to that day to get to him, to rescue him, to love him.

He poised his finger over the keypad. He could enter this world, but in doing so, he wondered if he would be leaving Mikaela behind. Moments passed, and the kind group member named Lily made a second request for him to share his story. Matt typed, "Gotta go, thanks," and closed the site.

He left his bed and found Mikaela on the sofa, pouring over a document on her laptop. As soon as she saw him, she set it aside, opening her arms to Matt who fell into her embrace, burying his face in the tangle of her dark hair.

"I love you," he whispered. "And I need you so much."

"Thank you for saying that." Her glassy eyes seemed a contradiction to the smile radiating across her face. "I needed to hear it."

Matt straightened and brushed her hair back from her face. "How can that be? I feel as if my needs crush you every day."

She framed his face in her hands. "Never think that. I love you, and I love helping you, because I love us."

CHAPTER ELEVEN

Mikaela saw positive changes in Matt every day. On the fifteenth, he was already up and dressed and kneeling beside her with the thermometer at the ready when Mikaela's alarm sounded. He organized his own meds, made breakfast, and washed a load of laundry before they left for the hospital that day. When they returned home, he slept for three hours, proof that the improvement was more about a shift in his attitude than an overnight increase in strength.

But that came too. After Mikaela's morning tests and chartings, Matt asked when they were going to plant the seeds. Excited by his interest, she pulled out all the supplies and they quickly planted every peat pot and set them in trays, placing them on the window sills. Two aspects of that activity caused Mikaela to marvel. First, Matt did it standing up for almost an entire hour, and he charted every pot—what was in it and when it was likely to sprout.

The chart wasn't rocket science, but Matt's willingness and ability to organize the data calmed a quiet fear that had picked at her peace about a change in Matt's personality and cognitive function. The normally resilient Matt had recently become confused and overwhelmed by games or puzzles, and he often seemed to check out during conversations. Unsure whether this development was physical or emotional, Mikaela asked the DVP guys to hold off on poker for a few weeks. She feared Matt's reaction if he suddenly couldn't remember the rules or keep track of the cards in each hand. But Matt seemed back again, and for that, she was grateful.

Another surprise awaited her on the morning of the seventeenth. Instead of waking to the beep of her normal alarm, her phone played the theme song from a spy movie. Lying on her nightstand beside her phone was the black plastic travel box for Matt's razor. Bold lettering, which she later discovered was done in white correction fluid, read, "Operation Ovulation." When she opened the lid, she found her ovulation meter and a love letter from Matt, who was playing possum and feigning sleep. She rolled over to face him and found him holding her thermometer at the ready.

After numbers were gathered and recorded, Mikaela climbed back in bed and snuggled into Matt's waiting arms. "How did you do all this? *When* did you do all this?"

"I climbed the stairs, Mikaela, twice!"

She rolled over to face him and saw pure joy brightening his eyes.

"How do you feel?"

"Like I could do it again. In fact"—he threw the covers off and stood with ease—"I'm going to!"

Over the course of the day, Matt conquered the stairs three more times, coming down with his step tracker the last time.

Building on his success, Dr. Marcosky turned him over to the occupational and physical therapists to build his strength and sharpen his cognitive functions. Of his own volition, Matt set up a walking circuit around the house. He started in the bedroom, turned right at the door, navigating around the living room/dining room, then into the kitchen, around the island and table, then down the hall and up the stairs. The course on the second floor was a straight line, up and down the hall, first side-stepping, then backward, then forward, and down the steps. Each circuit was a little under two hundred fifty steps.

Mikaela set the practice run to set up and take down the clinics for Thursday, when the DVP poker schedule was set to resume. Matt had already been through a tough round of therapy earlier in the day, and she hoped he'd rest until the guys arrived. Instead, she heard the theme from a boxing movie commence, and when she checked out the source, she found Matt at the top of the stairs wearing what appeared to be nothing but a plaid flannel robe and running shoes.

"What are you doing?" she asked between laughs.

Matt placed one hand on his hip and used the other to open one side of his robe, revealing a maroon and white track suit and a hauntingly bony leg.

"Do I dare ask where you got that getup?"

"I'll have you know that these are the proud colors of the St. Andrews Academy track team."

Mikaela covered her mouth and roared. "The shorts are a little . . . short. You look like a skinny Chippendale dancer."

"I'll take that as a compliment. And someday, I will again fill this outfit with my manly muscles. But today? It's short because I haven't worn this since I was fourteen."

She tried not to dim the moment with the shock of hearing that he was roughly the weight he was when he was fourteen. "And the plan worthy of this momentous outfit?"

"I want to show off my skills to the guys tonight."

"Your skills?"

"I'm going for three thousand steps, and I'm making them do it with me."

She dreaded missing the coming spectacle.

"I'm glad you're wearing your robe. Besides everything it adds to the ensemble, you need to stay warm."

"Yes, mother."

"Oh, a little sass, eh?" She smiled at his reemerging spunk. "Will you do me one favor and stay downstairs until the rest of the squad arrives?"

"Mikaela—"

"Please?"

He didn't argue further. Instead, he descended the steps Miss America-style, and walked straight into her arms. "Thanks for tolerating my high jinks. I can't tell you how great it is to feel a little like myself again."

"I understand, but you may be a few yards past normal on this one."

"I'll take that under advisement. Call me. A lot. Let me know when you're on your way home." He gave her another kiss. "You're not the only one who worries about the person they love."

With a final kiss, she left the house as a call came through from Kate.

"Daniel told me you were training volunteers tonight. Could you use one more?"

"Absolutely! I'll pick you up."

"No need. I'm right outside. I thought I'd sit and keep you company during the big game, but I'll go with you instead. Besides, I'd like to run the final designs past Bennett."

As if summoned, Bennett Sadler called as the women headed down the highway for Upper Marlboro. "Reverend

Coolidge confirmed that the shipment arrived, and I've got twelve volunteers coming at seven. The reverend says he invited a few congregants to come as well. People are excited to help."

Mikaela ended the call, and for the first time in a long time, her happiness wasn't tinged with fear or stress or dread about the next terrible morning or the next lab result. She knew there would still be bumps and bad days, but today was good, even great, and she wanted to bask in that. Her heart was light, and Kate noticed the change.

"What's come over you, Mikaela? You're like a thousand-watt bulb."

"Matt's doing great, and the clinic project is great, and life is . . ."

"Great?"

They both burst out in laughter. Kate turned the radio up loud, and the two sang whatever song played with full voice, whether they knew the words or not. Mikaela "got" Matt's crazed antics. It was the joy of life ebbing through them after months spent muscling along on sheer grit. Maybe she was more exhausted, mentally and emotionally, than she really knew.

She was nearly giddy when she arrived at the church and saw all the volunteers unboxing the new supplies. That bubbling happiness shocked Reverend Coolidge, who was the recipient of her enthusiastic hug. "Isn't this amazing!" she cheered. "You are all amazing!" she yelled out to the crowd.

Alaina Valerio was there with her three children. Mikaela rushed over and gave her a hug as well, adding, "Thank you for coming."

"Thank you for making this possible."

Mikaela pointed to Bennett who was chatting with Kate and smiling at Mikaela from afar. "He's the man who made this possible."

Alaina waved at Bennett, who ambled over with Kate in tow as Mikaela asked Alaina, "Are these your beautiful children?"

The pretty, young mother gathered her two oldest children close and gave her tattered stroller a little nudge forward. "This is David, Camilla, and Robert. Do you have children?"

Mikaela blushed. She simply said, "Not yet, but someday."

"Shall we begin?" asked the reverend. When Mikaela said yes, the reverend offered a prayer, and then Mikaela handed out a floor plan of where the tables, partitions, exam tables, file boxes, and chairs needed to be placed. She made it a game, using teams of four, running them through the set up, take down, and storage of each area's materials—the administrative center, the waiting area, and exam areas. By the end of the evening, these volunteers were pros at getting the clinic set up in under forty minutes, and they could take it down in under thirty. They were each assigned different churches where they would now go and train the local volunteers in those communities. After that, each church would be responsible for assuring that the clinics were operational on the days the doctors were scheduled to come.

When all the equipment and furnishings were stored away for the final time and the people were beginning to leave, an angry Hispanic man entered, searching every face in the room. Alaina froze, and her children cowered behind her whispering, "Papa."

All eyes followed the man's stare back to Alaina. She cradled her children around her as her embarrassed gaze swept left and right at the concerned people standing in tense circles in the room. Before the man reached her, she began pushing the stroller forward with one hand and guiding the children toward the exit with the other. The man grabbed her arm and pulled her along, as if she weren't moving fast enough.

Mikaela took a step forward to challenge the intruder, but

Alaina shot her a pleading look, begging her to withdraw. Bennett did not pick up on Alaina's plea for restraint, and he started toward the man until the reverend took his arm, urging him to stop. Mikaela seethed over the man's mistreatment of Alaina, but she did nothing and said nothing, as the family exited the building.

The room buzzed with concerned voices. The reverend said a few words of thanks for the volunteers' efforts and offered a prayer to send everyone home safely, but when the volunteers were gone, Mikaela could not be dismissed.

"Was that Alaina's husband?" she asked.

"Yes. Eduardo. The father of her children."

"He's a beast," said Kate.

"I should have called the police," added Bennett.

The reverend grew quiet and cast his eyes toward the door where the family had exited. "Tonight was a good night. A happy night. We made a good start on helping these people medically, but a clinic, for all it's amazing worth, can't and won't solve all these people's problems. If you're going to work with them, you need to understand that much of what you're going to see and hear may shock your suburban sensibilities. Wealth and status don't protect people from hard things. I know a little about your situation, Mrs. Grayken, so you understand what I'm saying, but wealth and status does guarantee the basic necessities of life—a safe and comfortable roof over your heads, nutritious food on your tables, and clothes on your back. It gives you choices and the ability to change your circumstances. Those are luxuries most of the people who come here will not have."

Mikaela suddenly saw the clinics as little more than a Band-Aid. "So how do we help them?"

"This *is* a good start. Every little bit helps. You can't fix everything. Just treat those who come to the clinics as you'd like to be treated. With respect."

The counsel hit Mikaela hard. For all the good she was trying to do, she wasn't prepared for failure or for another issue in her life where she felt powerless.

The rest of the volunteers resumed their chatter as they gathered their coats, and then Mikaela heard a somber voice beside her say, "It's easy to get caught up in your own woes and forget that everyone has something they're wrestling, isn't it?"

Mikaela turned and found Kate standing beside her, as silent and stone-faced as she was. Before she had a chance to formulate a response, she heard Bennett offer to take all the volunteers out for a late bite. Most of those remaining were his own employees, but he purposely made his way to Mikaela.

"Hey, why so glum?"

Mikaela managed a terse, tight smile. "I'm weighing what the reverend said."

Bennett took her by the shoulders. "Don't let Alaina's domestic troubles get to you. You can't save everyone from everything. You just do what you can do and you've done a lot."

"Thanks."

"Come out with us for a bite." He looked at Kate. "It'll do you both good to laugh."

The clinic volunteer in Mikaela weighed how an hour's lighthearted fun might ease the sting of futility settling over her. She looked at Kate and saw her eyes brighten, and then Mikaela's phone buzzed within her pocket. When she checked the message, she found a video clip awaiting her and a smile immediately tugged at her mouth.

"What is it?" asked Kate. "Is it Matt?"

"It's the whole gang. All the DVP guys. Look."

She hit play, and found Matt, still dressed in his prep school track suit, holding a trophy, most likely from the same trunk and era as the tiny track shorts. The sweaty, motley DVP crew was gathered around him as he held the trophy forward and said, "Hey, Baby. I hope everything went great with your clinic setup tonight. Just in case you didn't already know it, you're a champion in my book."

"Ours too!" yelled the crazy backup squad. "This is for you, Mikaela!" Then they broke into a cheer, complete with grunty shouts and swaggering arm motions.

When the road is rough,

and the going gets tough,

Who do you want in the game?

There's just one squad around,

Who can turn things around,

And we know that team by name.

Mi-kae-la! Mi-kae-la! Mi-kae-la!

Except one of the slightly inebriated guys slipped up and yelled, "St. Andrews!" and Mikaela assumed the cheer was yet another item resurrected from Matt's prep school foot locker. No, matter. It satisfied the guys' best intentions.

"They're all as crazy as a box of toads," said Kate with a laugh.

Mikaela considered how much she loved every one of those crazy guys, especially the bald, skinny guy in the middle.

Bennett's mouth twisted into a lopsided grin. "I'm assuming the answer is no?"

"Thanks for the offer, but I've got a squad of cheerleaders waiting for me at home. Kate?"

Kate bit her nail in thought and gave Bennett a wry smile. "It's tempting. I'd like to get out of my own head for a while, but I'd best go home with Mikaela. I'll incorporate your suggestions into the logos for the mobile clinics and call you when they're done. We can finalize them then."

Mikaela turned the radio volume down in the car for the half-hour ride home. It served as a curtain of white noise against the thoughts occupying her mind. She and Matt were finally enjoying some relief and hope. She didn't know how long it would last. Maybe Matt was on his way to a full cure or at least facing a period of solid remission. She hoped so, but whatever came next, tonight reminded her that lots of people had struggles of one kind or another. Cancer was the battle she and Matt had been called to fight, but whatever time they had, decades or years or months, she was grateful there was love in their home.

Her heart ached for Alaina and the wrestle she faced.

Mikaela watched Kate from the corner of her eye as her sister-in-law leaned her head against the window, staring forward.

"Is everything okay, Kate?"

A tepid smile preceded this veiled reply. "Just mullin' a few things over."

Mikaela laid her hand over Kate's and wondered if she was wrestling something too.

CHAPTER TWELVE

T he calendar page turned to March, and day sixty-six post-transplant rolled by. The seeds in the peat pots had long since sprouted and were nearly ready to be moved into the cold frames. Matt hovered over them, watering them and measuring their growth as he drew hope and inspiration from their burgeoning life. He told himself that the day would come when they would not be the limit of his contact with nature. He dreamed of being well enough to venture outside into the world of spores, urban pollution, and pollen to enjoy the great outdoors without its being a mortal threat to his well-being.

Then March sixth dawned bright and beautiful, along with more of the painful mouth sores, cracked lips, and throat inflammation Matt had come to accept as his new normal. He was slightly miserable when his wife dropped him off at the infusion center on her way to tour one of the clinics. Matt was nearly finished with his infusion when Dr. Marcosky popped by with some long-awaited news.

"It's taken us a little longer than I'd hoped, but I'm finally able to say that your immune system is strong enough for us to tackle this GvHD head on. I'm prescribing a high dose of steroids through your IV today, and I'll write a prescription for oral steroids to continue the treatment at home. Your mouth and throat should quickly feel better, which is important because you're going to need a healthy mouth and throat to keep up with the changes I expect to see in your appetite and energy levels."

Matt didn't register anything special about this announcement. In the past two months, there had been many changes in meds and procedures attached to pronouncements of hopeful outcomes that rarely met expectations. "Okay."

"Do you hear what I'm saying, Matt? It'll take months to fully restore your immune system, but it's responding very well. That surge of hunger and energy you've been feeling lately? It's going to continue. You're going to start picking up weight again, and to make sure we build your muscles back up, I'm ordering a PT schedule for you. What forms of exercise do you enjoy?"

Matt was hopeful as he said, "I ran and swam until this bout with AML."

Dr. Marcosky's face pinched, lowering Matt's rampant enthusiasm. "How do you feel about walking and using light weights?"

"Great. I've been walking around the house and tackling the stairs for two weeks."

"Good, good. Do you have a pedometer or step tracker?"

"Yes, I do."

"Great. I want you to track your number of steps each day and the number of minutes you exercise. If you don't already have some light weights, get some. Physical therapy will lay out some goals for you. How's that sound?"

Matt nodded. "Fine." He was, after all, quite proficient at filling out charts.

Dr. Marcosky leaned forward and placed his hands on Matt's shoulders. "You need to understand that an *improving* immune system is still compromised and not fully healthy, but if you promise to follow my instructions carefully, I'd be willing to free you from house arrest with certain precautions."

The words hung in the air like a whisper. Matt cocked his head, trying to replay the sounds of each syllable to be sure he'd heard correctly. "I can leave the house? Not just to come here?"

"With precautions. But yes. You'd still need to wear the protective mask when you're in close quarters with strangers or in large crowds or around potentially sick people, but Mikaela told me how much you miss being outdoors, so I think we can reintroduce you and your immune system to the world again."

The news hit Matt in ways he'd not expected. Tears burned behind his closed eyes. "Really? I can go outside." He broke down and cried openly. "I'm sorry. I've waited so long. I began to think I might nev—"

"No apology needed, Matt. I understand. You've been through a lot. I know it hasn't been easy, but you've come a long way. The road ahead won't be free of bumps and restrictions. Don't take unnecessary risks. Let the weather be your guide, but spring is around the corner. Go celebrate this milestone."

"Thank you!" Matt rose up to hug the doctor when he felt the tug of the port in his neck.

"Whoa, whoa, whoa," said Dr. Marcosky as he placed a hand on Matt's shoulder to ease him back down into the bed.

"Can I also get the port out?"

"Not yet, I'm afraid. That's why swimming and running are still off the table, but I'm tapering you down to two treatments a week instead of daily. We'll get that port out soon, okay?"

Matt pressed the heels of his hands into his moist eyes. "Thank you! Thank you." Another thought came to him. The barrier that separated him from being the husband he hungered to be once more. He bit his upper lip and asked, "What about . . . ?"

"Sex?" Again, Dr. Marcosky's face pinched. He pulled a chair up close and sat. "There's intimacy and there's sex. Hold your wife. Cuddle with her. You'll just have to enjoy that level of closeness, for now."

"Then when is it safe? What's the bar?"

"I know you feel better, but your platelet count needs to be around fifty thousand, and we're not there yet. If you continue as you are, it shouldn't be too much longer." He patted Matt's arm and stood again. "Hang in there, and don't let that restriction dilute the excitement of all the progress you're making."

Matt tried to put the disappointing news into perspective. An hour ago, when he arrived at the infusion center, he still felt like a patient with a long road ahead. This positive report made his spirits soar, but his body was still weak and easily drained. He would follow instructions and wait. "I need to call Mikaela."

"I almost considered waiting until she picked you up to tell you both, but I figured you'd enjoy telling her yourself."

"Two of the free clinics opened their doors today. She wanted to see how things went. I can't wait until she gets here so I can tell her the news."

"Better than that, you can take Mikaela out to dinner. Head back to work if you want, just don't overdo. Listen to your body."

Dr. Marcosky left, but Matt felt as if a filter had been peeled away, allowing the sun into his world again. AML would always be a threat, but the transplant had taken, and he was doing well. He was getting his life back by degrees. He would take it!

When Mikaela arrived to pick him up, Matt was ready and sitting in a chair in the almost empty lobby without his mask. Mikaela didn't notice the significance of his situation at first, until a wave of panic washed over her, followed by a smile that matched Matt's own. Her eyes glistened as he stood and walked to her, wrapping her up in his embrace. They stood there for several moments, rocking and crying and laughing. When Matt pulled back, he kissed her and whispered, "How about we head home and get dressed up? I'd like to take my wife to dinner, that is if you're available, Mrs. Grayken."

From that moment, Matt and Mikaela shed their old life and began living a life they previously dared only dream of. They kept up the regimen of taking Mikaela's temperature and plotting the data on charts with a new level of hope and anticipation while Matt charted the increases in his strength and endurance. They walked along the Tidal Basin, popping in at whatever café or museum they fancied that day, as they dreamed of April's return of spring and the cherry blossoms.

On Sunday, they shared the last pew at the old church three blocks down the street. Matt sat against the wall, and Mikaela took the guardian seat beside him, ready to hold all the loving but potentially germ-bearing well-wishers at bay. When they opened the bulletin, Mikaela pointed out a list where Matt's name sat among those for whom special prayers were needed.

"How long have they been doing this?" he asked.

"Every week since Thanksgiving."

Matt's lips quivered as he wiped his eyes. He'd grown accustomed to Mikaela's personal worship. The very sight of her reading her Bible or kneeling in prayer humbled and strengthened him, because he knew she was praying for him or finding passages to buoy him up. Their joint prayers created an intimacy between them and God that he had previously not imagined. Seeing his name listed in that bulletin expanded Matt's understanding of God's love even further, beyond the vending machine–like granting of uttered prayers to something more intimate, to a network of angels—human ones—who were His hands and His eyes and His lips, tangible emissaries of support and love.

"How can I thank everyone for praying for me all this time?"

Mikaela smiled at his childlike question. "Just do the same for these others."

"Like a chain."

"Exactly."

"At home. Every day. Remind me, okay?"

She clasped her hand in his and nodded as they let the organ prelude wash over them.

Matt listened to the sermon, really listened, even jotting down a few notes on his bulletin because he recognized that one of the most frightening side effects of treatment was the fog that muddled his thinking. He frequently weighed the value of beating cancer if it meant the door prize was dementia. That worry had been one of the roots of his depression and ebbing faith. He found it hard to recall information or to hold on to thoughts unless he wrote them down. Even the previously mastered functions of his computer and smartphone had begun to elude him.

Once the weekly poker games started up, Matt's clouded thinking made it impossible for him to keep track of the game. Despite the guys' efforts to encourage him and minimize his obvious cognitive struggles, Matt continued to be the consistent loser, leaving his collection of biddable toys rather depleted. As treatment progressed, and his energy returned, so too did his clarity and focus. March also brought him immeasurable peace as he began winning on Thursday nights, not only reclaiming some of his most prized treasures, but claiming a few of his friends' favorite pieces as well. It was a huge turning point in how he saw himself, and the same happiness was reflected on his friends' faces as well.

All the church-based clinics were up and running, but Mikaela continued popping in randomly, making sure they were well staffed and that supplies were replenished. With them humming along, her focus moved to preparing for the mobile clinics' delivery in May and their integration into the plan.

Matt began dropping by work an hour here and there. Ben, the board member and friend Matt had named acting president of Great Expectations during his illness, had kept Matt fully apprised of the company's projects and profits, even during the weeks when Matt could barely follow the spreadsheets and emails. The economy was strong, which boded well for Great Expectations, whose primary clientele were wealthy people seeking exotic vacations and once-in-a-lifetime experiences.

He still believed there was a need for the service Great Expectations provided, but his heart now yearned to fulfill the simple dreams of deserving people in the community. As CEO, Matt decided to leave Ben in the president's chair, managing the day-to-day operations, while he longed to work on this humanitarian side of the company.

He once again assembled a team of bright, hungry interns and met with them in the company's war room. "Ben told me the company gave its full support to Great Expectations' humanitarian push. I can't tell you how pleased I am. He's been waiting for me to take the reins, but frankly, I'm still running on low speed and I'll be here only part time for the next few months. I'm counting on you. I'll coach you, but I need you to spearhead this campaign. Brainstorm ways to find deserving individuals and families with a need we can grant, and then develop a plan to select the most deserving recipients. Talk to schools. PTAs, churches. Run a public campaign. Bring me any idea you come up with. I'll check back in a week. Let's see how many dreams we can grant using five percent of the company's monthly budget."

Matt no longer took the simple experiences for granted, things like taking the car for a drive alone, ordering food from a drive-through, picking up flowers from Gino's florist shop, an— the best piece of normalcy ever—simply coming home after spending time at the office. But nothing in his expanding world took precedence over the dates circled on the calendar.

He entered through the back door carrying a bouquet of calla lilies. Mikaela was on her phone, but she quickly ended the call and moved to Matt. "They're beautiful. And calla lilies? Just like my wedding bouquet. Thank you."

"Pinch me," said Matt. "Because this feels like a dream."

She obliged with a little pinch to his slightly fuller cheek. "This is real, Mr. Grayken. This is what you fought for, and this is your reward."

His hands framed her face, holding her in his gaze. "I'd do it all again for this moment. Thank you for hanging in there with me. I know I still don't look like much of a prize for all your sacrifice."

"You laid everything on the line for me, Matt. That's the greatest kind of love. And for the record, I kinda dig bald men. Have you seen my brothers? Crewcutted grunts? Very sexy."

"Sexy, eh?" Matt leaned against the counter and pulled Mikaela close. "Tell that to my platelets. Rev those boys up to fifty thousand."

"We've got plenty of excitement ahead. Give those platelets a break. You know what tomorrow is, right?"

"Your blood work and ultrasound." He inched his fingers up her back and drew her mouth to his, kissing her softly. "Even if I'm stuck in the waiting room, I'm just excited to be there."

"It's a busy lab. I think you should wear your mask for safety's sake."

"I'll wear a clown wig if that's what it takes. I don't want to miss a minute of this baby experience."

Mikaela sealed the moment with another kiss before saying, "I'd better put these flowers in water," and heading for the cupboard where the vases were kept.

"Who were you talking to on the phone when I came in?"

"Kate. She's heading to New York to sketch the mural for your parents. I'm kind of worried about her. She seemed troubled the night we did the practice setup at the clinic. Have you spoken to Daniel about how they're getting along?"

"Daniel hasn't said anything." Matt sank into a chair. "I'm failing at this brother gig. I've been so preoccupied with myself and my health that I've barely called or contacted her, and I get the feeling she prefers it that way."

Mikaela came over and sat on Matt's lap, wrapping her arm across his neck. "I think it's just the intensity of the situations you two have been thrust into—the adoption details, Hugh's death, your cancer. The only family she has left is a brother she just met and who is still somewhat of a stranger to her. I imagine she's trying to figure out where she fits in this scenario."

"Is that what she told you when you two talked at the church?"

"Not in so many words. Remember I told you about Alaina, the young mother with the three children, and how her husband came in and ordered her to leave. He was a real charmer, if you like your men tall, dark, and abusive. Anyway, after he drove Alaina and the children away, Kate said something about how it's easy to get caught up in your own woes and forget that everyone has something they're wrestling. When I tried to get her to talk about it, she clammed up."

MIKAELA WAS CALLED BACK PROMPTLY at ten for the thirty-minute test. Matt paced back and forth by the receptionist's station, asking for news every five minutes. After the third inquiry, Dr. Chapman came out.

"Mikaela's fine. She's getting dressed now."

"So, we're a go for this month?"

The doctor laughed at Matt's reference. "Yes, we're a go for insemination. I've got you two penciled in for some time between the twentieth and the twenty-second. Mikaela said you're the keeper of the chart. I'm sure you'll let me know when she's ovulating."

The same rush of emotion that overwhelmed Matt in Dr. Marcosky's office engulfed him again. Dreams were becoming realities, and he was a full partner instead of merely a spectator.

When Mikaela came out, Matt approached her with awkward concern. "Was the test painful? Do you feel okay? Do you need to lie down?"

Mikaela linked her arm in his and led him toward the exit. "Is this how you're going to be throughout the entire IUI process? Fussing over me, worrying about every little thing?"

When they reached the sidewalk, Matt lifted his mask and smiled. "I'm afraid so, since I figure it's my turn, right?"

"Good," said Mikaela as she pulled his mouth close to hers. "I like this protective side of you."

Matt held her tight in arms that were gaining strength every day. He kissed her long and deep, enjoying the pleasure of the passion that simple contact stirred in him. For the first time in months, he felt like a man.

When he pulled back after the kiss, he raised his eyebrows

and blew out a rush of air as if he was exhaling steam. "Come on fifty thousand!"

———

LIFE FELL into a blissful normalcy of time at work and time at home, charts, and fewer medical procedures. The day arrived for their first attempt at insemination on post-transplant day eighty-four. The procedure itself was quick and undramatic, but Dr. Chapman left the room and gave the couple privacy to process the milestone.

Matt held Mikaela's hand, bathing it with kisses as she rested on the table. With childlike wonder, he stood and stared down into her face. "We could have just made a baby."

Tears formed in Mikaela's eyes. "Wouldn't that be amazing?"

"Miraculous." He brushed her hair back from her face and touched his forehead to hers. "I love you so much, Mikaela. Thank you for keeping me going, even when I wanted to quit. And no matter what happens today, thank you for giving me this chance, even just the chance, to be a father."

Mikaela's breath shuddered as she drew it in. With a gentle, comical shove, she pushed Matt back and wiped her moist eyes. "Hey, hey there, Buster. If this time fails, we keep on trying. We have enough of your sperm for three more attempts, and if that doesn't work we still have so many options left to us. Even adop-tion." She sniffed and smiled, imbuing him with the hope that so radiated from within her. "Adoption worked out pretty well for you, right? It got us here."

Matt's thoughtful smile began to quiver. "It got me to you." He punctuated his affirmation with a soft, sweet kiss, reminding himself that whatever happened, having Mikaela was enough. A child would just make what they already had even more exquisite.

"And we're agreed that we're not telling anyone, right?" asked Mikaela.

"Just you and me, Babe."

The nurse knocked and came in to inform Mikaela that she could now dress and leave. Mikaela patiently bore Matt's fumbling efforts to hand her clothing items and zip and button things up. His fussing finally reached a point where she politely asked him to sit. He chuckled and blushed, realizing he might need to ratchet the support back a few notches.

Matt replaced his mask before they departed the room and made their way through the waiting area to the main exit. They left the facility hand in hand, with people's eyes on them.

"They see this black mask and wonder if I'm a medical threat or a terrorist."

"Terrorist. Definitely a terrorist . . . who stopped by for some fertility help."

"Yeah. Maybe just a medical threat."

Once outside on the sidewalk, Matt stopped and looked at Mikaela. "We need some way to mark this momentous day."

"We won't know if it was momentous for two weeks."

"Oh, no, Mrs. Grayken, this moment *is* momentous." Matt lifted his mask and set it atop his head. "And why, you ask?" He took her hand and twirled her to a bus stop bench near the corner, encouraging her to step up. Once she was stationed above him, a streetside Juliet to his curbside Romeo, he continued with, "Because right now, inside you, at this very second, a spark of my life is mingling with a spark of your life, and the prospect . . . nay, even the possibility of a new spark of life being formed by that union is"—he brought his fingers to his lips and sent them flying with a smack—"momentous!"

Mikaela laid her hand along his cheek. "You're right. So, what do you have in mind, Mr. Grayken?"

He took her by the waist and tried to help her down, but his will was greater than his strength, and his arms were unable to bear Mikaela's weight. She nimbly caught herself before stumbling. She then quickly steadied Matt before he landed in the busy city street.

Concern replaced the humor of the previous moment as Mikaela checked on Matt. "Are you okay? I think that was too much too fast."

"I'm an idiot." Flushing red, he sat on the bench and leaned over to settle his nerves. "I can see the message on my headstone now: "

Here lies Matt Grayken. The man who wasted a miracle. He survived cancer, then fell into oncoming traffic and died on the very day his child was conceived.

"It was a sweet moment . . . that is . . . until the near-death experience at the end, of course."

"Otherwise, a perfect ten on the suave scale?"

"Oh, at least." She kissed his cheek.

With a single sentence, Mikaela had restored Matt's humor and saved the moment.

"Now what was your idea for our celebration of this momentous day?"

"How about a crab cake sub, and then I want us to go home and transplant the seedlings into the cold frames."

"Seriously? Planting the seedlings is your idea of a momentous celebration?"

"It's life," said Matt. "Today is all about life."

CHAPTER THIRTEEN

Mikaela awoke with Matt smiling and staring at her. She returned his smile and closed her eyes to fall back asleep, but she could almost feel his gaze upon her. When she reopened one eye, she found that she'd been correct about being the focus of his staredown. With a harrumph, she asked, "What?"

"Nothing," he answered with an even bigger smile.

She rolled onto her side, facing away from him and asked. "Come on, Matt. It's only been three days. Are you going to stare at me every morning from now on?"

"You're agitated," came the reply. "Mood swings are common during pregnancy."

"Irritation is also common when one's husband is a maniac."

"Okay." He chuckled. "Have it your way." He swung his legs over the side of the bed and headed for the bathroom. "But mark my words, you're pregnant."

Mikaela waited until the bathroom door closed to allow her own hopes to giggle out. She ran her hands over her belly, knowing there would be no change there, but enjoying the dream of the day when a change might appear. She knew she was just as guilty as Matt for looking for some sign to support her hope. She searched for feelings of nausea, imagined that her breasts were tender, listened to her appetite for signs of cravings, and performed a little test for any evidence of dizziness. She closed her eyes, jiggled her head, and then opened her eyes again to see if increased blood pressure due to pregnancy might be causing the room to spin. No such symptom manifested itself, but something else did become apparent. Matt had reentered the room in time to stare at her again from the window seat.

Mikaela gasped at her silent observer and threw a pillow at him. "You're staring at me again." She laughed as he batted her weak pitch away.

"It's not staring. It's enjoying."

"Okay, that's even more lecherous."

Matt leaned back and pointed her way as he laughed. "You're just embarrassed because I caught you having the same thoughts you chastised me for having."

Mikaela grabbed another pillow, fell back, and used it to cover her face. "All right. I'm busted," she confessed in a muffled voice buried under a down filled mask. She lifted the pillow and sat up. "This is completely unproductive, and besides . . . I'm going to go crazy waiting for some sign that the procedure worked."

"First of all, can we please agree not to call this life-making miracle a procedure?"

Mikaela sat up and blanched. "Sorry."

"It's okay, but as the guy who needed a stand-in, it's a little cold."

"So, what shall we call it? Ooh . . . I know. How about 'our spark'?"

"*Our spark.* . . hmmm . . . I can live with that. In fact, I kind of like it."

"Great. So back to our initial issue. We've got to stay busy until we know whether our spark worked or we'll drive each other crazy. And it would be a terrible waste of suffering and sacrifice to get divorced at this point."

"True . . . true. So what's on your agenda for the day?"

"They're short one nurse at the Upper Marlboro clinic, and I offered to fill in."

"Isn't that the clinic in Alaina's neighborhood? The woman with the abusive husband?"

"Yeah, but it's good for me to see how the clinics actually function from the providers' perspective."

"Mikaela . . . look me in the eye and tell me you'd have volunteered just as quickly if it were any other clinic."

"I would have, Matt. Absolutely."

Matt didn't seem convinced. "You're getting too personally involved in this situation. You've brought her name up a dozen times since that night. I don't think it's a good idea to get this invested, especially with a person in a volatile relationship."

"I don't intend to linger and chat. Besides, I promised Dr. Gorman I'd stop by his office after the clinic closes and finalize the plans for the ribbon cutting when the new mobile clinics are delivered."

Matt arched an eyebrow her way in a clear signal that he was still dubious about the plan. He opened a drawer and fished around for a tee shirt. "I suppose Bennett Sadler will be at this meeting too?" he asked with his back to Mikaela.

"Yes. You need to meet him. He's really a pretty good guy."

Matt turned and said, "Oh . . . I'm sure he is."

Mikaela tossed the box of tissues at him. He reacted quickly in time to catch it, offering her a grunt in return. "What's that for?"

"So you can clean up your mess. You dripped a little sarcasm back there."

"Pardon me for not enjoying that another man keeps my wife on speed-dial."

Mikaela crawled across the bed catlike and hovered near Matt's corner. "Oohhh . . . misplaced, purposeless jealousy?"

Matt shook his head at her and gave her a pitiful glance. "Now you're just being hateful . . . teasing my underperforming platelets like that. And for your information, that only adds salt to the wound."

She sat on the edge of the bed and looked contrite. "Sorry. I'm just feeling a little out of sorts today. Kinda giddy."

Matt pointed to her and tilted his head her way. "See? Pregnant."

"Enough, Mr. Grayken. What's on your agenda today? I know you have your infusion at three. Are you starting the day at the office?"

"I'm meeting with the interns at ten to hear their ideas for granting deserving people's dreams."

She leapt to her feet and gave him a hug. "That's so exciting. I can't wait to hear what you guys decide. I bet most of the families who come to the clinics deserve to have a dream or two come true."

"Mikaela . . . "

"Just saying. . ."

She quickly dressed in nurse's scrubs and tied her hair up for the day. Before leaving the house, she slipped into the bathroom and opened the shower door to offer Matt a goodbye kiss.

"You'd better be careful about opening my shower door,"

Matt warned. "One day soon, I'll drag you right in here and hold you hostage."

Mikaela never spoke of how deeply she too longed for more than the altered touch Matt's health required. They'd had so very little time to fully love one another. She missed lying skin to skin with Matt's arms around her, but it was an invitation to longings that had to be ignored or denied, leaving both the giver and the receiver unsettled and unfulfilled.

She allowed her eyes to slip from his face to his shoulders. They were fleshing out again, as were his trapeziums and his neck. He wasn't the muscled swimmer she had met, but neither was he the rail-thin specter he'd been six weeks earlier. His cell-memory responded to his increased appetite and movement, rebuilding muscle, fattening up his hollow cheeks, and growing a halo of ducklike down on his head and chin. Her prayers had been answered. God was giving her back her husband by degrees. She could wait for his full return to her, but he needed to know she missed him as deeply as he missed her.

She placed her open palm on his wet chest and another behind his neck. When her lips were mere microns from his, she said, "I'll gladly be your hostage, Mr. Grayken." And with a playful change of mood to calm the rising tides, she rubbed his fuzzy head and added, "I think fuzzy is almost as sexy as bald."

Matt grabbed a towel, and before the snap bit into her leg, she squealed and ran for the door and on to the garage.

The adrenaline-rushing scene stayed with her during the first fifteen miles of her trip. It cheered her and left her hungry for more of the energy of life swirling around and within her. To the chagrin of the stalled drivers in either lane beside her, she cranked up the radio and bounced and sang happily as she sat in the bumper-to-bumper D.C. traffic.

As Mikaela pulled into the church parking lot, she saw

Alaina pushing her baby stroller with one hand and tugging her thin sweater more tightly around herself with the other. Before Mikaela could reach her, she had crossed through the doorway that led into the social hall, where the clinic was set up. Reverend Coolidge rushed over to Mikaela as soon as she entered the building. Problems greeted her before the helloes were even said.

"The files aren't here," said the reverend as he walked her over to Dr. Preneur, a retired M.D. and one of the day's two staff physician volunteers. "Dr. Soucy and his wife were going to be the permanent volunteers for this clinic. They planned to keep the records at their home."

"Were? Did they quit?" she asked. She remembered the couple.

Patients filled out a series of forms the first time they came to the clinic—a family health history, a personal questionnaire, insurance forms, and a privacy document. Each clinic needed a paid and licensed person or couple to securely handle these records and input the data into the computer. The Soucys had agreed to handle the Upper Marlboro clinic.

Dr. Preneur stepped forward. "Mrs. Soucy had a stroke. Dr. Soucy asked me to come in his stead today, but with all the chaos in his own life, he forgot to send the records and the computer."

"Oh, dear," answered Mikaela. "Are the records on the computer?"

"Not yet. Mrs. Soucy was going to input them and set us up electronically this week, but . . ."

"Oh, dear," she repeated. Mikaela understood that the reputation and integrity of the clinic project depended heavily on its professionalism and the quality of care it delivered. Knowing a patient's medical history was critical. So was privacy. "We'll have all the patients fill out new forms today, even those returning for follow-up. I suppose we need permanent replacements for the Soucys. I'll try to hire someone right away to handle this clinic's records."

"I can help," said Alaina. "I'm a very good typist."

Mikaela turned to face the woman who had entered from behind her. What she saw left her staring like a gawking child. Alaina's arms had several greenish bruises on them, and her cheek showed the same yellow-green tinge from behind her long dark hair.

"Alaina . . . I . . ."

"You said hire. That means there is pay?"

Mikaela took a breath and nodded. "Yes. But not very much. Just one hundred dollars each day the clinic is open and ten dollars an hour for any record entries you need to make after clinic hours."

Alaina's eye brightened. "So, at least two-hundred dollars a month?"

"Yes, but . . . but . . . Eduardo didn't seem very happy about you being here. I don't want to add any additional burden to your life."

Alaina looked at her children. "It's only two days a month. I can get away. Do you know how many gallons of milk two hundred dollars will buy? How many shoes? Or loaves of bread?"

Mikaela was ashamed that she had forgotten how much two hundred dollars meant to most people. "You'd have to sign a legally binding confidentiality agreement. You couldn't talk about the records . . . to anyone."

The young mother twisted her hands on her stroller's bar. "I know you're worried about what Eduardo might do to me or make me do, but I am not the mouse you think I am." She raised her head and tipped her chin Mikaela's way. "I obey him to a point, to give him respect, but there are lines he cannot make me cross. I am in church every Sunday whether Eduardo is home or not. And I help count the weekly offerings. Reverend Coolidge will vouch for me."

The reverend placed his hand on Alaina's shoulder. "It's true. And she gets the deposit right every week. Better than I do."

Alaina turned to gaze back at the reverend. "Can I leave my pay here in the church, with you, and get some when I need it?"

The reverend nodded and glanced quickly at Mikaela, who felt sicker about the situation with each passing minute. She remembered Matt's conversation earlier in the morning. He wouldn't like her getting more deeply involved in the dynamics of this family. She bit her lip and asked, "Where would we store the records and the laptop?"

"There's an extra closet in my office. It has a combination lock. I can show you," said the reverend.

Mikaela followed along, grateful that when Robert began crying, Alaina lingered behind to tend to him. When she and the reverend reached a quiet corner, she turned to him and asked, "You saw how Eduardo manhandled Alaina the other night. And how frightened the children were of him. And did you see Alaina's bruises?"

He leaned against the wall and allowed his chin to drop into his chest.

"Yes. I saw it all, but what if this is her chance to build a résumé for a better future or to simply make the food last until the end of the month? What if this is really about saving a little money so she can take her family away if she needs too. Ask yourself this. Would you hire Alaina if you'd never met Eduardo?"

Mikaela slumped into the wall. "Yes."

"Then I think you have your answer."

MATT COULDN'T STOP RUBBING his head ever since Mikaela made her point about his growing hair. He smiled, but smiles came more easily now. He felt an increasing want and need to repay the good fortune he was experiencing by doing good to others. And behind the war room door lay the team with which he was hoping to make that dream happen.

He swung the door open and set his eyes where the conference table was supposed to be. Instead, he saw six interns in white choir robes, wings, and halos holding a cardboard cutout of a white, city bus with a blue banner running along its side. The banner was filled with the image of an elongated, cartoonish flying angel and a caption that read, "Be Someone's Angel," The seventh angelically robed member of the team had a guitar strapped to his body. He was strumming and singing a little ditty that said:

Be someone's angel,
Make another's dream come true!

Blue posters and banners bearing the angelic logo adorned the room, and in the very back of the room were sample pamphlets and fliers ready for distribution after Matt's approval.

Matt's jaw dropped. He was wowed, and he broke into clapping as he walked his gaping, open smile from intern to intern, shaking hands and congratulating them on exceeding his expectations. The rush of excitement left him dizzied, so he pulled out a chair and took a seat, inviting all of them to sit as well.

"Phenomenal job, but I'd still like to hear the pitch and plan."

A blonde Cornell grad named Gretchen stepped up. "The

hardest part of this project was getting inside your head and imagining what you wanted this to be. We finally went to Ben, and he shared a conversation you had with him about your vision for Great Expectations. He said it was after your second fight with AML. Ben said you told him that life should be greater than doing more and collecting things. It should be about becoming more. You wanted to give people the opportunity to travel to amazing places and have once-in-a-lifetime experiences that would change them forever."

Brian Castro, a senior at George Washington University, picked up the conversation. "We came back in here and wrestled over the scope of the project. We figured we might be able to grant a few dozen wishes a year, but we started considering how we could maximize the impact, to create a program that would encourage service and goodness, blessing the giver and the receiver. An hour later, we had it all—the theme, the jingle, and a plan that wouldn't limit us to the dozens of wishes we could personally handle. Instead, we thought, why not inspire an army of people to fill each other's wishes and dreams? We'd furnish the funding, the project support, and the critical connections and contacts they'd need, but we'd inspire and empower members of the community to name the recipients, come up with the ideas, and provide most of the manpower."

Matt caught their vision, which was greater than even he had imagined for the program.

Another intern added, "We'll plaster these banners on city buses, and then we hope to hit the local radio and cable stations to spread the word. Our website is up and running. People can go there to fill out applications for the grants."

"And who will decide which projects we fund?" asked Matt.

"We knew you wanted to stay involved, so it will be you and a committee of fifteen community leaders," said Maggie as she slid the list Matt's way. "They've already committed to convene once a month to select candidates based on funding."

"You've thought of everything," said Matt. "Well done. Let's launch this right away."

THE CLOUD that hung over Mikaela's morning followed her into the afternoon. She hired Alaina despite serious misgivings, and then Bennett texted his regrets about the afternoon meeting with Dr. Gorman, so the good doctor decided to cancel the meeting altogether and rubberstamp anything Mikaela decided. Now all the big decisions about the ribbon cutting of the mobile clinics fell to her.

Needing someone to console her, she headed to the infusion clinic to sit with Matt. As she approached the reception desk, she saw one of the regular shift nurses inserting a glittering number fifty into a beautifully decorated cupcake, which she then carried into one of the infusion suites. The remaining nurse gasped and then smiled when she saw Mikaela.

"We weren't expecting you today."

"My afternoon meeting got canceled so I decided to come and sit with Matt. Which suite is he in?"

The nurse's smile became pinched, and her eyes widened as if she had been caught eating candy from someone else's Halloween bag. "Suite seven. I'll buzz you in."

When the door buzzed and opened, Mikaela expected to hear the strains of "Happy birthday," ringing down the hall. Instead, she saw the nurse hand the cupcake off to Dr. Marcosky, who thanked her before slipping into infusion suite seven. "Fifty?" she muttered loud enough for the cupcake bearer to hear. "Are Matt's platelets up over fifty thousand?"

The nurse held a thumbs-up sign close to her chest. "You didn't hear that from me."

Mikaela floated to the doorway to hear the conversation ensuing between Dr. Marcosky and Matt. She saw the pure delight on the doctor's face and heard Matt's emotional voice repeat, "The port is coming out? Thank you, thank you."

She too wanted to cry. It had often been difficult to separate the optimistic cheering she did to rally Matt's spirits from real, medically supported health. But this number was a major milestone, and its quick rise was further confirmation that Matt's general health was solid. These were the blessings they'd prayed for, and they were coming true. She clutched her hands to her chest and closed her eyes, whispering "Thank you, Father. Thank you, thank you, thank you."

As silently as she arrived, she left the infusion suite area and swore the nurses to secrecy about her arrival as she hurried out of the clinic.

As a rule, Matt hated shopping, but this shopping trip ranked among the most delightful experiences of his life. He parked the car in the garage and exited with his bag and more radiant joy and pent-up excitement than he could remember.

He and Mikaela had shared a few exquisite nights together, but they were sorrow tinged by the tick of the clock measuring the decline of his remaining time. No sorrow hovered over this night. Dr. Marcosky said there were no guarantees about how long this reprieve would last, but neither were there any reasons to assume it would be brief. So, hope was the watchword, and to mark the triumphant return of hope, he had purchased a few celebratory items.

He figured he had at least an hour or two before Mikaela arrived from her second meeting, but as soon as he opened the back door that led to the kitchen, he caught a whiff from Mikaela's favorite candle. Candlelight flickered in several corners of the house, aided only by the tiny lights of the Christmas tree. Matt's favorite folksy jazz CD was playing on the stereo, and the table was set with lit tapers and their best china. Matt set his bag down on the counter, somewhat disappointed that his surprise was not to be, but more intrigued by the welcome he was receiving. *Did she know? But how?*

"Mikaela?" He stepped into the living room and called to her again. "I didn't see your car."

"I didn't want you to see it," she replied from the bedroom, whose door was only slightly ajar.

Prickles rose on Matt's skin as his imagination went into hyperdrive, inspiring his heart rate and breathing to do the same. "Did you happen to stop by the infusion clinic this afternoon?"

"I may have," his tomboyish wife answered, in a voice as soft and warm as suede.

Matt felt his palms sweat. He unbuttoned the top button of his shirt and released his tie until it hung loosely around this collarbone. The bedroom door opened slowly, revealing Mikaela, with her tousled hair loosely gathered upon her head and a touch of color on her lips and cheeks. She was dressed in the black satin gown she had worn to the Irish Embassy Ball the previous fall, the night they had nearly fought their way into annulling their marriage but ended up making love for the first time.

The first time . . . The words resonated over and over in Matt's mind. There had been too few nights afterward, before illness separated them again. Hope swept the sad memories away. Time was on their side now. It was finally their ally.

He walked to her, his arms sliding around her in one single, seamless motion, melding them body to body, hands to backs, cheek to cheek. Matt closed his eyes and breathed in the smell of her, no longer fearful of where his mind or will would take them. He felt her heart beat against his chest, her breaths warm his ear, her muscles melt into his own.

He brushed his lips across her brow, trailing his lip down her cheek until he found her mouth. His legs faltered, and Mikaela drew back, worried.

He cupped her face in his hands and said, "I'm still a little bruised, but no longer broken."

"Just lean in to me. I've got you, Mr. Grayken."

"I never doubted it, Mrs. Grayken. Not for a second."

Conversation seemed a chore. He had spent weeks, months making small talk about anything that kept his mind off death. Now he wanted to feel life. He wanted to feel it surge through him, even to the point of leaving him feeling breathless and weak from its power. He marveled over the unique capacity of a kiss to do that, to move beyond the mere touch of lips, sending sensual shockwaves to far-off limbs, leaving legs shaky and arms like rubber.

He thought he might never waste his lips on speech again, and then Mikaela said, "I picked up dinner."

"Me too," he replied before pressing his lips back down on hers.

She moaned in pleasure and pulled back. "And tiramisu. Your favorite."

"You are my favorite right now," he joked, drawing her mouth back to his.

"This is supposed to be a romantic dinner at home. You just had your port removed."

He smiled down at her. "Then let's explore some alternative dessert options."

"Matt. . ." she implored, but he would not be redirected or dissuaded. Mikaela slid her hands around his neck and took hold of his tie. "Welcome home, Mr. Grayken."

NEITHER SET of entrees were eaten that night. Instead, they ate Mikaela's chilled tiramisu and Matt's soggy crème brûlée as they talked in bed, wrapped in sheets and folksy jazz.

"How did you get home so early?" asked Matt as he spooned another bite of crème brûlée into Mikaela's mouth.

"Bennett bailed on the meeting to catch a flight. Something about wining and dining a client or an investor in New York, or something."

"He sounds like a flake."

"He's not . . . usually. But all the plans for the ribbon cutting of the mobile clinics have now defaulted to me."

"If he walks like a flake and acts like a flake . . ."

"Your opinion has been noted. How was your meeting with the interns?"

Matt leaned up on one elbow and set his plate to the side. "It was actually phenomenal. They exceeded all expectations."

"That's great! I can't wait to hear."

He shared the highlights of the plan and then asked, "And how did it feel to return to the world of nursing today?"

Mikaela paused and made a few hmms and umms while putting an excessive amount of effort into chewing a bite of the custard. "It was good. I enjoyed helping people again. I've missed that."

"Did Alaina show up today?"

Mikaela quickly scooped another large spoonful of her dessert into her mouth.

"You're chewing crème brûlée. You're stalling. Oh my gosh." Matt flopped back against the bed." Something happened today. You're getting more involved in Alaina's life, aren't you?"

"I wasn't trying to, but the lead couple for that clinic backed out and I needed to hire someone to handle the recordkeeping, and yes, Alaina applied."

"How do you think the abusive husband will like this change?"

"What could I do, Matt? She overheard me talking to the reverend about needing a new paid volunteer, and she jumped on the chance. What could I do?"

Matt spread his arm out and she lay back into the curve of his shoulder. "I trust your judgment, Mikaela. All I'm asking is that you trust mine too."

"I do, but your worry goes a little overboard sometimes."

"Like with Bennett?"

"He's not a threat."

"It's not just a husband's jealousy that makes me mistrust Bennett. I've read a lot of articles about him, including the interview he gave. He gets what he wants. End of story. There's no way he couldn't foresee how jacking up prescription costs on that heart medicine would hurt patients. But he did it anyway, because he wanted to kick up profits to fund more billion-dollar breakthroughs."

"That allowed him to produce some drugs below cost."

"Drops in the bucket. His profits this quarter are soaring."

She bolted to her knees. "Which he used to fund our clinic project."

Matt likewise moved into a sit. "Which put him in good

graces with the city council and wealthy philanthropists with whom I predict he'll soon be doing business."

Mikaela sat back on her heels in defeat. "I don't want to argue with you."

Matt lay back down and covered his eyes with his arm. "And I don't want to lose you."

"Do you hear how ridiculous you're being? Even if Bennett Sadler were crazy in love with me, which he's not, it wouldn't matter, because I don't have feelings for him, got it? For currently unfathomable reasons, I'm already in love with my pigheaded, jealous husband."

Matt lifted his arm and stretched it out to her. After a long stink-eyed look and a sigh, she returned to her spot in the curve of his shoulder, but his cheek was not warmed by another kiss.

Long after Mikaela had fallen asleep, Matt stared at the ceiling, castigating himself. Why on this day of all days, the day when he was celebrating, if not the defeat, then at least the temporary banishment of death, the greatest of all threats, did he continue to see new threats around every corner? But he could not shake the unease that crept into his heart each time he thought about Bennett Sadler, and a faceless man he knew only as Eduardo.

CHAPTER FOURTEEN

Monday, April ninth, was a huge day with three circles on the calendar page, one in blue, one in red, and one in green. The blue circle marked day one hundred post-transplant, a major milestone complete with results from another painful but worthwhile bone marrow biopsy confirming that Matt was in remission.

The green circle, Matt's favorite color, marked his thirtieth birthday, which they celebrated with his parents over the weekend, and the bright red circle, added by Matt on the morning of the ninth, marked two things—the fourth day Mikaela's period was late, and the first time she threw up her breakfast.

Matt accepted her unwillingness to take his leap of faith and declare those clues as evidence of pregnancy, so he decided to offer her another previously unacceptable option. After opening his birthday present from her, he handed her one, a small box awkwardly wrapped in floral paper and tied with a lopsided purple bow.

"A pregnancy test?"

"You'll know once and for all."

Mikaela bit her thumbnail. "That's just it. Right now, I have the unconfirmed joy of believing I'm pregnant. What if I'm not? What if my fear of it not being true is what's throwing my cycle off and making me nauseated? Then it's gone. It's all gone."

Matt pulled her to himself. "Then we start again."

She slumped against him and lay still there for several long seconds before meeting his expectant eyes. "I don't know if this will make sense to you, but in a very small way, a miniscule way, this waiting game had helped me understand your experience with cancer. I want to be pregnant so desperately and yet I'm so afraid I won't get the answer I want. That's how you felt every time you did your labs, isn't it? Wanting so desperately to get good news but terrified the news would be bad. Does that make sense?"

Somehow hearing her say that made him feel both peaceful and sad. "Perfect sense."

"It makes my heart break for you, imagining how a lab test, something completely out of your control, can have so much power over your life. I'm sorry if I didn't fully 'get that' before." She leaned her head into his shoulder. When she again looked up, she saw him smiling. "What?"

"If I say it, you might hit me."

"What?"

"Emotional mood swings are—"

She punched him in the arm.

Matt framed her face in his hands and kissed her. "Just take the test. Please? It'll be all right. Whatever it tells us, *we* will be all right."

She nodded and headed into the bathroom. A minute later, she came out without the stick and crawled into the waiting warmth of Matt's arms. She jabbered on about their upcoming trip to New York to spend a week with his parents and about her plans for the mobile clinic ribbon cutting, and an autumn gala to raise enough local money to sustain the units for several years. Matt feigned listening while his mind raced on to what he would say if the test was positive and what he would do for Mikaela if it wasn't. All the while, he watched the clock mark the passing minutes. When seven minutes had passed, he found a break in her nervous ramblings and said, "It's time."

He placed his hands over her eyes and walked her to the sink. His heart raced, knowing that if this test proved negative, their possible number of future tries was limited. And then he saw the stick. And two undeniable pink lines! Tears burned behind his eyes as he allowed his arms to slide around Mikaela's shoulders.

"Congratulations, Mrs. Grayken. You're going to be a momma."

Her breaths came in ragged shudders as she checked for herself. Once assured of the results, she slumped against Matt and cried into his chest. It struck him that he held more than Mikaela within his arms. He was holding his wife *and* his child. His *family*. A new sense of responsibility washed over him, filling him with gratitude. He closed his eyes, welcoming the new feelings of indebtedness to God for this gift. He kissed Mikaela's head and whispered, "Thank you, Father," understanding the love and power embodied in that name as never before.

Matt called the office to say he'd be late, and they headed back to bed for an hour to hold each other and allow the news to settle in. Everything in those moments changed, as if the earth had been moved from her regular orbit into a new place, a heavenly place of peace and gentleness, where every nuanced glance and touch held the secret only they knew. A baby was coming!

Daniel and the DVP guys came early for poker the following Thursday to help celebrate Matt's clean bill of health by moving the Graykens' bedroom out of the study and into the upstairs master. Matt recognized that Mikaela needed an actual office to manage the increasing demands of the clinics, so he asked the guys to help with a few other moving jobs. They hauled the extra bed and dresser out of the study and into the garage for donation to a charity, before moving a new desk and a daybed back into the room. Now the office would also serve as a guest room for company. No one but Matt and Mikaela knew the plans for the former guest room down the upstairs hall, where pastel paint chips and fabric swatches were already spread across the floor.

Matt pulled Daniel aside and asked if he'd heard from Kate.

"We talk every day. Just not about anything meaningful. She's hard to understand. Some days she sounds excited to answer my calls. Other days, I'm certain she's avoiding them."

"Mine too. I'm sorry you've been hurt because of her difficulties dealing with me. I admit that I've been so preoccupied with the adjustments in my own life that I haven't reached out to her as I should."

"I think you get a pass, under the circumstances."

"Maybe so, but I owe her my life."

Daniel stepped up to Matt. "That attitude is part of the problem. She doesn't need your undying gratitude. She needs your friendship. Sibling love will follow. You just need to relax and get to know her."

It made sense, and doubled Matt's guilt that he hadn't bonded with her as he wanted. "Mikaela and I are headed up to New York soon. Seeing Kate is a big reason why."

"I'm glad to hear that because she's made it clear she doesn't want me 'in her space' while she's working. I'm glad the mural she painted on your parents' wall is almost finished. It'll be great to get her back."

"She's finished?" Another wave of guilt hit Matt. "I should have known that."

"Maybe you should have called her."

"I definitely should have asked. I've just had my mind on other things."

"Call her. Right now."

Matt pulled out his phone and dialed her number, but she didn't pick up. He then called his parents, who said that Kate was out. In frustration, he texted Kate.

Hey, I miss my sis. Call when you can. I'm excited to see the mural.

Love, Matt.

THREE ATTEMPTS WERE MADE to enjoy the spectacular beauty of the capital's Cherry Blossom Festival along the Tidal Basin, but Mikaela's nausea forced them to either cancel their plans or leave early each time.

Her first OB-GYN appointment was set three weeks out, but she called for help with the nausea as soon as she became a registered patient. Mornings were rough, afternoons were rough, and even nights were hard. While the minty flavor of the toothpaste was soothing, the toothbrush became Mikaela's mortal enemy, causing her to gag and wretch every time she brushed her teeth. She couldn't bear the smell of eggs or raw chicken or meat. At the first sizzle, fried foods sent her running for the commode, where she'd be found sweaty and hunched over. Matt held her hair back out of the vomit and placed cold, wet rags on her neck. His efforts to make light of the situation with a joke about the strong constitution or personality of the growing child were not appreciated, and he often dodged glaring looks which were generally followed by apologies and tears. On one particularly hard day, Matt appeared incapable of doing anything right or, at least, of doing anything to ease Mikaela's discomfort. He was about to exit and leave her alone to her suffering when she reached a hand to him and asked him to stay.

"I'm sorry," she said between heaves. "This is like an out-of-body experience. I'm just not myself."

He sat beside her and gathered her hair up. "It's okay. I understand."

"Thank you for being patient with me."

"It's my turn," he said, kissing the back of her neck as she hung over the porcelain toilet bowl. "My cancer gives me some insight into this phase of pregnancy. No one enjoys having their body go rogue on them, so you have my complete support and sympathy, just as you gave them to me."

As sick as she was, she knew his fight with cancer and the level of illness it caused him were more pardonable than morning sickness. "But you weren't mean to me. I've been sniping and complaining. And how do women gain pregnancy weight when everything makes you sick?"

"I was grumpy. And I think that lack of appetite will change. Remember me? The skinny rat of a man?" He tapped his stomach. "I'm up thirty pounds. I need to put more time in swimming laps at the pool."

She lifted her head, and he handed her a towel to wipe her mouth. "I know I don't always say it enough or act like it, but I really do love you."

"Ooh . . . let me get a pencil and write that down."

She hit him with the towel. "Not funny, mister. Give me back that sensitive guy you just mentioned."

He chuckled and pressed his lips to her sweaty temple. "I promise that he's the guy who'll be escorting you to the ribbon cutting this afternoon."

"And you'll be pleased to know who else will be there."

"Please don't say Bennett Sadler."

"Your sarcasm is showing again. Of course, he's coming. You need to get over that right now. And while I'm thinking about it, I'm going to need another promise that you'll bring my sensitive, civilized, confident, knows-he's-being-an-idiot husband to the gala next month, when Bennett gets his award from the Inter-faith Coalition of Churches."

"That's asking a lot."

"Promise me."

He huffed comically. "I promise. Now tell me who else is coming, and please let it be someone I actually want to see?"

"Kate. She arrived last week. A signage company turned her drawing into twenty-foot vinyl graphics that will hold up better than paint. She insisted she had to be at the ribbon cutting in case a sign tore during installation and needed to be touched up."

Matt sat back against the wall, weighing the news against what Daniel had told him. "Daniel thought she was still in New York, finishing up my parents' mural."

"Daniel probably assumed she was still in New York. She didn't tell him otherwise because she didn't want him to know she was back in town. He'd want to get together, and she wanted to focus all her time and attention on the work."

"She contacted you but not me?"

Mikaela heard the hurt in his voice. "Please don't take it personally, Matt, or read too much into it. My relationship with her is simple and new and clean. No history. No baggage. You two have almost thirty years of messy history between you. It's going to take some time."

"You're right. I'm glad she's back. I need to see her. She and I really need to talk."

"Then you'd better leave so you can get to the lab for your blood work and still hit the gym before the ceremony." She patted his stomach. "Only one of us is allowed to get fat this summer."

THE PACE of his recovery was slow and frustrating, but Matt was grateful to be back in the pool. He missed the rush of slicing through the water like a beam of light and feeling his body respond when he called for more speed or for the endurance to flip and turn and sail through one more lap. Swimming was not nearly the same experience now. He slapped the water and gasped for air at the end of every half-lap, and his legs no longer moved with grace. More bent than straight, his kick testified to the muscle atrophy he'd experienced over the months in bed. After his last bout with AML, every hour not spent at work was dedicated to rebuilding his strength and speed. But those were old priorities when his life was his own. His goal now was simple—to get stronger and to increase his endurance. His need to be the best in athletic endeavors had been replaced with dreams of new bests—to be the best husband, the best father, and the best person he could be.

Famished after his swim, he hurried to the lab, hoping the line was short so he could get out of there and to the closest food source he could find. He checked in at the front desk where the technician pulled up his file. "Found you. Also, just a reminder that your next bone-marrow biopsy is in three weeks. Do you need a copy of the lab slip?"

Just the mention of the biopsy made a knot form in Matt's stomach. He felt great, but he wondered if he'd ever feel fully clear of leukemia again. "No thanks. Dr. Marcosky's office mailed me a copy."

"Okay. Well, since you missed the morning rush, I can take you straight back."

He was in and out in under ten minutes, but it took an hour to shake loose from the nervous knot caused by the mention of the upcoming biopsy. He grabbed an apple and a protein drink at the hospital food cart and headed to the office. Five of the interns were waiting for him in the lobby.

"Are you as excited as we are?" asked the normally reserved intern named Maggie.

"About what?" asked Matt.

Her jaw nearly dropped into the foam on her cappuccino. "With all due respect, Mr. Grayken, you've got to be kidding, right?"

Matt shot her a pistol point and smiled. "Right. And just call me Matt. We're a team. Now fill me in as we walk to the war room."

She hurriedly capped her beverage and began her report. "We placed the trial banner on a single bus and we've already received eighteen online applications! We're sifting through them to make sure they're all legit, but we thought you'd be excited to see the level of response."

Matt stopped walking and glanced into the faces of his seven-person dream team. "I am. I'm very excited by the progress you've made. How else are we reaching the public?"

Matt started walking again, and the interns rushed along around him.

"Well get this," said another intern named Brian. "Some rich philanthropist saw the bus banner, and he offered to kick in a half-mil to fund the project."

Matt stopped cold and turned to the freckled young man. "What was his name?"

"Bennett Sadler. He's the president of some big pharma—"

"Stick to the budget I gave you, got it?" snarled Matt. He caught himself when he saw shock and fear register on the intern's face. "I- I-I'm sorry, Brian. Forgive me. You didn't do anything wrong. I have personal issues with Sadler. I don't approve of how he runs his company, and I don't want this project to be impacted by any controversy surrounding him. You're doing great. I just want to keep this Angel project completely in-house for now, okay?"

Sadler's reach into yet another corner of Matt's world galled him. Despite a productive meeting with the interns, anger continued to seethe through him as he headed for the ribbon-cutting ceremony at the Congressional Concourse Shopping Plaza in the middle of the district the units would serve. He arrived early and met Mikaela near the aluminum grandstand set up between the two units.

Her hands were tucked under her chin, and she was nearly skipping toward him. "Aren't they gorgeous? And wait until you look inside! They're mini emergency rooms!"

As angry as he was at Sadler, he had to admit that the man had funded two impressive medical clinics. Each long side of the navy blue buses had Kate's design bonded to their sides—three large, white letters, MMP, painted in Kate's graceful lettering, with smaller letters, spelling out Metro Mercy Project, trailing after the larger ones. A tour of the interiors made Matt think of his favorite TV sci-fi series. He all but expected an alien doctor to walk out from one of the three treatment bays.

Matt had never wanted for money, but neither had he ever envied others for having more than he did, until this moment. He wished he could have been the man to fund Mikaela's dream. He had offered, of course, but his offering would have been nothing like this. Mikaela was right about him. He was jealous of Bennett Sadler, and that admission stung worse than he could have imagined.

Kate slipped in just seconds before the commencement of the dedicatory program, where the vehicles would officially be given to the greater D.C. community for the good of its citizens. Kate took her seat on the stand with Mikaela, Bennett, Dr. Gorman, and a few local leaders. Matt took his reserved seat, and Mikaela rose to give her speech, thanking Bennett and all the community and religious leaders who had contributed to the clinic program's success. Matt saw Mikaela's eyes shift, and then she smiled at a spot in the back of the crowd. Matt turned and noticed a young Hispanic mother arriving from the direction of the bus stop with a toddler, a baby, and a ragged umbrella stroller. He watched as she and her children moved to the front of the crowd, where seats were also reserved for them. He noticed how she received smiles and hugs from some of the guests seated near her in the front row. Matt felt certain this was Alaina.

Bennett's speech was the shortest of those given by the four speakers, ending the program earlier than expected. When the applause died, people lined up for tours of the buses. Mikaela, Kate, Bennett, and other special guests were quickly swept up by photographers, so Matt headed for the refreshment table.

He found Alaina standing in a small group with a collared reverend. Her eyes nervously darted to the street where they finally froze. Matt followed her gaze and saw a black Suburban stopped in traffic at the light. When the light changed, the SUV with darkened windows moved on, as did Alaina, who rapidly pushed her stroller away from the scene. There was no proof that the driver was the infamous Eduardo, but Matt was unwilling to take any chances. He searched for Mikaela, anxious to leave this place before the car returned. He found her at the head of a long line of waiting visitors. Stressed and unsettled as he was, Matt knew his wife. Mikaela wouldn't leave until the last guest had been received, so he moved to the refreshment table and relieved his stress by downing a few catered cookies.

A new reason for stress approached in the form of Bennett Sadler, whose hand was outstretched. Matt longed to make a quick escape, but that was not an option. Guilt swept over him, followed by a determination to prove he was a bigger man than his jealous nature might suggest. He smiled and accepted Bennett's gesture.

"Hello, Matt. So nice to finally meet you." Bennett shrank back and put his hands forward, as if he had caused an offense. "May I call you Matt? I feel as if we're old friends. Mikaela talks about you all the time."

Matt caught the man's need to ingratiate himself. Matt was also irked by Bennett's effort to identify his connection to Mikaela. "Of course, you can call me Matt, *Bennett*."

"Great. Great. You're looking good, considering everything you've been through."

Matt snagged another cookie and nodded. As much as he loathed the idea, giving the guy an attaboy seemed a more palatable option than discussing his own near death, or possible future death, with a guy he felt pretty certain was auditioning as his replacement. "You've done a good thing for the community. These buses are amazing."

The man dipped his shoulder modestly. "It was Mikaela's vision."

Matt screwed the toe of his shoe into the blacktop. "Yes, it was."

"It's been an honor to work with her."

"And now you're done and free to move on to other projects. I hear you have an interest in my company's 'Be Someone's Angel' project."

"Yes. So, you've heard."

"It actually came to my attention this morning, but unfortunately, it's a personal project. I'm funding it in-house."

Bennett leaned in and smiled a toothy grin. "I'd love to help you take it to the next level."

Matt straightened to his full six-foot height and faced Bennett squarely. "I'm completely content with the level we're on, Bennett, with this project and every aspect of my life. But thank you."

The taller man allowed a tepid smile to curl the corners of his mouth. "Then I assume you realize what a lucky man you are."

"I know I'm a very blessed man, but I don't count any of it as luck. Luck is transitory, Bennett. Success, friendships, family, love. These are gifts upon which you build something strong and tenacious and enduring."

A pause that seemed more like a standoff ensued between the two men. Bennett finally broke the silence, saying, "I understand. I admire you, the battles you've fought, what you've built. I've heard Mikaela speak of her superhero brothers and about your DVP group. I envy you two with all that love and support."

For a moment, Matt felt guilty about shoving his blessings in Bennett Sadler's face. He swallowed and tried to come up with a way to backpedal out of his arrogance, but before he could answer, Bennett drained the glass of sparkling water in his hand and smiled, tipping the empty glass Matt's way.

"Friends and family are good, but you never know when you . . . or Mikaela might need an extra friend. So I'll be around. Just in case."

Matt's hand curled into a fist as the man of the hour moved away, but relief approached in a yellow dress as Kate made her way through the crowds to Matt. He watched the awkward way her head dipped each time they made eye contact, and deciding that the best opening was overt love, he met her halfway and swept her into a hug. She didn't fight his embrace, but her muscled back and arms remained tight until he released her.

"I've missed you," he began. "How was New York?"

"Lovely. Fun. I think I gained eight pounds, what with all the wining and dining your parents threw at me. They're grand folks, Matthew. I think the gods smiled on you when they sent you to them."

"I'd have to agree, though I'm still grateful to add a sister to my family. When can we get together?" He took one of her hands. "Now that I'm feeling more like myself, Mikaela and I can't wait to show you around the city and take you to some of our favorite places."

She listened with interest, her eyes growing wider with each point.

Matt pressed further. "I know Daniel has missed you. How are things going between you two?"

Her head bobbed left then right. "I've been playing a bit of dodge with him."

"That's what he said. I love Daniel. He's like a brother to me, but being close to me doesn't mean you have to love my friend."

Her shoulders rounded, and she looked up at the sky. "Thank you for saying that." She gave Matt another hug. "I do care for Daniel. He's kind and good and smart. It's just . . . something isn't clicking quite right between us. It might not be him. It might be me. Probably is, actually. My mind is so jumbled with ideas and notions. I came here to meet my brother and to help him if I could, but in truth, I'm not done grieving Hugh yet because I never properly grieved for Mum or Da or you. I just kept running from one heartache to another. Being with your parents was painfully lovely. Your Da was always asking me if I needed anything, and your Mum made food or bought me things before I knew I needed them. It was . . ."

"Overwhelming? Suffocating? Stifling?" Matt laughed.

"Yes," she answered with a hearty laugh. "But also wonderful. The idea of having someone fend for you instead of always fending for everyone else. I confess I wet my pillow more than once."

Matt wanted to scoop her close and move her back home again. "You have me now, Kate. I can't imagine you ever needing my help, but if you do, I'll fend for you."

Her smile spread from ear to ear. "You're a lamb, Matthew, and I love you already, but I feel as if I've got nothing to give anyone right now, not even myself. And the emptiness isn't something someone else can fill. I need to go home."

Somehow the news wasn't unexpected, but it saddened Matt. He thought of Mikaela's excitement over having a sister, and their news about the coming baby. He longed to tell her now, but he held back, not wanting to impose upon her yet again. "To Ireland?"

"Aye. It was inevitable. I can't live here mooching off the likes of my baby brother's family forever." She laughed again and squeezed Matt's hand before letting it go. "I don't have a work visa, but my need is more than financial. I'm a bit broken inside, and I need to go home where my ghosts lie, say goodbye once and for all, and heal awhile."

"I understand, but I hope you'll come back soon. Autumn in

the east is gorgeous, and I assumed we'd be together for the holidays."

"I'll try, all right? I'll give it a good try."

"When will you be leaving?"

"This afternoon. I'm already booked, and I've said my piece to Mikaela."

"So soon? You need to at least call Daniel."

"I will. From the airport. I'm not one for long goodbyes."

She kissed each cheek and held his hand until her steps carried her beyond his reach. Matt watched her disappear into the throng. Once she got past the buses, he lost sight of her once and for all.

Kate's departure felt like another failure somehow. Life felt smaller again. He felt small again. Small and weak at a time when his and Mikaela's world seemed to be in constant flux and swarming with predators—like Bennett Sadler and a man named Eduardo.

CHAPTER FIFTEEN

Matt filled the calendar page with notes about a flurry of firsts—the first dreams granted by the angel team and their community partners, the setting of the first seedlings in the vegetable garden, Matt's first post-transplant haircut/fuzzcut, and Mikaela's first OB/GYN appointment, which ended with the most exciting moment of Matt's life, the first sonogram image of their child. Another harrowing, nail-biting, bone-marrow biopsy passed with good results, a painful rash flare-up proved to be a medicine reaction and not GvHD, and Mikaela found a cure for her morning sickness, baked potatoes, which became her new breakfast staple. In honor of the coming Memorial Day holiday and the summer season, Mikaela changed the ornaments on the tree to a patriotic red-white-and-blue motif.

At Mikaela's June OB/GYN appointment, Dr. Chapman presented the couple with the option to know the baby's gender. Matt immediately leapt at the idea. Mikaela's eyes lit up and then quickly dimmed.

"Don't you want to know so we can ponder names and prepare the nursery?" asked Matt.

"Yellow works for boys or girls. You know how I love butter yellow."

Matt sensed that she was hedging. He asked the doctor if he and Mikaela could have a moment alone. Once the doctor left, Matt took Mikaela's hand and gave her a one-eyed wince. "What's the real reason you don't want to know if we're having a boy or a girl?"

Mikaela removed her hand from Matt's and fumbled with her fingers. "I think the expectation will be good for us."

"For us? I think you really mean it will be good *for me*." He waited until his silence brought her eyes to his. "Knowing or not knowing the baby's gender isn't going to affect the stakes of my fight. I'm not fighting to know if I'm having a boy or girl. I'm fighting to raise this little person with you."

Mikaela's eyes began to shine. "Okay."

"Let's compromise. Let's have the doctor write the gender on a card, and we'll give it to . . . Daniel to hold for us. If we need to know before the baby's born, he'll tell us. Otherwise, we'll paint the room yellow for Sparkle or Sparky."

The couple left that day with the news in a pink-and-blue-striped envelope, and they focused on how to tell Matt's parents and friends about the pregnancy. They choose the weekend of Mikaela's birthday, June 16, to share the news, and made arrangements with a local restaurant for a special dinner at five with Matt's parents. When the food came, everything Mikaela ordered was doubled. Two bread plates arrived with two rolls, along with two beverages and two salads. Catherine kept calling for the waiter to amend the error, but Donovan's eyes shifted from Mikaela to Matt, who seemed completely calm while Mikaela happily and deliberately ate from both sets of food.

With a loud laugh, Donovan slapped his hand on the table and grabbed Catherine's arm. "Don't you get it, Catherine? She's eating for two!" Matt and Mikaela burst into laughter while Catherine and Donovan jumped up and hugged them both.

Informing Mikaela's brothers was also fun. They lined up peat pots with sticks and name holders on the table. The first held a tomato plant, the second a marigold, the third a pepper plant, and the last held a sonogram they printed off the Internet. Matt photographed the bunch, and Mikaela emailed the photo with this caption: "Something's sprouting at the Graykens' house." Within minutes, loving text messages and video calls began pouring in.

The sprout setup was also used to inform the DVP gang as they arrived with dates for the party. Their reactions were filled with pride and joy equal to that of the family members, and Mikaela understood, once again, that love bound Matt and Mikaela to these guys to as much as blood or law bound them to any family members.

In a covert moment, Matt and Mikaela cornered Daniel and handed him the envelope with the baby's gender. "We want the news to be a surprise, so we're entrusting you with this envelope to prevent us from grabbing a peek."

Daniel scowled. "I don't get why you wrote it down at all."

Mikaela touched Matt's arm and walked away leaving the reply to him.

"We just felt it would be good to have handy, in case the worst should happen. In the event I'd like to know who I'd be waiting to meet someday."

It was apparent that Daniel felt the honor and weight of the request. He had arrived alone, and yet he still managed to appear happy for Gunther Knudsen when this DVP brother announced his engagement to Constance, a woman he'd been dating for six weeks. When the guys pulled him aside to question the wisdom of marrying someone he'd known for such a short time, Gunther pointed to Matt and Mikaela's success, and the comments ceased, at least for the evening.

Daniel wandered over to the nacho bar, where he drowned his sorrows by dipping one chip after another into hot queso. Matt sauntered over and dipped a chip.

"I take it you're thinking about Kate?"

After plunging a final chip from the dip to his mouth, he shot Matt a look of pure despair.

"I'm sorry, brother."

Daniel shook off Matt's pity and leaned against the island. "You started this, you know." Matt began to protest, and Daniel hurried on. "Not the Kate thing. I rushed into that, but probably in part because of you. You braved the passage out of our eternal boyhood. You showed us it's time to be men, and you made marriage look better than playing around and being alone. Now Gunther wants what you have, Matt. I want what you have. I thought that maybe . . . just maybe Kate was someone I could have that with." When Matt didn't offer a comment, Daniel continued. "Maybe I didn't make my feelings clear. We had fun together."

"I don't think it's you, Daniel. I think Kate's still dealing with a lot of baggage from her past."

"But why did she leave without even giving me a chance to plead my case?"

"She said she's not good at goodbyes."

Daniel huffed. "That's an understatement."

"Only one question matters now. Do you love her or just like her?"

Daniel hung his head and stared at the floor. "How do I know?"

Matt looked across the room at Mikaela, whose hand kept moving to her belly and whose eyes kept moving back to meet Matt's. He thought about all she had endured to support him, all the tears and prayers and sleepless nights. He also considered how he had surrendered his own will in order to fight the cancer for her . . . for them. They still lived out on a limb, in a fragile space that defied reason.

He turned, placed his hands on Daniel's shoulders, and looked him in the eye. "You'll know, Daniel, but don't fight for her and complicate her life until you do."

Daniel nodded. "Understood. Have you told her about the baby yet?"

"We're video-conferencing with her tonight. Morning her time. Why?"

"Just tell her I miss her, okay?"

MATT CAUGHT his mother moving quietly through the guests, chatting privately with this person and that. Soon thereafter, everyone began saying their goodbyes and heading for the door. She sent Mikaela and Matt up to bed to rest while she and Matt's dad tidied up. Mikaela hugged her in-laws and happily obeyed. Matt hung around a few extra minutes to enjoy some time with his folks.

"I saw you giving the guests the old five-minute warning. Thanks for calling 'end-of-game' on the party, Mom. We've been running on adrenaline, but we both started to crash about nine." He stretched his neck to kiss his mother's cheek as she washed a platter. Then he pulled out a barstool and sat down.

"That was my first and most important grandma gift. To keep my grandbaby's parents healthy."

And then it hit Matt. A new understanding. A new clarity.

"That's what you've been doing all my life. Fighting for me, sometimes with me, even sometimes against my wishes, to keep me healthy so I could someday know what you've known all along. The love of a family of my own."

Matt's dad was drying dishes, but he froze, and his eyes misted. "Aye, boy. Aye," he said before turning for the cupboard to replace the glass he'd been drying.

"I haven't always appreciated what you went through for me. I'm sorry, Da and Mum."

His mother's lips quivered through her smile. "Your Da got it right most of the time, even when I didn't exercise the greatest tact, but I swear to you that love was always at the root of what we did."

"I know that. At least I do now, and I have only the tiniest inkling of what a parent feels. But I know that I already love this child. That I would do anything, find whoever I needed to find, to protect him or her and keep this child well."

He rose from his seat and moved near the sink, beside his mother and an arm's length from his father. He pressed his fingers to his lips to still them before saying, "It can't have been easy for you to meet Kate and have the story of my birth and adoption rehashed so openly. And through it all, you were so kind to her, and you made her feel that she still has a family with us if she wants it. Thank you for making it possible for me to have you and have her too."

"Of course, we would, Matthew. She's easy to love, and we'd do anything for you."

"I know that." He could hear the emotion strengthening the influence of his brogue. "And I want you to know that hearing about Kate's life, the life I would have had . . . well . . . it's made me ever more grateful that I was blessed to come to you. I haven't been very good about telling you that, but I love you both. Very much."

There were tearful hugs. Matt stayed downstairs with his parents, tidying the great room and putting away food, just to have an excuse to be near them. He marveled at how easy conversation came that evening, how their opinions mattered more to him and their advice seemed more profound. He knew they hadn't changed in mere hours. He had. He was going to be a father. A father . . . The responsibility filled him with inexpressible joy and weighed upon him like a pink and blue anvil as he climbed the stairs for the bedroom.

Matt found Mikaela lying on her side, scrolling through her phone. She sat up as soon as he entered the room. "I thought you'd have been asleep an hour ago."

"My mind is racing. I've been looking at baby furniture and reading articles about infant care." She threw her hands to her head. "Does this parenthood thing scare you?"

Matt sat beside her and smiled. "A little. Does it scare you?"

Her arms slipped around Matt's shoulders, and the two bent until their heads touched. "A little."

"I think you'd feel better if your parents were still here. I just spent an hour talking to mine. It was great."

"I'm glad. So . . . what great wisdom did they impart?"

Contentment bubbled up inside Matt, breaking free through his smile. "Just that they love us and that they have confidence in us."

"And that made you feel better?"

Matt chuckled. "Yep. Because in the last hour, they became the most brilliant people I know."

"Then you think we'll be okay?"

Matt turned and kissed her temple. "You bet we will, Mrs. Grayken. No doubt."

CHAPTER SIXTEEN

Mikaela hit her stride in July. She felt great and had her energy back. While her road seemed smooth, Matt's continued to be fraught with bumps and potholes. His immune system rebelled each time Dr. Marcosky attempted a medicine adjustment or a steroid taper, slingshotting him from a normal energy level to spirit-draining fatigue and causing a series of rashes and GvHD scares. Mikaela worried about the mounting strain his unstable health was taking on him.

She drafted him into readying the nursery. They discussed hiring someone, but Matt bought her notion that going the DIY route would be more personal and therapeutic. She signed them both up for Saturday morning classes at a home improvement store and bought decorating books and power tools. Matt nailed prefinished white shiplap boards to the bottom third of the walls, while only suffering two notable wounds—a smashed thumb and punctured index finger. He removed old wallpaper and painted a primer on the upper walls in preparation for Kate's planned November arrival, which Mikaela insisted would provide Kate with plenty of time to paint a magnificent, whimsical mural around the room.

They bought a crib that required no less than ten hours of mind-bending assembly, disassembly, and reassembly, punctuated by breaks that kept Matt from declaring the pieces tinder and setting fire to them in the backyard. When the crib was finally operational, Mikaela bestowed the title "handyman," upon her hubby. He celebrated with a one-way trip to bed and a well-deserved nap.

Mikaela balanced being available for Matt's widely varying needs against her responsibility to fine-tune the clinic project. The Interfaith Coalition of Churches met the first Monday of each month to evaluate the successes of the clinics and to address arising needs. Since funding was always a priority issue, budget issues and the planned gala were the primary topics at the August meeting.

Another issue was raised. As grateful as everyone was for Bennett Sadler's magnanimous initial donation, his appearances at meetings and his involvement in the project generally, had dramatically dropped off. Reverend Coolidge and the committee were therefore anxious to fund the clinics locally so their future success would not depend on one generous donor.

Mikaela was surprised to hear that no one else on the committee was receiving contact from Bennett. He continued to text her nearly daily with some question loosely related to the clinic project or to gather information for a wealthy friend who might be interested in funding a similar project in another state.

How are our patient numbers this month?

Can you send me the contact info for the mobile clinic company for an interested colleague?

Let me know if I can help with prescriptions. Remember, I DO have contacts in pharmaceuticals.

Each professional text or call somehow always turned social, with inquiries into her health, Matt's health, or the baby's. The conversations seemed normal at the time, but his lack of contact and failure to return the calls of other committee members seemed curious. He was the president of a billion-dollar pharmaceutical company after all, and perhaps he considered his involvement in the clinic project complete. It made sense. So why was he still contacting her?

"Mikaela? Mikaela? Mrs. Grayken . . . ?"

Alaina nudged Mikaela and brought her back into the conversation.

"Excuse me?"

"The gala?" asked the reverend. "We'd like to hear your plans, please?"

"Of course. Let me just pull them up." As Mikaela scrolled through her computer files, Alaina leaned close and smiled. "I often daydreamed when I was pregnant too."

Mikaela noticed that Alaina was wearing long sleeves on a sweltering day, and she saw the edge of a bruise peeking out above her wrist.

She turned to Alaina and said, "I'd like to talk to you after the meeting if you have time."

Alaina looked at the clock on the wall and bit her lip. "I'll try."

With the file loaded, Mikaela began explaining her plans for the Metro Mercy Project's Fall Ball and Charity Auction set on October twentieth at the elegant Baylor Hotel and Convention Center overlooking the National Harbor. Then she handed out donation forms and tickets to every committee member, asking each of them to secure at least ten high-ticket auction items or services donated from their community, and to sell at least fifty of the one hundred-dollar tickets each.

She hurriedly answered questions, hoping to end the meeting quickly enough to catch Alaina before she left to meet the three o'clock bus. After the prayer, she leapt from her seat to catch the worried mom who was already headed for the door with her baby and stroller.

"Alaina, I don't mean to be nosey, but . . . I saw the bruises on your arm. Did Eduardo do that?"

Alaina's eyes flashed panic and then embarrassment. "I have to go. You don't understand."

Mikaela grabbed her hand, and Alaina shrank, leaving Mikaela feeling like another bully in the woman's world. She released the hand and stepped back. "Let me help you. I can get you and your children someplace safe."

A light of hope shone in the young woman's eyes and then went out. "He would find us. No. It's not possible."

"I promise you that it's possible. We can find a way."

Alaina swallowed and stared blankly out the window as the bus pulled up to the stop. Panic again twisted her face as she began racing down the hall to the exit, reaching the sidewalk too late to signal the driver. Tears sprang to her eyes. "The children walk home from school and pre-K. I must be home before the children!"

"I'll take you."

"Then we must hurry."

Little was said on the ride to Alaina's neighborhood. She asked to be dropped off a block south and around the corner from the bus stop, saying she could make her own way home from there before the children arrived. Mikaela stood by the car door as Alaina placed the baby in the stroller. The young mother paused for several seconds before turning back to say goodbye.

"Thank you for the ride. And for caring." Then she

hurriedly pushed her stroller down the street and away from Mikaela's view.

Some high school boys began whistling and catcalling, not at the obviously pregnant Mikaela as much as at her pricey Range Rover. She felt overtly conspicuous and thoughtless, driving her expensive vehicle in Alaina's struggling neighborhood. She quickly put the vehicle in gear and drove away, passing an equally conspicuous vehicle, a black Suburban with darkened windows, parked on the corner. Looking back in her rearview mirror, she saw a passenger exit the black vehicle and use his phone to take a photo in her car's direction. As she turned the corner, she saw that man head off in Alaina's direction, and she prayed the mother wouldn't pay a price because Mikaela had given her a ride.

CHAPTER SEVENTEEN

Matt had rehearsed his pitch a dozen times before heading into Dr. Marcosky's office for his consult. On a wing and a prayer, he'd asked Ben and the Great Expectations staff to pull off a once-in-a-lifetime, first-anniversary trip for Mikaela. He wanted to dazzle his longsuffering wife and show her some of his favorite corners of the world. The plans were set. The tickets booked. All he needed was for Dr. Marcosky to clear him for the eighteen-day escape, and with that dream in mind, he made his plea.

"Absolutely not."

The finality of the no staggered Matt. "Is there something you're not telling me? Is my immune system more than just weak? Is the cancer back?"

The doctor's hands flew before him like two five-fingered fans. "No. but . . . but listen to yourself . . . to your plans. Japan? Burma? Tanzania? Your immune system is barely ready for an unmasked stroll through the hardware store. We can't possibly immunize you or risk exposing you to what you'd encounter in international travel. Choose something local. People travel from all over the world to visit D.C. to see what's in your own backyard. Make it less about the place and more about what you do."

He drove home, bemoaning the fact that all his elaborate anniversary plans were dashed to pieces. He wanted to take Mikaela to dinner in Baltimore tonight, to the same Italian bistro where they'd shared their first August date a year ago. He prearranged the same meal—two bowls of Italian wedding soup, with extra meatballs and spinach—and then he planned to hand her the packet with the tickets and itineraries. They would have left September ninth, and spent their anniversary in places of great wonder and beauty. He would have shown her the places and people that shaped him and his ideas, eventually bringing him to her.

Now what?

He dragged himself into the house and found Mikaela dressed in a blue floral maternity dress. The knit hugged her adorable bump like a second skin, ending in a tight skirt that fell below her knees. She twirled and ended the floorshow by framing the baby bump with her open hands.

"New dress?" he asked.

"I wanted to take Sparkle or Sparky along on our big date," she teased.

"You glow, Mrs. Grayken. You absolutely glow." He pulled her close and pressed his head to hers.

"You seem pretty glum for a man who's got a date with a thousand-watt babe."

"Just a little disappointed. Let's go. Our reservation awaits." He offered a meager hint of a smile and swept his arm forward in a weakly playful gesture.

Mikaela sat on the edge of the table, her own smile dimmed. "What's going on?"

Matt tossed his keys onto the island and leaned into it. "You don't have to clear your September calendar after all. Dr. Marcosky killed our trip."

"For medical need or to be cautious?"

"He's being cautious." He pushed away from the counter. "Let's go."

She walked to him and laid her arms across his neck. "I'm sorry, Matt, but I'm not surprised."

"My world's a little bigger than it was last month, but I'm starting to think I'm never going to really get it back."

Mikaela's arms dropped to her sides as she slumped into one hip and glowered.

"What?"

"I'm just wondering what part of that life you'd want back so badly? As I recall, you were living in a half-empty house, estranged from your parents, and afraid to share your medical situation with even your closest friends."

Mikaela's characterization of his former self struck a tender nerve. "I'm just saying that I miss being able to travel past the beltway without having to get my medical team to sign a decree. I want to enter a public venue that holds more than ten people without the need to wear a mask that makes me look like I'm harboring a deadly disease."

She took a deep breath and put her hands on her hips. "I know this is hard, Matt, but—"

"I'm sorry, but please don't queue up another 'the cup is half full' pep talk. I can't handle it tonight." He leaned back against the fridge. "Let me just wallow in my self-pity for a few moments. Please."

"Fine." She turned and headed up the stairs.

Hearing her obvious stomps, Matt moved to the bottom of

the stairs and asked, "Where are you going? We have reservations."

She glared down at him from the fourth step. "I'm giving you space to wallow."

"Well, thanks for understanding," he snapped back. "All I wanted was to take you somewhere very special to me for our anniversary. Forgive me for being disappointed that I dared to hope for something normal."

She huffed and shook her head. "Normal? Does *normal* seem like a step *up* to you?" She laughed sadly. "See . . . I feel like normal is a step down, because I think we've been living in a world of miracles that makes normal seem like a downgrade." She placed her hand on her belly. "You think this baby is just normal? A child conceived by a dying man because someone had the foresight to prepare for an eventuality where he might miraculously get a reprieve from cancer and live to father a child?"

She descended two steps and paused as her body hitched. She sucked in a sudden breath. Concern raced through Matt, but she froze him in place with her glare. "You know why I was excited about this special evening? I wasn't dying to hear about our extravagant trip. I wanted to take your hands and set them over this moving, living baby, and let you feel the reality of this miracle, this spark of life we created. See, this baby is so beyond normal. The fact that you're standing in our kitchen is so beyond normal. I'm sorry if you can't appreciate the wonder of our imperfect but miraculous life."

She hurried up the stairs, her muffled cries echoing behind. Matt tried to follow, but he heard the door slam shut and the lock turn.

He slept in the den that night and found Mikaela disinterested in the apology he offered the next day. She said he missed the point, as she hurried out the door to work at one of the clinics that was down a nurse. Matt wondered if the shift was prescheduled or a convenient escape from him.

He replayed their argument in his mind a dozen times, and while he conceded that he'd been petulant and childish, he was also wounded over the accusations and hurtful analysis she'd launched at him. Of course, he loved her. Loved the baby. Loved his life. Why couldn't she understand that he loved all those elements of the present while still longing for the health and freedom of the past?

Nonetheless he bought flowers, sent texts, made dinner, and ate crow, but Mikaela returned home unmoved. Once Matt got past his wounded pride, he headed to a quiet corner and prayed to know what to do or say to bring trust back into his marriage. No lightning bolts of wisdom came. Just a reminder of the basic element of their union—that he desperately loved his wife.

"Will you please talk to me?" he asked through another closed door.

She opened it slightly and came into the hall.

"I love you," he said with a mix of tenderness and fear. "This isn't us. We don't shut each other out, Mikaela. Please, help me fix us."

Her eyes welled with tears. "I'm tired, Matt. Tired of always having to be the optimist and bearer of sunshine. The other day you said I glow. Well, that doesn't always come naturally. Sometimes it requires a force of sheer will because I feel as if I'm on my own here."

"How can you say that?"

"Because most days, I wait until you decide what kind of day you're having before I know what kind of day I'm going to have. You say you feel as if you have no control? I feel that way too . . . every day. Is Matt happy? Is Matt sick? Is he angry or bitter or sad? Is he going to work so I can work, or is he staying at home with the covers pulled over his head, waiting for me to cheer him up?"

Matt knotted up until he could barely breathe.

"I know you're scared. I know the threat of a bad lab test hangs over you every day. Well, newsflash." She began to cry and tapped her chest. "It hangs over me too. As a wife. As a mother. Where do I take my fear? I can't share it with you because then I'll have to pull us both up. So I carry it around in me, praying for a day of joy from you or a week of positive attitude so I can breathe before the next hard thing comes."

Matt shrank upon hearing Mikaela's assessment of him. Embarrassment, anger, hurt, and shame scalded him, but he set those feelings aside and focused on the terror that consumed him at the thought that he'd pushed Mikaela beyond her breaking point. "I'm sorry." The words slipped from his mouth like dispassionate, lukewarm water.

Mikaela slid down the doorjamb to the floor where her head crumpled. Seeing her there, spent and small, killed Matt. She was also hurting, and for the first time, Matt feared they were in the middle of a crisis from which there might be no complete return or reprieve. He had violated a tenet of his fundamental promise to her—to never give up. However unwittingly, he had surrendered to his despair leaving tired, pregnant, overburdened Mikaela to pull her weight and his.

"This has been my greatest fear," muttered Matt. "That you'd wear out. That I'd *burn* you out. And now with the added concerns of the baby?" Matt joined her on the floor. "This is my fault. I'm sorry."

She reached a timid hand to him. "I'm sorry too. It's not all on you. I'm not myself. And I'm not being completely truthful. It's not just your mood swings. It's everything. I've overextended myself with the gala and the clinics and Alaina. The things that once made me happy and made me feel needed are crushing me."

"I haven't been much of a partner."

She leaned her head against the wall. "Kate's gone. Bennett's pulled back. I feel like the Council of Churches is depending on me alone now, and the baby's coming in three months."

The pain in her voice cut Matt. She needed him, and he hadn't been there for her. "I'm willing to help."

When she looked up, a plea was in her eyes. "The best help you can give me is to figure out what you need. See someone about your depression. Whatever it takes to help you pull out of this spiral, because I need you stable and engaged."

Matt swallowed hard to push that dose of reality down. "All right," he conceded. "Just please don't give up on us."

"That's exactly what I'm asking of you."

They fell into a polite, dangerous two-step over the next weeks. Matt withheld his fears and feelings from Mikaela, and she carried the guilt of his silence every day. He attended counseling with someone Dr. Marcosky suggested, and Mikaela was invited in for every other session. Dinner conversation was centered on the day's work rather than on the couple's dreams, and they slept side by side, lulled to sleep by worry, fatigue, and fear. Their grand anniversary plans had deteriorated to, at best, marking the occasion with a simple dinner out.

Until Matt finally had enough.

The idea struck him on the day of their anniversary, when he and the angel team were finalizing a plan to send a soldier mother and her children to Orlando for the holidays, so they could make memories before she was deployed again.

Memories . . . It was as if his dim-wattage bulb finally switched into high beam. He turned the remainder of the Orlando details over to the now-employed former interns and headed to his office for a little personal brainstorming session. The hour passed in a bliss-filled rush, energizing parts of him that had become numbed and complacent. After an hour, he took his list and left the office with a plan of his own.

The necessary shopping was a delight, and each purchase sent his spirits soaring higher until his enthusiasm for the evening's plans threatened to burst like a bubble in the wind. Before his nerves overtook his boyish joy, he hurried home to Mikaela.

She was at her desk in the den, finalizing the gala's menu, when he arrived. He set his box in the great room and pulled Mikaela away from her work, begging her to sit on the sofa.

She looked at the box with cool skepticism, asking, "What's this?"

Matt sat on the coffee table, directly across from Mikaela. "I'm taking us back to the beginning. To our wonderful, beautiful, miraculous beginning. What is the moment when you knew you were falling in love with me?"

Mikaela's shoulders sagged, as if she was uncomfortable offering her tender answer.

"Please," he urged.

She took a breath and rolled her lips. "All right. It was at Meriwether's . . . the sandwich shop in Baltimore. The place was crazy busy, but there you were, sitting at that tiny, pink table with loud, hard rock music blaring. You were clearly uncomfortable, dressed in your three-piece suit, but you were there, waiting for me. That's when I knew you were a man of your word. That's when I knew you were a man I could count on."

The memory that initially made him chuckle, left him mellow and sad. Mikaela was telling him what she loved about him. His stability and strength. This was what she still needed from him. He prayed that what he brought would help her see him as that man again.

"I knew I *could* love you from the first day I watched you in Prospect's infusion center, but the first time I knew I *would allow myself* to love you was at the Christmas Shop downtown, when you chose those ornaments and helped me see a future worth fighting for. A future of unknown duration but of inestimable possibilities. I keep losing sight of that, and I'm sorry, but I think I found it today. I want to show you what I've finally managed to remember about the past year."

He opened the box, revealing several tissue-wrapped bundles. He handed Mikaela the first one. "Open it."

She carefully unwrapped the tissue paper, revealing a crystal snowflake dangling from a nylon thread.

"I remember you waking me up on December 26th, the day the transplant prep began, and telling me about the miracle of the Christmas snow that had fallen overnight. You said it was a good omen, and you were right. Look at where we are."

He handed her another bundle, which proved to be a blown-glass strawberry. "Remember the strawberry air freshener you brought me because I couldn't have a real berry? You made me laugh that day. You always find a way to make the hardest things bearable."

He handed her bundle after bundle—a busty dancer in honor of the day she had to gown up, a tiny box garden representing her gift of the seeds to keep him focused on life, and a crystal candle representing the baby spark they began in Dr. Chapman's office. On and on the ornaments came, twelve in all, each a reminder of a beautiful miracle Mikaela had given him over the year.

She was weeping before the last ornament, a small figurine

of expectant parents standing beside an empty cradle, was opened. She choked out a "thank you" and wiped her eyes.

Matt buried his face in her lap, his emotions on overload as he said, "I love our imperfect, miraculous life, and I'm sorry I sometimes lose sight of it. I'm going to try to do better, to be that man again, that awkward but steady guy you knew you could count on."

CHAPTER EIGHTEEN

M att loved to arise before Mikaela and stare at her as she slept. Her silhouette reminded him of a master's sculpture. Her dark hair tumbled along the white sheets that fell in folds along her motherly curves. Her face was serene, no longer pinched with worry and fear. The two of them were one again, in every way, not without effort, but precisely because of the effort each was investing in the marriage again.

His hand naturally reached for her belly now, attaching him in some corporeal way to the child he would soon meet. He marveled at the power of the tiny being who, like an alien force, shifted his mother's abdomen, sending identifiable footprints through her belly's wall. He laughed out loud, and talked and sang to the child, sharing the little Irish ditties his Mum sang to him. He loved this baby. He loved his wife. In short, Matthew Grayken loved his precious life.

He was working harder to focus on the good rather than on the restrictions and festering nuisances of post-transplant life. He moussed his still-thin hair to give it some semblance of style, smeared lip balm on his dry, cracked lips, and quietly down-played his lost interest in exercise caused by the ache in his limbs and the bone-deep fatigue besetting him. Still, he ignored these little worries and carried on, until he found himself awaking in a fevered sweat on Friday, October 19th.

He debated whether to reveal his symptoms or hide them until after Mikaela left for the Baylor Hotel to oversee final preparations for the next day's gala. Choosing the latter option, he slipped out of bed, intending to bathe his body in cool water, but on the way to the bathroom, he felt dizzy and weak and fell onto the edge of the bed, sliding to the floor.

Mikaela heard his groan and lumbered to him. "You've got a fever. Matt, you're sick."

He didn't have the strength to stand, and his dead weight was too much for Mikaela, so an ambulance was called. Mikaela dressed quickly and arrived at the hospital a few minutes behind. Fortunately, St. George Hospital was served by the ambulance company. The Emergency Room staff paged Dr. Marcosky soon after pulling up Matt's records and completing his vitals.

Mikaela reverted into nurse mode, asking questions of the staff and studying the monitors. She never mentioned the next day's gala, but Matt could feel the dual responsibilities tearing her apart. She was the primary host for the event that would fund the clinics for the coming year, and yet she was loyally by his bedside, supporting him. Matt reached for her hand. "They're going to be running tests for hours. There's nothing you can do here. Go to the hotel and oversee the setup."

She laid a hand by Matt's cheek. "When did the symptoms begin?"

"A few days ago. I thought it was just a rough patch. I didn't know I was sick."

"You should have talked to me."

"I was trying to avoid being a wuss."

She groaned and pressed her cheek to his. "Oh, Matt. Now you're afraid to be honest with me? We're still not getting this right."

"I didn't want to add to your stress before the gala . . ."

Mikaela rolled her eyes and chuckled.

". . . like I'm doing right now by being rushed to the ER. Go to Baylor. I'll just hang around here."

She didn't laugh, nor did she budge. Then Dr. Marcosky arrived.

"What do you think could be causing Matt's fever?" she asked.

"It could be any number of things . . . including all the normal culprits. Just because Matt had a stem-cell transplant doesn't mean he can't also get the flu. Go, Mikaela. I hear you're hosting a big gala tomorrow. Matt's in good hands. Go."

DREAD FILLED her as she drove away from the hospital. No matter what she did, she knew she was letting someone down. Thankfully, Alaina proved to be a godsend. She had arrived with a copy of the floor plan and was directing the banquet staff to correct a mistake in the table setup.

Mikaela hugged and thanked her. "Where's the baby?"

"Eduardo took him so I could come here and talk with you."

Mikaela felt her expression sour over the mention of the man's name. Alaina's sunny disposition shifted in response.

"You dislike him, but there are things you don't know about Eduardo."

Alaina's defense of the man sent Mikaela off into a rant. "I know he hurts you and orders you about. I know the children are afraid of him and you feel you need to hide your money from him so you can save it for the children's needs."

The young mother stood up to Mikaela. "You don't know the why."

"I don't need to know."

"Because you don't want to. You see the problem you want to solve, not necessarily the ones that need solving. You said you could get me and my family to safety. Did you mean that?"

Alaina's accusation and request pummeled Mikaela. She intended to help when she offered. She just didn't know how she would make it happen. "Yes."

"And what about Eduardo? He's in the most danger."

A worker dropped a banquet chair against another with a loud bang. Alaina jumped, launching Mikaela's next point. "I see how jumpy and fearful *you* are, Alaina. Not Eduardo. You'll have a hard time convincing me that he's a victim."

"But he is. He's afraid of Joaquin."

"Who's Joaquin?"

"He runs the biggest chop shop in the area. Some of his guys steal cars and the others tear them down for parts so they can be shipped without detection or sold in pieces."

"Eduardo works for Joaquin?"

"Not by choice. Remember I told you how David fell down and cut his leg when we arrived in town? It was worse than that. I was pregnant with him by the time we graduated from high school, so we left Texas and headed here to make a fresh start together. Eduardo was good with cars, and I planned to work in a government office when the baby got a little older. Joaquin welcomed us, helped us find an apartment, and gave Eduardo a job in his garage. A year later, when David was barely walking, he fell down a flight of concrete steps. He was so badly hurt. I finally had to take him to the ER. Joaquin paid for everything. It was then that we realized the cost of being in his debt."

"He wanted more than interest on his money?"

"He said he now owned Eduardo."

"Can't he quit? Move away?"

Mikaela's legs felt heavy, so she dropped into a chair. Alaina slumped into a chair nearby and said, "No one walks away from Joaquin alive."

"What? Not even you or the kids?"

"Family is the leverage he holds over Eduardo and the other fathers."

"But I've seen Eduardo grab you. And I've seen the bruises on your arms. He's not innocent either."

"Yes, he grabs me because I disobey his warnings. Eduardo is afraid for me. Joaquin discourages his workers and their families from attending Reverend Coolidge's church because the reverend helps the community break free of Joaquin's slavery. Joaquin also doesn't want his gang families to have other jobs or any support not provided by him. He supplies everything for his 'team.' He is their brother, their mother, and their father, rolled into one."

"To keep everyone dependent on him."

"Yes. The only way we could ever get away would be to suddenly leave everything we own behind and get to a city where he can't find us."

"Have you considered going to the police to report Joaquin?"

Terror twisted Alaina's face. "We can't take that risk. Joaquin would frame Eduardo, and *he* would walk. No. No police. Can you help us?"

Mikaela looked into Alaina's trusting eyes while remembering what she had just told Matt about feeling buried and drowning. Matt had been so worried about her needs that he'd hidden his own illness, ending up in the Emergency Room. She dropped her worried head into her hands and considered the numbers, the details, and the talk she'd need to have with Matt.

Alaina touched her shoulder. "Please, Mikaela. You are good friends with Bennett Sadler. I see how he looks at you. He would do anything for you. Perhaps you could talk to him. He's very rich. Ask him to help us."

Alaina's description of Bennett's feelings for Mikaela made her flush with guilt and naïveté. Yes, Bennett could easily afford to arrange Alaina's escape with her family. So could Matt, the man whose very life might be in peril because he didn't want to add to her burden. The question was, who did she dare ask?

She looked up at Alaina's expectant face. "I don't know how yet, but I'll find a way."

CHAPTER NINETEEN

Mikaela wished handling Alaina's problems were as simple as handling the concerns about the gala. After going over last-minute details with the Baylor Hotel's special events manager, she felt confident she could walk away from the setup without worries. She wished she had equal confidence in her ability to manage Alaina's request.

Pregnancy made everything more difficult. She was struggling to slip her arm into her coat sleeve when two hands arrived to assist. Startled, she looked over her shoulder, coming eye to eye with Bennett Sadler.

"Bennett!" she stammered. "Don't sneak up on me like that. You'll have me delivering this baby early, right here on the grand ballroom floor."

"As I've told you before, Mikaela, you can count on me for anything. If need be, that offer includes the emergency delivery of babies." He pulled her collar up tight under her chin. "I'd enjoy being the first one to meet this new little person."

His gaze sent nervous shivers down Mikaela's spine, and she

quickly stepped back to extricate herself and her coat from his helpful grasp. She began fastening the large buttons.

"How are the preparations going?" he asked.

"Good. They're good. Really . . ."

"Good?" He added a chuckle. "Which makes me think something may not be as good as you say." He did a quick search of the room. "Matt's not here? I assumed he'd be your right-hand man today of all days."

"He's . . . under the weather."

"Then I'm doubly glad I'm here."

"Thank you, but everything is under control. The committee actually hasn't seen much of you these past few months, so we didn't count on your help for the gala."

"I . . . have been . . . traveling quite a bit in recent months."

"So, I've heard."

"Heard? From who?"

"Mostly the magazine rack at the grocery. You've been abroad right?"

"Abroad. Yes. Expanding our markets. But surely you knew I'd be here for the gala. I wouldn't miss your big night."

"It's not my night, Bennett. It's the Metro Mercy Project's big night."

"Of course, I just know how exciting it is to launch an event you've worked so hard for. As far as I'm concerned, this is your night."

Before she was able to formulate a response, Bennett moved on to a new, less controversial topic. "The room looks beautiful. You knocked it out of the park with the autumn palette you chose for the color scheme."

"Thank you," she said as she picked up her purse and fumbled for her keys.

"I don't want to keep you, but . . . may I tell you how much I admire you, Mikaela? Not many women would be able or even willing to set aside their own needs, which in your current situation, are many, to manage the crushing burden of an invalid husband. And on top of it all, you still have the ability to see and address the concerns of others. A person like you could do so much good in the world, but I worry about you. People with far less on their plates burn out all the time. You need a little pampering. You need someone who can pull the load beside you and for you when you need a break."

She'd heard these thoughts before. They'd been her own a few weeks ago when she lost it with Matt, but she also recalled hearing Bennett speak similarly in the past months, doling out sympathy and compliments about her strength and selflessness. She realized how deeply they had penetrated into her, soothing tiring days, assuaging feelings of defeat. She had admired him for building up her sagging self-esteem, but on this day, his words came back to her like the unwelcome echo of criticisms she had thrown at Matt. Bennett had negatively colored her attitudes and view of her marriage, and that needed to end.

The phone rang in her pocket. Matt's face filled the screen. She felt like the fulcrum on a scale where one side held ease and compliments and the other was hard news and a rollercoaster of emotions. She took the call.

"Hi, honey. What are the doctors saying?"

"I don't have any results yet, but in the craziness of the morning I forgot to tell you my surprise. In fact, they're ready to take me back for an endoscopy, so I've only got a minute. I proposed that Great Expectations offer two auction items for your gala. Ben and the board approved them. One is a two-week African Safari for six. The other is a River Cruise on the Thames for six. They should pull in some hefty donations. I just wanted you to know."

She rolled her lips in and smiled. "You're heading back for an endoscopy and that's what's on your mind?"

"No. You were on my mind. The auction items were secondary."

"Well, they're amazing. Thank you so much. I love you, Mr. Grayken. I'm on my way."

"I love you, Mrs. Grayken. I'm on my way too . . . to endoscopy."

When the call ended, Bennett remained silent, his expression best defined as awed and flummoxed. Mikaela slung her purse strap over her shoulder and said, "I'm sorry, Bennett. What were we discussing?" When he didn't answer, she said, "See you tomorrow night at the gala."

Dr. Surinaj, an ER doctor, was with Matt when Mikaela arrived. "Matt has had MRSA for some time, but it's flared up. We knew that early on, but we didn't want to miss a second infection because we leaped to that conclusion alone. Now we can treat him with IV antibiotics, and he should be well in a few days."

The impact of the news hit her. "An IV?"

"Yes. He'll be out soon and feeling as good as new, but we'll keep him here for just a few days. Admissions will send an agent to get his information, and transport will be here soon to move him upstairs."

They thanked the doctor, who left through the curtain partition.

"No gala," said Matt.

"It's okay." Mikaela kissed him. "I've already got your donations."

"Gee, thanks." Matt's eyes crinkled as he laughed, revealing the extent of his pain.

"How did setup go?"

"Very well. Alaina was already there, handling the early problems."

Matt's expression grew sheepish. "She's proven to be an asset to you. I'm sorry I've been so skeptical about her."

There was never any real question about who Mikaela most trusted to help her meet Alaina's needs, but she'd been reluctant to add another complication to Matt's life or to hers. But now that Matt had provided an opening, she decided to pursue it. "Would you say you're now on Team Alaina?"

"She requires a team?"

Mikaela became solemn. A family's safety hung on the outcome of the coming conversation, and Mikaela needed Matt to feel the full weight of what she was about to ask. "I may have been wrong about Eduardo, Matt. He's being controlled by a criminal who's not only threatening him, but Alaina and the children too. They're all in danger. She needs a team who can work a miracle for her family."

Matt lay back into his pillow as his eyes scanned Mikaela's face. "Are you serious?"

"Very serious, Matt."

"If Alaina's story is true, the people who help them will also be in danger." He bit the side of his mouth in thought and then said, "I feel how earnest you are, Mikaela, and I'd like to help your friend, but there's no way I'm getting involved in a situation that could put you in danger."

Mikaela laid her head on his chest. "There has to be a way we can help them anonymously." She looked up and knew he was at least mulling over her request.

"Maybe there is," he muttered, as if the words were thoughts he had not intended to voice. Then in a louder voice, he affirmed the statement. "I think there might be a way. I am in the dream-granting business, after all."

They talked and planned until the transport aide moved Matt to his room, and then they ran and reran the plan long into the afternoon thinking through every obstacle to be sure their decisions were covert and safe for all the people they would need to involve. They would need some allies, one with financial connections and someone with contacts in a remote town where Alaina and her family could make a new start.

Matt had connections with several of the community's bank managers and merchants who had supported some of his angel projects. He called them up and asked for their help with yet another very confidential dream come true. Mikaela felt inspired to call Reverend Coolidge, who already knew Alaina's plight. He agreed to contact a few out-of-state pastor friends whom he had met at the church's national conference, to see if any of them could help the family safely relocate.

Matt included these discreet men of God in the plan and ran through his and Mikaela's part of the plan once more, aloud.

"We'll cover the costs personally, but we'll run the funds through several banks so the money can't be traced back to us. The president of First Trust Bank will be the final contact. He'll think the Be Someone's Angel Fund is partnering with Reverend Coolidge's church, so he'll know nothing about Alaina or her family. The money will be placed on a preloaded credit card, which the bank will send to the reverend via a courier, and our part will be complete. After that, everything else depends on Reverend Coolidge and whatever pastor he finds to help them on the other end."

"How do we get them out of town?"

"The reverend will pass the card on to Alaina on the day the family is scheduled to leave. He told me he'll find someone to discreetly transport them to the Philly airport for their flights. No one will expect them to head there."

"That's what I'm hoping. The amount on the card should be enough to buy their tickets and leave a reserve large enough to tide them over until they find work. They can stay at a motel in Philly for one night, buy their tickets online, and leave the next day."

"How soon will the money be available?"

"A week or so." He looked at his IV. "I'm a little tied up right now."

"I'm sorry. I should be babying you instead of adding to your stress."

"Our part is easy. Everything hinges on Reverend Coolidge and his colleagues."

A nurse walked in to change the bag of IV antibiotic. Mikaela stood and walked to the window, rubbing the prickles that rose on her arms.

When they were alone, Matt asked, "Are you okay?"

She sat on the window bench and nodded. "I'm not cut out for this cloak-and-dagger stuff."

Matt extended his free arm to her, and she drew close and rested her head on his chest.

"You know what I'm thinking?" asked Matt.

She shook her head. "What?"

"That our concerns seem small compared to Alaina's."

"I've been thinking the same thing."

Matt kissed her head and kept his lips pressed there for several seconds, enjoying the weight of her upon his chest while her scent filtered into him with every breath.

"It's good to stop and remember how blessed we are sometimes," she added.

Matt couldn't have agreed more.

Mikaela was too far along in her pregnancy to sleep comfortably in the thinly padded recliner in Matt's room. She returned in the morning for a few hours to help him pass the time while tethered to his IV pole, and then she headed home to shower and dress. More than anything, he wished to be like Cinderella, granted a few hours' reprieve from reality to attend the grand ball, but it was not to be. The notion gave him another idea, however, one he could make come true, and he set about making phone calls to set the plan into motion.

Mikaela returned at four, dressed simply in an elegant beige gown that gathered above her baby bump, falling into soft gathers around her feet. She wore her long dark hair down in soft waves. The effect was elegant and understated.

He placed his fist over his chest, as if he were driving a dagger into his own heart. "You, Mrs. Grayken, are killing me. You look like a princess."

She curtsied slightly. "Thank you, kind sir. But what about the hair? Up or down? I like up, but it starts to sag like melting ice cream after a few hours."

He had no idea what hair went with what. He loved her hair up in that messy way she bundled it, but up left her sexy neck bare, and she would probably be dancing with other men tonight. His childish insecurities won the fight. "Down looks perfect. Definitely down for tonight."

"Thank you."

"You know what else would look great with that dress?" Matt asked. "Your wedding necklace. Some of the capital's wealthiest and most powerful will be your guests tonight."

"Are you trying to make sure everyone knows my generous, rich husband may be absent tonight, but he's not forgotten?"

A look of wounded innocence set his mouth in a pout. "*Moi?*"

"Uh huh. You're forgiven. I actually thought about wearing it, but tonight I'm representing the clinic clients, the host churches, and their communities. I doubt they will be coming in diamonds and sapphires."

"Well said." He loved her simplicity and confidence and the way she always got it right. "Are you and the reverend planning to share the exit strategy with Alaina tonight?"

"If she asks. I'd rather wait for a quieter moment, but thank you for making the financial arrangements."

"Anything for you."

"I wish I could stay longer, Matt, but I want to be at the Baylor at five to be sure everything is perfect. Wish me luck." She closed her eyes, fisted her hands, and said, "My goal is two hundred fifty thousand dollars."

A snarky comment passed through Matt's head. *Bennett will probably toss that out as an opening bid.* He was grateful it did not pass through his lips. After a dramatic pause, as if to provide time for the delivery of the wish, Mikaela bent down to kiss Matt goodbye.

He spent the hour after Mikaela left his bedside writing and rewriting his message. He knew something special about the Baylor that Mikaela didn't know, and at six thirty, before the guests arrived and her stress increased, he would send her this simple text.

I wish I could be beside you, but take a stroll in the atrium. I've arranged a little magic for you tonight. Good luck, Mrs. Grayken. I'm so very proud of you.

Matt

MIKAELA HAD NEVER BEEN MORE nervous. All the technical aspects of the evening were set. The special events manager had followed her plans to a tee from the menu to the music to the dining table décor and extra tables draped and laden with the spectacular auction donations. But galas and parties for corporate giants, senators, and their wives? She had no experience in such things. This was Matt's world, and like a little girl playing dress-up in her mother's shoes, she felt wobbly without him by her side. He was supposed to be there, clearing the social flotsam from before her. But ready or not, she was solo. On her own.

While the waitstaff attended to final details, members of the committee began filtering in. Reverend Coolidge and his wife gushed over the ballroom's beautiful decorations, telling Mikaela that this was the fanciest event they'd ever attended. As they strolled away, panic hit Mikaela hard as she began second-guessing herself. Was it too fancy? Too extravagant? She wondered if she was guilty of the same thing a movie star had been slammed for when she held a gluttonous one-thousand-dollar-a-plate banquet to raise funds for starving children who would have been better served if the banquet had been scrubbed and the cost of the food thrown into the donation. She found a quiet corner and pressed her fingers into her temples to calm the pounding there.

As she leaned forward, staring at the floor, two hands appeared in her view. One held two acetaminophens. The other, a glass of cold water. She looked up and found Bennett coming to her rescue. "You look a little pale. How can I help?"

"I'm fine," she argued, shaking as she spoke.

"You're clearly not. You need to sit."

"I need to greet the guests as they arrive."

"Would it help if I stood with you to help you greet them?"

She was certain the optics of Bennett as her escort would have driven Matt to the brink, but Matt wasn't there, and she needed someone to catch her if she started to fall. "I'd appreciate that," she answered.

They moved to the main entrance of the ballroom and sat at the closest table, where she could rise to greet the early arrivers, while sparing her legs until the guests entered en masse. They chatted about random things. She noticed how he intentionally skirted any questions about his European travels, leaving her to wonder if the trips there were extremely personal or painful.

Her phone buzzed in her bag. She tried to ignore it, but the persistent buzzing set her on alert about Matt. "I need to get this. It might be the hospital."

The tension in her body turned to curiosity as she read the text and stood.

"Is everything all right," Bennett asked.

"It's Matt. He wants me to walk through the atrium right now."

Without waiting for a response from Bennett, she headed into the grand atrium, a large glass-topped courtyard filled with lush greenery and lighted trees planted along the walkways. Shops and eateries ringed the perimeter, while a quaint little cottage sat in the center. A stream meandered through the middle, trailing into a waterfall and pool, where a pump recirculated the water back to the beginning. The outer wall was also made of glass panels, providing a spectacular view of the lights along the Potomac River walkway and of those on boats and ferries moving people from the Maryland shore to Alexandria, Virginia, and neighboring ports. Standing within the atrium garden made her forget that she was in the belly of a massive luxury hotel and conference center.

Mikaela checked her watch and looked back nervously in the direction of the ballroom. "Hurry, Matt," she whispered to herself. "I should be greeting my guests."

Bennett took her elbow and led her to a small wrought-iron bench. He indicated for her to sit, and once she did, he sat beside her. "I'm very grateful to have a quiet moment alone with you. I'd like your opinion on something."

"This sounds serious."

"It's funny how I never thought so before. And then I met you."

The atrium clock chimed, and excited people hurried from the shops and restaurants with their eyes focused upward at the ceiling in wondrous expectation. Mikaela heard the swoons and likewise gazed up, and then she saw the cause of their wonder as snow began spraying from obscure jets in the ceiling. She stood in childlike pleasure, with her arms extended and her face upward, hoping to catch the flakes in her open hands and on her face. As the cold dotted her cheeks, she turned in a circle and laughed, feeling as if she were standing in a shaken snow globe. The marvel of the moment caused the evening's stress to ebb from her, and that feeling of peace increased as she overheard a conversation between two hotel workers discussing the reason for the evening's snow.

"Is this a system check? I heard the chiming. I didn't think we turned the jets on until Thanksgiving night, to signal the official start of the Christmas season."

"Someone has pull with the manager. Word is, this was a special request."

Mikaela knew who made it snow early, creating this whimsical miracle. Her phone buzzed again, this time with a call. Her hands shook as she hit the button. "Matt, did you make it snow?" she asked.

"That depends on whether or not you like it."

"I love it!"

"I'm so glad, because I reserved ten suites on the sixth floor for Thanksgiving weekend."

"Here? For the entire family? When did you do that?"

The pleasure in his voice made her ache to be with him. "Weeks ago. I wanted cabins at Deep Creek Lake, but Dr. Marcosky suggested I plan to stay locally . . . just in case."

Mikaela refused to allow the caution in his plans to diminish their wonder. "Oh, Matt! I can't imagine a more magical place for Thanksgiving!"

He sighed with audible joy. "I'm glad it makes you happy. And Thanksgiving dinner will be catered in the small ballroom. All you have to do is set the menu."

"You're my hero."

"I'm just glad I still have a few tricks up my sleeve. Tonight, I was really just testing a theory."

"A theory?"

"Yes, that love-sent snow is almost as magical as Christmas snow."

Her mouth trembled as the snowfall and his devotion overwhelmed her fragile emotions. "You can take it on good authority that it is. It absolutely is. Thank you, Matt. I wish you were here with me, right now."

"But I am. There in that snow. Brushing against your cheeks. Kissing your nose. My love is in each flake."

"I love you."

"Hurry back and tell me all about tonight. Every detail. I'm so proud of you, Mikaela."

She pressed the phone to her chest and gazed up, welcoming each icy drop descending upon her face. She had all but forgotten about Bennett until he rose and stood beside her.

"He gave you snow."

"Yes, he did."

"Amazing. Mikaela, it may shock you to hear this, but for all his hardships and suffering, I've envied your husband . . . because he had you."

"Bennett . . ."

"I asked myself whether love is always like this?" He held his hand out to welcome the snow, then he turned and looked at Mikaela with awe in his eyes. "And then I realized that it's not just you. It's him too. The whole is much more than the sum of its parts with you two. Does loving someone always change the calculus between individuals, making each other more . . . somehow better?"

Mikaela cheeks flushed as she considered the comment. "I don't know, but I hope you find that with someone. I really do."

Bennett laid his hand on her shoulder. "Thank you. I hope so too."

Mikaela caught sight of Alaina near the entrance to the ballroom. Panic was written on the Hispanic woman's face. With a hurried goodbye to Bennett, Mikaela crossed the footbridge and returned to the ballroom. Alaina was standing by the doorway dressed in a lovely red formal. Mikaela caught her attention and smiled as she wrapped her up in a hug. "You look beautiful!"

"Thank you. I bought it at a consignment shop. It was only worn once."

"Is Eduardo with you?"

"No. He planned to, but he's with the children." Alaina's eyes darted left and right, and then her voice lowered to a whisper. "Joaquin called him on a job tonight. Eduardo didn't want to go, but rather than confront Joaquin, he lied. He said one of the children was sick, and he had to stay home with them because I had to attend this event. Joaquin wasn't happy. I think

Eduardo was afraid to leave the children with the neighbor tonight."

"Surely Joaquin wouldn't hurt your children."

"I don't think he would," she answered without assurance, "but I think he sent someone to follow me. A black SUV followed every bus change I made, and it's parked outside in the lot. How soon do you think we can leave town?"

Mikaela's mind was still focused on the black SUV in the lot. "The financial arrangements to relocate you are being finalized but we're still waiting on housing. It shouldn't be more than a few weeks."

Alaina drew in a long slow breath. "Thank you. The sooner the better. Eduardo is different now that he has hope of getting out from under Joaquin's control. I think Joaquin senses the changes in him. Maybe he fears Eduardo will go to the police. He's watching every move we make now."

Mikaela admitted to a bit of trepidation when she asked, "How are you getting home tonight?"

The young mother pulled nervously at her fingers as she answered. "The bus, I suppose."

Mikaela wanted to offer her a ride, but she kept thinking about that black SUV. "If you can wait until the end of the event, I'll take you home."

"Then Joaquin's men will know your car. I can't ask that of you."

"Then let me pay for a car to drive you home."

Relief flooded over Alaina. "Thank you. I owe you so much. I'll stay for an hour, then I'd like to get home."

Mikaela made the Uber arrangements and paid in advance. When the transaction was set, she took Alaina by the arms and smiled hope into the woman. "Hang on a little longer, Alaina. Tell Eduardo we have a plan."

CHAPTER TWENTY

Mikaela had cause to be on cloud nine after the gala. The event netted over three hundred thousand dollars, enough money to operate the clinics for months. Plus, the following Monday's special committee meeting, called to evaluate the gala's success, was actually a surprise baby shower for Mikaela. Doctors, nurses, patients and committee members all greeted her with hugs and gifts for the baby whose due date was less than eight weeks away.

Alaina's gift was a knitted afghan she had made herself. As beautiful and appreciated as that gift was, the better gift was the peace on the woman's face.

"Reverend Coolidge said two of his friends have offered to help us. They're both looking for apartments and work for us. We could be safe by Christmas."

When Mikaela left the shower, her heart was fuller than her car, which was packed to the roof. She called Matt to tell him about the party.

"So many of the gifts were beautiful knitted and crocheted blankets and adorable quits. This baby will never be cold."

"It sounds wonderful. I'm sorry I missed it." Mikaela heard that false optimism he used to mask his depression.

"Me too. Has Dr. Marcosky been in to see you today?"

"Yeah. He brought some good news and some hard news. I'm out of here on Thursday."

"That's great!"

"But my immune system took a hit, so I have to wear the mask in public places again."

Mikaela's natural inclination was to find some funny reply or put a positive spin on the situation, but she knew Matt didn't want or need cheering right then. He needed to acknowledgment another loss of normalcy and control, however small it might be, and grieve for a moment.

"I'm so sorry, Matt. I know this must feel like another step backwards."

He didn't answer for several moments, and when he did his voice was mellow and low. "Do you feel like it's a setback?"

She scrambled to interpret his need and formulate a suitable response. "No. These things are to be expected."

"I just . . . I worry that . . ."

"Matt, this is a blip. I'm not afraid of blips. Got it?"

"But what if I end up in sterile protocol again, and I can't be there when the baby is b—"

"Stop." Mikaela cut him off. "Let's not look for hard things that aren't there, okay?"

"Okay."

When she got off the phone, she called Daniel, whose voice sounded much like Matt's.

"Hey, Daniel, I take it there's been no word from Kate."

"She said we need to talk when she comes back to paint the mural in the baby's room."

Mikaela took a deep breath and prepared to deliver another emotional lift, this time to Daniel. "Talking could be good," Mikaela said, offering her advice in a voice that mirrored Matt's false optimism.

"Or it could be the end."

"It sounds like you could use a pick-me-up. Wanna help me plan a surprise for Matt?"

"Sure." His voice sounded only slightly more enthused than a dieter's when ordering a lettuce salad, and then he perked up. "What did you have in mind?"

"Something hilarious."

THE IRRITATION and frustration Matt felt over his discharge instructions bored holes in his psyche. Mikaela seemed attuned to his need for solitude. She cupped her hand over his and drove home in relative silence.

An unexpected but welcome gift was waiting for him as they drove up the street. Kate was sitting outside in a rental. Instead of parking in the garage, Mikaela also parked at the curb so Matt could get out and greet his sister.

"You still have a key. Why didn't you just go in?" he asked as he pulled her into his arms for a hug, forgetting the mask that hung around his neck at the ready.

"I heard you hit another rough patch," said Kate as she fingered the mask. "How are you, baby brother?"

Matt brushed her worries aside as Mikaela also grabbed a hug. "Pop the trunk and I'll get your bags."

"No, no, no." Kate's refusal was emphatic, and Matt poised for rebuttal.

"My immune system is weak. My arms and legs are fine. I can carry your bags."

Kate brushed a lock of hair back and glanced up, clearly buying time. "It's not that. I'm not planning on staying here."

"You're staying with Daniel?" Matt asked with curious amusement.

"No. On my own. I'm not without my own resources, little brother. In fact, Hugh and I traveled the whole of Europe on a dime by staying in hostels and such."

"I won't hear of it," argued Matt as he moved to the trunk. "Pop the lock."

"No, Matt," both women said in tandem.

Mikaela laid a hand on Matt's arm and gave him a squeeze, drawing his steely gaze. "Matt, she knows she's welcome here. She's doing what makes her feel most comfortable. It's her choice."

"But she's going to be working in the nursery. It just makes sense for her to—" And then he got the message. It was him. The woman who saved his life still wasn't comfortable around him. "I see," he said as he walked back to his car. "I understand. You girls go in. I'll park the car, Mikaela."

Kate caught his arm and pulled him back. "It's nothing you've done, Matt. And it's not for lack of caring about you. I'm not one to jump into the pool all at once. I stick my toe in before deciding whether or not to go further. I jumped in all at once, happily, to help you, but I need to pull back a bit and figure out who I am without Hugh and who I am with you. I need to move slowly, at my own pace. I hope you can understand."

He nodded, but he didn't understand. Not really.

They spent the month in semiconfinement at the house.

Matt painted the base colors where Kate told him while she added the artistry that brought her joyful mural to life. Mikaela spent most of their work hours in her office with fans running and a window open to alleviate the fumes. The downtime the threesome spent was pleasant and jovial, but Matt envied the friendship the women shared—how naturally their conversations slipped into laughter and, more painful for him, how they could talk about meaningful things as if they had been friends forever. He and Kate didn't share that same ease. She retreated when he laid a brotherly arm across her shoulder, and he still noticed the sad expression her face slipped into when she gazed at him.

Mikaela caught him staring off at Kate's taillights as she pulled away one night. She moved behind him, laying her folded arms across his shoulders. "Give it time, Matt."

He leaned his forehead against the cool glass. "I just want us to share what you have with your brothers."

"I know, but we built those relationships over years. You've barely had one together."

"I just feel like there's a wall between us. I wish I knew what it was, but she won't talk to me about anything personal." He turned around and held Mikaela. "Has she said anything to you?"

"I know she's very proud of you. For the person you are and all you've achieved."

He pulled back and checked Mikaela's expression. "Really?"

"Really, but"—Mikaela stepped back and held his hands as she eyed him with trepidation—"can I give you some honest advice? Even if it stings a bit?"

"I take it I'm not going to like this?"

"Probably not, but it might help your relationship with Kate."

Matt straightened, bracing for a solid dose of hard truth. "Swing away."

"You've got to stop looking at things as if you're the only one who's hurting."

He dropped Mikaela's hands as the indictment burned into him. "You think I do that?"

Mikaela moved to a kitchen chair and sat down. "Remember last fall when George took emergency leave to visit? You were in the hospital, so very sick, and your parents were furious and cold to me. I couldn't understand why they were turning on me. He helped me understand their anger and fear. He's seen a lot of grief and loss in the military. He told me trauma changes people, carves us into someone new. Sometimes we're better, stronger for it. Sometimes it cuts too deep, and we break. It's not right or wrong, and it's not fair. We're all just doing our best."

Matt's insecurities ramped up. "What are you saying? You think being sick has changed me?"

"Trauma changes everyone, Matt. Imagine all *Kate's* been through. I think all her losses have cut her deeply. Trust what she said. Be patient. Give her time."

More patience wasn't the answer he wanted. He caught himself proving Mikaela's point. *The answer he wanted* . . . He sounded self-centered, even to himself. He would give Kate time. But what of the changes Mikaela saw in him? He didn't pursue the topic. He simply said, "Thanks for the tip," and walked away, brushing a tentative hand over her arm as he made his way to the office to nurse his bruised ego.

He applied Mikaela's advice when Kate returned the next day, keeping the conversation light and avoiding awkward pauses that he previously filled with probing questions about her childhood. Evasiveness paid off with a relaxed day, and he repeated the exercise throughout the project. Still, when the last scene was painted and after the praise and cheers simmered down, Kate cleaned her last brush, said her goodbyes, and began toting her supplies to her car.

"Wait, wait!" said Matt. "We need to celebrate. How about letting us take you out to eat—" And then he choked on his words as he remembered his restrictions. It was impossible to eat in a public restaurant while wearing a mask.

"It's all right, Matt. This baby is a part of me as well. Painting that mural was a delight."

Though Matt was moved that she mentioned her own attachment to the coming child, she again moved to the door, prompting Matt's need to clarify her exit. "But you're still joining us for Thanksgiving, aren't you? The whole family will be together."

Kate's glance shot to Mikaela as if seeking support, but Mikaela's eyes were as filled with expectation as Matt's. Kate slowly teared up and she blurted, "I can't. I'm sorry. I'll call you soon."

Without further word, she was gone. Matt sensed something dreadfully final in the closing of that door. "What did I do? What did I say?" he asked in flat, hopeless tones.

Mikaela laid a limp hand on his arm, seeming as shocked by the situation as he was. "You didn't do anything wrong. You've been great. It's her. She's struggling with something big."

"And she won't let me in."

There wasn't time to grieve over Kate's declined invitation for Thanksgiving. Daniel's heart had been badly harrowed by her refusal to be alone with him, and Matt spent the next evening preventing his best friend from drowning his ex-boyfriend sorrows in every bottle of bourbon in his home bar. Daniel's hurt mingled with Matt's own, settling into anger aimed at Kate.

Mikaela kept Matt busy, inviting his parents down the weekend before Thanksgiving to help them prep for the holiday and the Compton clan's invasion. Matt and Donovan walked along the National Harbor, taking obscure photos of sites and buildings, both downtown and along the river walk, for a planned photo scavenger hunt for the families. Mikaela and Catherine spent their time packing snack baskets for each family's suite. Tickets were purchased for *Icefest*, the Baylor's annual show of magnificent ice carvings that transformed the atrium into a brightly glowing marvel of frozen characters, architecture, and beauty. They counted on the capital's own magic to fill the remainder of the holiday entertainment.

The Compton clan began arriving the Tuesday before Thanksgiving. The Baylor's shuttle buses made multiple runs to Reagan International Airport to pick up arriving families. Matt, Mikaela, and Matt's parents greeted each family as they arrived, and by Wednesday afternoon, everyone had gathered. It was the first time all thirty-three cousins had been together, and the first time many of them had ever been in a five-star hotel. Matt drew immense joy from their comments about spending Thanksgiving in a palace, and he chuckled as they gawked at the red-suited doormen and valets. The younger children were initially put off by Matt's immunity mask, but as the holiday wore on, Matt won them over or took risks and lowered the mask long enough to charm a reluctant little niece or nephew.

Matt's heart surrendered to one little imp in particular, Rylee, a two-year-old niece whose every outfit was somehow adorned with glitter. Her elfin chatter and wide-eyed smiles captivated his imagination, making fatherhood seem tangible.

He soaked in the love the Compton family members lavished on him and his parents as they drew each Grayken as tightly into their circle as any of their own. But it was the loving way they swarmed around Mikaela that caused his eyes to mist. She seemed to slump into their waiting support, as if she'd been running on fumes and ready to drop before they arrived. They served her in diverse small ways that drew little notice from anyone but Matt—hugs, pats to her protruding belly, a gentle squeeze on her shoulder as they passed by, smiles sent across the room, whispered jokes or shared memories that set her off, into a titter of laughter. Matt watched them nurse the light back into her tired eyes and ease the furrow lines parked upon her brow.

A family church service was a priority for Mikaela. Transportation was arranged to haul the entire Grayken/Compton party to the stone church near Matt and Mikaela's home. That congregation had become the couple's sanctuary and support. The family arrived thirty minutes early and barely found seats in time for the service because of all the introductions and welcomes dished out by the friendly congregants. Matt noticed how Mikaela's eyes swept up and down pews crowded with loved ones, and he could only imagine that she was carried back to her own sweet family-and faith-filled childhood. His heart warmed at the knowledge that God and Sunday worship were also part of their marriage, and soon they would bring their child here and worship together as a family.

The adults and older children rented Segways to add to the fun of their D.C. tour. The small children's favorite game was chasing one another up and down the hotel corridors and elevators, forcing warning calls from hotel management. After a week of feasting, playing, and memory making, everyone loaded their bags back into shuttles and returned to real life. Matt and Mikaela bid the last family goodbye and then hugged the Graykens before they caught an Uber for a ride to the train station. Matt was amazed at the letdown he felt as he noticed errant glitter on his sweater from darling Rylee's parting hug before her family departed. He could only imagine Mikaela's disappointment as the holiday ended. He studied her face carefully as the eighth flood of goodbye tears traced down her cheeks.

"It went by too fast," he said with a little cough as they stood under the Baylor's portico, watching other families' vacation adventures beginning, as theirs ended.

"Yes, but it was perfect." Mikaela leaned into him, pressing her cheek against his arm. "I can't begin to tell you how much this meant to them, or to me."

He coughed again, and Mikaela gave him a worried glance. "I think you caught a cold from one of the children."

"It's just a tickle, and even if I did catch a cold, I'd do it all again." He took Mikaela's hand and led her into the Baylor's lobby and over to the railing for a final glimpse of its spectacular atrium. Matt bent to kiss the top of Mikaela's head as he danced around an observation he feared to raise. "You're different when you're with your family."

"Different? How?"

Matt shrugged to delay answering. "Calmer. More relaxed. Peaceful. Your laughter comes so easily. I felt as if I was seeing who you were."

"As compared to . . .?"

He rubbed circles into her hand. "My cancer makes everything hard. My health has taken its toll on both of us, but when I saw you with your family, carefree and happy, it's impact on you was so obvious."

Her brow wrinkled like a Shar-Pei's, dismissing his comment. "Of course I was relaxed and happy. But it wasn't because I was with them versus being with you. It was vacation versus real life. They all felt it too, the ability to set their troubles aside for a few days and just draw a long breath. As it turns out, we're not the only ones dealing with hard things. My family may keep in touch with weekly video chats, but they aren't good at opening up. George might need to make a career change because he was diagnosed with degenerative arthritis. And Thomas's son Brenden has been identified as autistic."

"I had no idea."

"No one did, evidently. My family is wonderful in their own way, but I have a bunch of proud brothers who aren't good at sharing their feelings. I need to do a better job of reaching out to my sisters-in-law."

"Circle the wagons."

"Exactly. The guys loved hanging out with your dad. His advice and his fatherly perspective reminded them of time spent with our dad. Sadly, the boys had so little time with our folks once they enlisted. Being with Donovan was a comfort to them, and your mom was the perfect grandma to all the children. They've missed that on my side."

"I hadn't really thought of all that. I can assure you that my parents loved it equally. I've never seen them so happy."

"And you, Mr. Grayken. You're the one who made this possible. I know it cost a small fortune, but I don't think you can understand what a gift you gave my family and me. Not only flying them all in, but into this amazing place?"

"I wanted to give them a special experience. I'm glad they loved it, but we might need to get part-time jobs if this becomes a family tradition."

"We'll start tossing our change into the sugar bowl every night."

"I thought that was the plan for the baby's college fund."

"Oh, dear. We'd better start scouring the help-wanted ads in the morning." She elbow-jabbed him again. "All silliness aside, thank you for arranging this. I love my family, and we try to stay in touch, but we haven't made getting together a priority before. But you made it happen. And now, they're determined to make more of an effort to pull off a family gathering every year. You did that."

Once again, Mikaela was making Matt's small efforts seem grand. He just wanted to get her home and pamper her for the next three weeks and beyond. "Thank you, but it's time to get you off your feet."

Mikaela squared herself to Matt. "You refuse to accept that you did something great here."

"If I did, then I'm glad. You have an extraordinary family."

"*We* have an extraordinary family. The Compton clan loved the Graykens."

Matt chuckled sadly. "All three of us?"

With a slight harrumph, Mikaela included herself in the Grayken count and corrected the number to four. "And you've got to stop seeing yourself as less because you had a nontraditional start. Did you ever stop to consider that God knew where you were and what was happening to you every step of the way?"

He had not, but the idea intrigued him.

"You've had more miracles than most people, Matt. You see yourself as damaged or less because you were abandoned, adopted, raised alone, and then presented with cancer, but what if you opened your eyes and recognized that each of those events guided you to someone you were meant to find?"

His throat became tight from emotions confirming what Mikaela was saying. "Like my parents and you?"

"And the DVP guys and even back to Kate. Maybe your life is actually charmed—not easy, but blessed beyond what you can see."

His eyes stung with happy tears as he drew her palm to his mouth, placing a kiss in the hollow there.

"Trust that God has used everything you've experienced—the struggles and victories, every loss and every joy—to shape you, temper you. Don't wish a moment of your life away, because each has contributed to making you this compassionate, tender, loving man. Not an only child or an abandoned child, an adopted child or a man with cancer. You're a very special person, Matthew Murray Grayken. You made dreams come true this week." She laid his hand on her moving belly. "You've made our dreams come true."

He pressed his forehead to Mikaela's and drew in a long, slow breath. "I want to hold on to this feeling right now."

Mikaela pulled back and set her gaze upon his shoulder where the few errant bits of Rylee's glitter remained. She cupped her hand there and brushed the sparkling bits into her palm, then raising that hand above Matt's head she whispered, "Then all you need is a little magic, and the courage to believe." She released the sparkles into his hair while saying, "Believe, Matthew Murray Grayken, that you are a very special man. A very loved man. Now let's go home so we can prepare to welcome a little miracle who's going to love you more than you can imagine."

CHAPTER TWENTY-ONE

Fatigue slammed Mikaela when she and Matt arrived home. Matt sent her to bed to rest while he unloaded the car. She didn't argue, not even when his coughing increased. Instead, she agreed that this would be her day to rest her puffy ankles, tender hip, and aching back, knowing that tomorrow, Wednesday, they'd be back at Dr. Marcosky's office for Matt.

She prayed he wouldn't be admitted again. Not after she needled Daniel into throwing Matt a daddy-shower on Thursday, in lieu of the regular poker night. She hoped the surprise party would distract her hubby during his confinement and refocus his energy on the joy of the baby's arrival. Planning the event had also proven therapeutic for Daniel, who needed a distraction of his own to ease the pain of Kate's aloofness and departure. Still, Mikaela accepted that the crazy party would survive and perhaps even be enhanced by a forced change of venue from home to hospital, if need be.

She lay down and picked up her phone to attend to the task she'd avoided for the past few days. Alaina had sent an increasingly panicked series of texts, and Mikaela staved off the long-impending conversation over the holiday by promising to get back to her soon. The truth, Mikaela reluctantly admitted, was that she'd made promises to Alaina—promises Alaina was counting on—and despite all the effort she and Matt and Reverend Coolidge spent fulfilling them, things weren't resolving as they'd hoped. Matt and Mikaela completed their part. The preloaded bank cards were delivered to Reverend Coolidge, but the hosting pastors had been so busy with the winter and holiday needs in their own communities that neither of them had yet come through with a plan for Alaina's family to relocate.

Mikaela rubbed her massive belly. She was tired, and anxious to focus on her coming baby. She needed to get Alaina's problems resolved. With that in mind, she texted:

Alaina, I'll come to the clinic Thursday morning. Let's talk then.

Having delayed the inevitable conversation a few more days, Mikaela called down for Matt to bring her a pint of butter brickle ice cream, and she settled in like a slug.

Morning arrived too soon and, with it, a trip to see Dr. Marcosky about Matt. Sure enough, the cold set Matt back to full house arrest until the baby was born to give his immune system a chance to recover. He bore the news well, and Mikaela was thrilled because at least the party could proceed as planned.

All baby-prep details were complete. Catherine saw to what little remained when she was in town, preparing for Thanksgiving. A cleaning company had been employed weeks earlier to keep the house sanitized for Matt's sake. With the house under control, Catherine turned her attention to washing, folding, and arranging the baby's tiny clothes and blankets in the dresser. Every possible supply was purchased, washed, and stored for future need. Literal cases baby wipes, and of diapers, in various sizes, were stuffed into closets and under beds, and Mikaela's hospital bag was packed and in the foyer. All they needed was for baby Grayken to make his or her appearance.

Baby Grayken . . . She and Matt had narrowed the baby's names down to two favorites, neither or which was Sparkle or Sparky. They shared their favorites with no one, intending to wait until they met their child to see if the names fit the little newcomer. She ran them through her mind a dozen times a day until they were so familiar to her that she felt she already knew their child.

Since all baby prep was complete, they turned their energy to Christmas décor, which they agreed to keep to a minimum— their beautiful tree and ornaments, candles in all the windows, a few knickknacks placed in the house, and a garland of fresh evergreen boughs and lights over the front door. She lit a cranberry and apple candle, and Matt made a fire, and then they settled in for a quiet evening playing "The Ornament Game." They took turns pulling an ornament off the tree and challenging the other person to name the life event that inspired its purchase. Picnic baskets, red lips, a lace star, and dozens of other ornaments, some tacky, some lovely, all memorable, were pulled down and replaced after stories and laughter and even a few tears.

Mikaela giggled with excitement Wednesday night, driving Matt crazy as she refused to disclose the reason for the excitement bubbling within her. By Thursday morning, his frustration over the guys' cancellation of poker night, and her secret, left him miffed, but Mikaela didn't care. This surprise shower would be worth a few hours of Matt's grumpy begging.

As she dressed for her trip to the clinic, Matt popped his head in the doorway. "How long are you going to be at the clinic today?"

"An hour or two. Reverend Coolidge and I are going to have a conference call with these other pastors to get some commitments about if and when they can help Alaina."

"We've done our part, Mikaela, and I'm not comfortable with you getting involved any further. Alaina's husband is running with a scary bunch. We agreed not to leave a trail of help back to our home and family."

"It's one phone call."

"That the reverend could make."

She slumped into one hip and eyed her husband. "I don't want her to think I've abandoned her. The reverend and his friends are handling the relocation. I just want to hold her hand and let her know she's not forgotten. Our baby is arriving to such a life of peace and safety. These are the same things Alaina wants for her children. It's hard for me not to feel a little guilty."

Matt pressed his forehead into the doorjamb. "Mikaela . . ."

She kissed his cheek as she passed by and out of the room. "I need to do this."

Matt called to her as she descended the stairs. "So I suppose this surprise isn't going to happen until you get home, right?"

"Maybe, maybe not," she threw back as she continued downstairs.

"Any info on attire would be helpful. You know, I could take a nap and miss the doorbell ring or walk into a room of guests dressed only in boxers."

"Nice try, Sherlock."

She breathed a sigh of relief as she heard a muffled moan and the bathroom door click shut. Her phone rang, and she tensed when she checked the caller I.D. The call was unexpected, and the caller could be bringing good news or a message that could derail Matt and all the hard-laid plans for the day.

With a quick groan and bite of her lip, she stepped into the office and took the call.

Within minutes, she wished she hadn't.

———

Worry over Mikaela's deepening involvement in Alaina's situation nagged at Matt's peace. As a shut-in, he was powerless to protect her or even to watch over her. She'd hate the notion that he felt she needed his watchcare or protection, but the man, the husband, and the father in him accepted his Cro-Magnon mentalities and worried nonetheless.

He headed downstairs to make his case once more and went searching for Mikaela. From behind the study door, he could hear her voice, tense and emotional, as she carried on a conversation. He began to walk away, but something in her voice—sadness, fear perhaps—held him in place, and he listened in as his own anxiety ramped up.

"I can't," he heard Mikaela cry. "Do you know what this will do to Matt?"

The mention of his name and Mikaela's tone sent chills up his arms. Several moments of silence ensued, and then Mikaela responded once again.

"You're asking me to help you rip his heart out. I can't. Yes, I love you, but I can't do this. I'm sorry."

Matt fell back against the wall, barely able to breathe. Devastating assumptions raced through his mind, validating his fears. He knew Mikaela loved him, but did she also love someone else? Had his perpetual illnesses, seclusions, and whining finally worn her down? Tears burned behind his closed lids, and then the door opened, setting Mikaela's horrified eyes on his.

"Matt!" she blurted. Her eyes nearly popped from their

sockets, darting everywhere before returning to him. "What . . . how much of that did you hear?"

He couldn't form any words to reply, fearing that any syllable, any movement, would begin a reaction that would alter his beautiful life as he knew it.

He remembered a case of water left in the garage on a night when the temperatures dipped below thirty-two degrees. When he picked up a bottle from the case, it was still liquid, but it shook slightly as he twisted the cap, and one tiny ice crystal inside began a chain reaction that turned the entire bottle into crystalline mush before his eyes. He felt that way. That paralyzed. As if any movement of his lips or eyes would transform his world into useless mush.

When the silence wore on, Mikaela spoke up. "I'm so sorry, Matt. I didn't see this coming either. I know you dislike Bennett Sadler, and how devastated you must feel right now, but Kate loves you. She isn't trying to hurt y—"

A wake-up bell rang in his brain, tossing him a life ring and telling him to grab it—quick! "Kate?"

"Evidently she and Bennett saw each other in New York when she was painting that mural for your parents, and he traveled to Ireland to see her when she went home."

"*Kate* and Bennett?" he muttered, barely able to put more than three words together in a thought.

Mikaela stepped to him, placing her comforting hands on his arms. "Yes. She said she fought the attraction because she knew Bennett riled you, and that choosing to be with him could cause a rift between you and her, but she loves him."

"Kate called to tell you she's marrying Bennett?" Matt began making sense of the conversation. "Is that why she's been pulling away from me?"

"I'm afraid so. Guilt has been eating at her. She knew you wouldn't approve."

"And Bennett loves *her*? I thought he was in love with—."

Mikaela cocked her head to the side and smiled as he caught his tongue. "It wasn't me. It was us. He said something to me the night of the gala, about how he realized that what he wanted was what we had together. I suppose he thinks he's found it with Kate. She said he needs to be loved, and she needs to be needed. That's about all you and I started with."

Matt wrapped his arms around Mikaela and drew her to his chest as relief flooded over him, leaving him shaky but grateful. "Mikaela . . . my heart stopped . . . literally stopped in my chest when I overheard you. I thought everything I love was on the line . . . that I had finally ground you down and lost you."

"Oh, Matt." Her disappointment was apparent but tinged with forgiveness.

"I know. I'm sorry. Forgive me. In that moment, I hated myself for the time I squandered bemoaning my difficulties instead of being grateful for more time with you and this baby. I love you so much. Maybe I still need to see someone professionally. I shouldn't have canceled appointments with that counselor. I'm not dealing with this cancer as well as I'd hoped. Everything feels threatening. I don't know how to pull out of this spiral."

"Then you or we will return to counseling. Okay?"

"Okay."

"And what shall I tell Kate?"

"Tell her I'll welcome him into the family. I'm not letting go of anyone I love because I have problems with Bennett. Especially you. Kate can have Bennett with my blessing. You're my everything. My world."

She hugged him tight and smiled. "Never forget this, Mr. Grayken. When love is on the line, I'll always choose us. Got it?"

"Got it." He pressed his lips to hers and felt an intoxicating mix of warmth and gratitude wash over and through him.

Mikaela smiled into his face. "But I do need to leave you for a few hours. I want to head to the clinic so I can get home early this afternoon." She wriggled her eyebrows, reminding him about the planned surprise.

"I don't care about surprises. I just want peace. And you."

THE CLINIC WAS ESPECIALLY busy with rows of patients waiting to be seen. Mikaela headed straight for Reverend Coolidge's office, but he wasn't there. She was anxious to hear whether there had been any solid offers of help from his colleagues. In the meantime, she decided to be useful and help with the patient load. She placed her purse in the cupboard set aside for volunteers during clinic hours and headed out to process new patients until the reverend arrived.

The steady flow of work kept her occupied until nearly two when Reverend Coolidge appeared, walking into an ambush of two angry families dragging their teens, demanding his intervention in a conflict. The poor reverend looked ready to drop, but he led the group into a classroom for counseling. Mikaela managed to catch his eye before he closed the door. He held up a hand with spread fingers, begging her to hold on for a few more minutes, so she carried on, keeping an eye on the clock as she determined what time she would need to depart to make it home for Matt's party.

A mother arrived with a sick infant. The chubby little cherub was feverish and crying, and the worry on the young mother's face caused Mikaela to triage the child immediately and place her next in line to see the doctor. When ten minutes passed without a doctor becoming free, Mikaela took matters into her own hands and stripped the child down to begin the preliminary exam. Her attention was so completely focused on this child that she didn't notice Alaina's arrival. At some point, she saw her off in a corner, biting a nail, as she stood by the stairs leading to the reverend's office. Mikaela waved to her as she treated the child, receiving a weak flap of a hand in return. The next time she looked up, Alaina was gone. A moment later, she was haranguing the reverend on the stairs, and then the pair disappeared.

Something in Alaina's situation had changed, and from the nervous panic in Alaina's eyes, Mikaela had a feeling the news wasn't good. As soon as the baby was safely in the care of a doctor, Mikaela headed for the reverend's office.

Alaina was pacing back and forth in front of the desk where the reverend sat, head in his hands, as he spoke on the phone. "What's going on?" asked Mikaela.

She squared her body to Mikaela's and said, "We're out of time. We need to leave now."

Shivers snaked down Mikaela's spine over Alaina's dread-filled tone. "Why? What's changed?"

"Joaquin has planned a big job for tonight. Very high risk with a big payoff for him if it works. Prison or worse for the men if it fails. Eduardo said we must leave today. It's our only hope"

Mikaela looked at the reverend, who shook his head and said, "I've made calls, but many of my friends are dealing with the aftermaths of floods in the south. The others have so many needs in their own communities this time of the year. They are already helping dozens of families with needs like Alaina's, and they haven't been able to make arrangements for her family yet. My hands are tied."

Fear like that of a cornered animal swept over Alaina's face. She backed against the desk in defeat and then rushed to Mikaela. "Surely you can do something. You promised!"

All of Matt's warnings and concerns about getting more involved in this dangerous situation flooded over Mikaela. Matt's concerns played in one ear, and Alaina's played in the other. No matter what she decided, she'd be letting someone down. Failing someone. And she had only minutes to decide.

CHAPTER TWENTY-TWO

Mikaela had left home for the clinic about eleven, leaving Matt without a planned arrival time, except for the vague promise to be home early for whatever surprise she'd planned. Around one p.m., he received a text from her explaining that they were shorthanded at the clinic and she decided to do patient care. All Matt wanted was to see her safely home. Instead, he texted, "Love and miss you," and after a long video conference with the Great Expectations board, he rattled around in the house, missing her and wishing she'd walk through the door.

He began cooking a stew and jumped in the shower about four o'clock in case Mikaela's surprise included company and/or photos that would be improved by his looking clean and shaven. When he exited the shower, he checked the phone and found that he'd missed another text from Mikaela sent fifteen minutes earlier, explaining that she'd be later getting home than she hoped. Matt called but there was no answer.

The doorbell rang around 5:00. Daniel arrived, dressed head to toe in a yellow hazmat suit.

Half-laughing, half-astonished, Matt asked, "What the heck?"

"This is haute couture for the occasion, sir."

"I thought poker was canceled."

"This is much better than poker, my friend." Daniel smiled and tossed Matt a plastic bag containing another yellow suit. "Hurry and change while I unload a few things."

Matt was excited to see what craziness Daniel and the guys had planned for the evening. Just the suits portended that it would be an evening to remember. By the time he finished changing, Daniel had unloaded three extra-large pizzas and a giant box wrapped in pastel paper. A banner stretched across the wall that read, "Happy Baby-Daddy Day."

When it hit him that this was a daddy baby shower, Matt's heart swelled, and he laughed from deep in his belly. He rushed over to Daniel and wrapped him in a hug. "Oh, man! This is awesome! Was this your idea or Mikaela's?"

Daniel hugged him back and laughed in return. "The idea for the party was Mikaela's, but the details are pure DVP."

Matt clapped his hands knowing something radically crazy was about to begin.

"Where is Mikaela?" asked Daniel. "She was going to be the official photographer."

Matt hid his worry over Mikaela's lateness, her involvement with Alaina, and her travel through the crime-ridden neighborhood housing the clinic. After his misunderstanding in the morning, he fought his innate urge to see threats and danger in every situation. Trusting in his wife's judgment, he simply said, "They were shorthanded at one of the clinics today, so she took a shift."

The doorbell rang again as Nelson, Gunther, Jacob, Russell,

Porter, and Miguel showed up in their own hazmat attire, with gifts in hand. Matt welcomed the crazily dressed crew and looked at the clock—five thirty. He excused himself and quickly called Mikaela. Again there was no answer and no new message, and once again, Matt fought the urge to fret and worry. Instead he resorted to logic, running the clinic schedule through his mind. *The official last-patient appointment is set for four thirty and takedown and cleanup require between thirty minutes and an hour,* he told himself. *The drive home in D.C.'s notorious rush hour slog can easily vary from another thirty minutes to an hour. If every worst scenario takes place, Mikaela's arrival time could be as late as six thirty.*

Comforted, he returned to his guests as Daniel called out, "Let's do this, Matt. Maybe we can still get in a few hands of poker."

All seven of the guys were eating pizza and anxious to share their gifts. Daniel stood and cleared his throat. "Matt, we confess that we were shocked and dismayed when you broke from the group and married Mikaela, but in time, you and she proved that getting hitched was not only right, but a brilliant move that made you happier than we've ever seen you. And if truth be told, we were and remain a little jealous of you. We hope we all find a Mikaela of our own."

A round of Hear, hear! and other words of assent were murmured through the group before Daniel continued.

"But fatherhood? To a tiny, messy, noisy, needy baby?" Daniel's face took on a somber, professorial expression as he grabbed handfuls of the suit's fabric and scowled at the future father. "We aren't questioning your decision, just your readiness for this next step, and to this end, we have come here tonight to see that you're properly prepared for this looming adventure."

Daniel sat Matt in a chair and handed him a large, heavy

bag. Matt unwrapped the gift, revealing a military-grade ruck-sack. "What the heck is this for?" Matt asked between bouts of laughter.

"That, my friend, is a battle-tested daddy diaper bag. This thing is waterproof, milkproof, and peeproof. It's also been used to carry ammo, so we feel confident that it will stand up to your future needs. And see? It has compartments for all the necessary gear you'll be carrying from here on out. This is a diaper bag a man can carry with pride."

Matt's phone rang, and he hurriedly picked it up, hoping to hear from Mikaela, but the number was unidentified, so he silenced the call and returned to the party.

Nelson stood up and handed Matt his box. Inside was a pair of heavy green, chemical resistant utility gloves that extended past Matt's elbows. It took Matt quite a while to slither into the rubbery gloves, and as he did, Nelson explained the gift.

"These are dual purpose gloves, Matt. Their slip-resistant texture should help you hold on to the baby during bath time, and the chem-resistant feature means that you are protected, no matter what shows up from either end of that baby."

One by one, the guys presented similar gag gifts. Jacob brought safety goggles, which he explained would come in particularly handy if the baby was a boy. Matt added them to the ensemble. Miguel's gift was a very long set of barbecue tongs, perfect for the seizure and disposal of toxic diaper waste. Gunther's gift was a case of disposable face masks. Russell gave Matt a small electric power washer to be used on either baby or daddy as needed, and Gunther brought an air purifier from an airline catalog.

Nelson placed headphones on Matt's head. "The final preparatory step is auditory training. Can you remain calm and execute good judgment while being subjected to auditory distress?" Porter played with his phone until a track of baby cries played so loud the other guys could hear the sound leaking from the headphones. Matt laughed through the first ten seconds of blaring chaos before pulling the phones off. Porter fidgeted with his phone again and said, "I just emailed you that crying track. That's my gift to you, brother. Play it every night from midnight to three a.m. until the baby arrives. He or she will take it from there."

With all the gifts opened, the guys posed Matt for photos either wearing or holding every item. The group was still hooting and laughing when a knock sounded on the door.

"I'll get it," said Daniel. "You're still on sterile protocol."

It was then that the pulsing red and blue lights drew Matt's attention outside, beyond the window. He slid the goggles from his face and studied the eerie glow from the curb a few meters past his door. His body froze in place while every molecule within him turned to the slushy muck he'd so feared earlier in the day.

The silly gifts fell from Matt's hands as Daniel opened the door revealing a uniformed police officer. The two men who exchanged a few words before Matt's ashen-faced friend turned to Matt, inviting the officer in.

Matt tried to rise but slumped back down on the first attempt. Pairs of loving hands supported him, pulled him to his feet on the second effort, and held him up when his doughy legs refused. He drew his next breath, expelling it in a single haggard, shredded whisper—"Mikaela."

He measured his life in a microsecond. Nothing held the poignancy or importance it had moments earlier. No success or joy had current meaning. No loss or threat loomed as terrifying as the fear that now coursed through him. Mikaela was his anchor. His purpose. She and their child . . .

"Mr. Grayken—"

Matt heard the sober greeting from the officer, but his mouth remained inoperable.

"Does a Mikaela Grayken reside here?"

When Matt failed to answer. Daniel blinked rapidly and drew in a shuddering breath that released in a ragged, "Yes."

"I'm very sorry to report that there's been an accident. Your wife's purse and I.D. were recovered at the scene. She and several other accident victims have been flown to shock trauma."

Eight pairs of eyes darted back and forth to Matt and to each other as they weighed the information. "Mikaela's alive?"

The officer nodded cautiously. "The woman was badly injured but stable at the scene."

"Matt, did you hear that? Mikaela's alive! She's a fighter."

Matt was still registering all the information as the officer continued to speak. *Badly injured . . . other victims.*

"Mr. Grayken, I'm here to transport you to the hospital."

Images of Mikaela, hurt and alone, swarmed in on Matt. Desperate to reach her, he began ripping free of the hazmat suit.

"Matt . . . wait." Daniel turned to the officer. "Matt . . . Mr. Grayken . . . is a leukemia patient. He can't go. I'll go. I'll check on—"

"I'm going," Matt said as he gathered his wallet and phone.

Daniel moved to him and took him by the shoulders. "Think this through, Matt. Mikaela's going to need you healthy and strong."

Matt removed his friend's hands and glared. "I know you mean well, Daniel, but nothing's going to keep me from being with her."

Daniel paced and then asked the officer, "What hospital has she been flown to?"

"The accident happened on I-95, so she's been sent to The

University of Maryland Shock Trauma. The children were flown to Johns Hopkins Children's Hospital."

"Children?" asked Matt.

"Yes. Three of them. All stable," replied the officer. "I take it that they're not yours?"

"No, but my wife is very pregnant. Was the woman in the accident pregnant?"

"I don't think so."

Matt remembered his morning conversation with Mikaela about Alaina. He walked to the wall and pulled a photo of Mikaela down. "Was this the woman in the vehicle?"

The officer studied the photo and pulled back with uncertainty on his face. "She had dark hair and eyes like this woman, but there was a lot of blood from a large cut over her forehead. I didn't see her features very clearly."

"Was there a man in the vehicle also?"

"Yes. About thirty years or so. A witness said a black SUV rammed his door at full speed and then drove off when the vehicle flipped. Paramedics were working on him at the scene. I'm not sure of his condition."

In that moment, the door flew open, and like a dream, Mikaela rushed in with utter panic on her face as she headed straight for Matt. His jaw fell slack as he stared at her, wondering if he was crazy or had dropped dead to join this conversation from the other side of the veil.

"Are you all right?" she asked as she held his arms and scanned him from head to toe. "I saw the flashing lights and thought it was an ambulance. I was terrified that something happened to you, but it's a police cruiser. Is this about my car being stolen?"

"Your car was stolen," Matt whispered as that bit of information jiggled all the other odd details into a semblance of reason.

He pressed his lips to her face and clung to her as the reality of her presence, there in the house, in his arms, swept away his lingering doubts. Tears spilled from his eyes. "There was an accident. Witnesses say a black SUV intentionally rammed the car at full speed and then drove off. They found your purse and I.D. at the scene. I thought . . . we all thought . . ."

Her hand flew to her mouth and she shrieked, "Oh, Matt! I'm so sorry. I'm so sorry."

A new horror filled her eyes. "I think Alaina stole my purse and car. She was right. Joaquin or his men would rather kill them than let them go. She was so panicked about the job Joaquin lined up for tonight. She begged me to drive her family to Philadelphia. I told her I'd hire a taxi to take her family to the train station and I'd have train tickets to Philly reserved for them. She agreed to the plan and then she disappeared. I assumed she went home to pack a few things, but she never returned, and when I finally went to leave the clinic, my purse was missing from Reverend Coolidge's office, along with my keys, my wallet, and my phone. So were the bank cards. We figured it was Alaina."

"No wonder you didn't pick up when I called. I just couldn't shake this nervous feeling I've felt all afternoon."

"I tried calling you too, on the reverend's phone, even though I knew you wouldn't recognize the number. Reverend Coolidge drove me home."

Because you knew I couldn't come for you. Matt refused to give in to those negative voices again. "I'm grateful to him."

"Alaina must have felt desperate to do what she did. And then there was an accident?" Her lips trembled as her eyes filled. "Is Alaina—"

"No. She's badly hurt. She and the children were airlifted to trauma centers."

Mikaela leaned into Matt and cried. "I've made such a mess

of everything. I gave her hope I couldn't deliver, and she took matters into her own hands. Now what's going to happen to her and her family?"

They gave the officer the actual names of the passengers in the car and offered general information about the danger Alaina and her family were attempting to flee. The officer was sympathetic to their plight but not to their choices. He said someone would be in touch about the car and Mikaela's purse, and then he left.

Daniel and the guys stayed just long enough to be sure there was nothing they could do for their friends, and then, with long hugs for both Matt and Mikaela, they too left.

Matt led Mikaela to the sofa and sat, drawing her down to lean against his chest. He buried his face in her hair and remained that way until the last of the nervous shakes left their bodies. When he finally felt still and in control, he leaned his head back and stared at the ceiling until he pulled enough of his thoughts together to speak.

"Nearly every night, since the day you accepted my proposal, I fell asleep replaying the same dream, imagining you going on alone. Now, I face dreams of you and our baby building a life without me, but never once have I imagined a life where I go on without you. Until tonight. That scenario terrified me a hundred times more than the thought of dying."

Mikaela threaded her fingers between his and squeezed. "You saved me today."

"How?"

"If this situation with Alaina had happened before I met you, I would have been in that car, driving her wherever she wanted to go. But I thought of the promise I made to you, and I offered to help Alaina in a way that didn't violate that promise. I chose you. I chose us."

CHAPTER TWENTY-THREE

Two detectives arrived to get Mikaela's full statement about how her car and belongings ended up at the scene. When she hesitated in answering, one detective explained some details that gave her hope for Alaina and Eduardo's future.

"The driver of the SUV was injured in the accident. We picked him up when he checked in at the ER in Rockville, Maryland. To save his own neck, he gladly fingered Joaquin as the man who ordered the hit on this family. If Eduardo testifies about the chop shop ring, we might be able to make the car theft charges disappear, along with probation for his part in stealing and dismantling all those cars."

Mikaela and Matt visited Alaina in the hospital to verify the good news. Alaina cried tears of regret tangled with apologies when she saw Mikaela. She begged forgiveness and explained her panic-driven choices.

"I know you meant well with your offer to call a car to take us to the train station, but Joaquin's men were already watching our house. I knew he would do anything to stop us, so

I needed to act quickly. I called Eduardo and told him to take the children to the park. Then I stole your purse and keys and picked them up. I swear I planned to leave your car and belongings at the train station. You've done so much to help. I wouldn't have stolen your things. Just borrowed them. Now I've lost everything, even my children, unless Eduardo testifies."

The talk relieved both the women. Alaina knew Mikaela still cared about her, and Mikaela knew the law would provide them the second chance they sought.

Heaven seemed to understand the Graykens' need for peace and calm, and it delivered two weeks of quiet healing as they prepared for their baby's arrival. Mikaela's water broke in the early hours of December fourteenth. As promised, Dr. Chapman arranged a private, sterile suite where Mikaela could labor and deliver with Matt safely by her side. Their chubby baby arrived by six p.m. without drama except for the child's exquisite welcoming cry, like the harkening of angels announcing a miraculous arrival from heaven. Plump and purplish, the child wriggled and kicked at the hands attending to it. The announcement, "You have a son!" came as Matt stood by Mikaela's head.

"We have a son," Matt repeated, as his tears mingled with Mikaela's during a kiss.

Dr. Chapman swaddled the newborn and laid him against Mikaela's body. The inquisitive, shaky little bundle instantly calmed. Matt marveled at how the child, less than a minute old, was already blinking and staring at the lights and sounds. Dr. Chapman called Matt to her side and handed him the scissors to sever his newborn son's umbilical cord between two clamps. The miraculous being, an invisible stranger mere moments earlier, was now clearly their son, a child with Mikaela's curly dark hair,

Matt's nose and deep-set eyes, and a full array of opinions, wants, and needs.

While nurses took him to bathe him and attend to his birth census—weight, length, eye color, etc., in readiness for his pediatrician's exam, other nurses attended to Mikaela, whose sweat-soaked hair and body somehow relegated her to a new level of beauty. Matt felt his chest tighten with emotion at the wonder of birth. He couldn't imagine any gift or service or words that could adequately thank her for giving him a son.

Once Mikaela was declared healthy and well, and their son was bathed and swaddled in a clear infant bed tagged with the name Baby Boy Grayken, Matt felt an indescribable hunger to see his parents, to share this experience with them. There was no confusion over who he was or to whom he belonged. He was a Grayken, and it was to them, the parents who raised him, that he longed to show his bonnie boy.

His phone beeped soon after the last nurse cleared the room. "Maybe your parents are here," said Mikaela.

As she predicted, his mother was the source of the text, informing them that they were in a taxi on their way from the train station.

As Mikaela attempted to get the baby to suckle, Matt could only imagine how she longed for her own mother and father at this moment, to share her joy and marvel over their own baby's leap into motherhood.

"I imagine you must miss your parents terribly right now."

She bit a trembling lip and smiled. "I wish they were here, but I feel them close, and your parents make me feel like a real daughter."

Matt had never loved his parents more than on that night as their awe over the baby knew no bounds. Tears flowed freely as the Graykens' cell phone cameras clicked off a thousand photos.

They hovered over Mikaela as if she were their own, while the love and pride in their eyes when they looked at Matt was a language he was just beginning to understand, linking a parent to a child and beyond, like a chain of love without beginning or end. Matt was home in every way.

That night, when the lights were low and the hospital sounds had eased into soft hums, Matt and Mikaela studied their tiny son to see if the name they had chosen for him was a good fit.

"What do you think, Mikaela?"

"Donovan Benjamin Grayken. It honors both grandpas. I think it suits him."

"And Benji or Donnie for short?"

"Donnie. My father will understand, and yours will burst his buttons."

Matt had gotten his wish. "Donnie it is. Welcome to the family Donovan Benjamin Grayken."

AFTER TWO DAYS, their little family headed home. Matt's restrictions were lifted, allowing him to fully return to the world again. He was fascinated by the fact that the home, which seemed so confining and limited when he was on sterile protocol, was now the only place he wanted to be.

He found himself staring at his sleeping babe, drawing the greatest pleasure from every twitch and blink. Mikaela had never seemed more exhausted or content. Matt rose for every feeding, his physical helpfulness limited to handing Mikaela the baby and changing Donnie between nursing on one side or the other. But his emotional investment and shared exhaustion gave

Mikaela a morale boost. He held her while she held the baby, as the sleepless trio struggled through to a new day.

He dreaded his return to work. He and Mikaela still had a healthy portfolio of resources by most family's account, but the past year had bitten deeply into their reserves, and the other Great Expectations employees needed the security of Matt's involvement.

He loved coming home and encountering evidence of Donnie's arrival. The humid warmth of the dryer, lavender bath lotion, and baby powder perpetually infused the air. Stacks of diapers and wipes filled drawers and shelves where CDs and DVDs once lived. Matt marveled over the abundance of fabric squares in every size. Warm fuzzy blankets, thin swaddling blankets, flannel spit-up squares, quilts, and play mats lay everywhere, giving the house the feel of a home.

Christmas arrived with little fanfare because the greatest gift had arrived weeks earlier, but the anticipated arrival of family and friends took on the new delight of watching adults turn into babbling idiots in the presence of the baby.

The house emptied of guests about eight, except for Matt's parents, who were staying for a few days. Matt heard a knock at the door and opened it to find Kate standing there, nervous and fumbling, with Bennett by her side. Matt opened his arms and drew her in, extending his hand to Bennett with a smile that came surprisingly easy. "Welcome to the family," he said to his new brother-in-law, who truly seemed to love the status of newlywed.

January dawned under a thick blanket of snow, shutting down the city and forcing the bustling capital to nestle in for a quiet welcome to the new year. Matt found it a perfect way to ring in what he saw as the best year of his life.

Mikaela set steaming cups of cocoa on the coffee table in

front of Matt as he held the baby. "Ready for a break?" she asked.

Matt shifted Donnie into one arm and extended the other to Mikaela. "I never want a break."

"You really are happy, aren't you? I've never seen you so content."

He gave that notion some thought. "I can't explain it, but I am content. Maybe the accident helped me face the truth about how fragile life is. Not just for me, but for anyone. Or maybe becoming a father has reset my priorities. All I know is I don't care about the past. I accept where I came from and to whom I belong. And I don't want to waste any more time worrying about the future, or what may or may not happen. I just want to live in this moment. To be fully present every second I have."

Mikaela reached up and drew his mouth to hers. "I'd say the ability to love life in the present is true happiness, Mr. Grayken."

"Then I'm the happiest man on earth, Mrs. Grayken."

– THE END –

ACKNOWLEDGMENTS

Writing a sequel to *Love on a Limb*, a book that resonated so deeply with readers, was a daunting task. Readers asked for it. They didn't want the story to end where it did, but I knew the bar was set high for a continuation of Matt and Mikaela's story. The reviews of *Love on a Limb* were the best for any book I'd ever written, and I dreaded the thought of falling short or of leaving readers wanting or disappointed.

A sequel would have to tackle more hard topics, and I'd need to get the medical details and the emotions just right, so I found an on-line support group for people with AML. I was so amazed by the strength and love I found there. These brave warriors, many of them veterans of several recurrences of cancer, lifted one another, and cheered victories while consoling those new to the disease or facing a new fight.

I told them I was an author, and I asked them if they'd mind me lurking around their page to better understand the fight they were engaged in. To my surprise and honor, they welcomed me in. They said they wanted their story told, because AML leukemia doesn't have a good PR campaign like some cancers, nor does it get the research funding other cancers receive, and they wanted to come out of the darkness and be understood.

Several individuals reached out to me privately to share their personal stories. Chris and Dana Heisler invited me to follow their daily journal. Chris is a loving husband and father who candidly chronicled their leukemia fight. I say "their" because Dana was also a warrior, fighting by Chris's side. This couple and their unyielding faith inspired me, and their journal kept *Love on the Line* honest and accurate.

Content, even stirring content, falls flat without great editing. My enormously talented friend and editor, Elizabeth Petty Bentley, who edited *Love on a Limb* and most of my recent books, set her own brilliant writing aside once more to edit *Love on the Line*. She pushes me and talks straight to me when I get lazy. I'm incalculably grateful for her nudges, her wit, and her command of her craft. Thank you, Beth!

Talented cover artist, Sheri McGathy designed the beautiful cover. It was a struggle to create a cover that featured Mikaela without revealing too much of the storyline. Sheri persevered despite my constant insecurities and vacillating opinions. Honestly, she's a saint. A gifted saint. Thanks, Sheri!

Lastly, many thanks to Ray Hoy and his team at The Fiction Works in Alaska. I usually send him my manuscript days before the launch and beg him to get it formatted for every possible reading experience within hours of going live. He has become a great friend and virtual hand-holder. Thanks, Ray!

I have great beta readers who let me know what's working and what's not in a developing manuscript. Some of them read multiple iterations of the story to help me get it just right. Their help is immeasurable and I'm so grateful for their support. My beta heroes on this project were Bruce Morse, Lisa Lee. Pam

Dove, Shauna Joesten, Khadra Michaelson, Babs Hightower, Debbie Paisie, and Jacklyn Good. Thank you so much!

Lastly, thanks and great love go to my daughter, Amanda. Our family had its own transplant experience during the writing of this book. Last fall, after thirteen years of great health and the births of three amazing children, Amanda, a kidney transplant patient, went into rejection. Once again, we were thrust into the miraculous and frightening world of transplantation. Thanks to Johns Hopkins Hospital's amazing transplant team, breakthroughs in nephrology, Amanda's courage and grit, and answered prayers by a loving God, she is once again enjoying good health. Still, we were reminded that health is a fragile gift that often requires a bit of courage. Amanda's courage, like the Heislers' inspired the emotional impact of this book.

Thank you, my readers, for inspiring me every day.

I'm very proud of *Love on the Line,* and I hope readers of *Love on a Limb* will find it a sequel worthy of book one. My wish is that anyone struggling with something hard, be it medical, or financial, or a crisis of love or faith, will find within these pages some inspiration to face their mountain with hope and determination, and to protect what and whom they treasure.

Because love, even a great love, can be taken for granted, and end up on the line.

Much Love,

— *Laurie Lewis*

ABOUT THE AUTHOR

Laurie (L.C.) Lewis will always be a Marylander at heart—a weather-whining lover of crabs, American history, and the sea. She admits to being craft-challenged, particularly lethal with a glue gun, and a devotee of sappy movies. *Love on the Line* is Laurie's eleventh published  novel. Her women's fiction/romance novels include *Awakening Avery,* (2018), Love on a Limb, (2017), *Sweet Water,* (2017), *The Dragons of Alsace Farm* (2016), and *Unspoken* (2004), written as Laurie Lewis. Using the pen name L.C. Lewis, she wrote the five volumes of her award-winning *FREE MEN and DREAMERS* historical romance series, set against the backdrop of the War of 1812: *Dark Sky at Dawn* (2007), *Twilight's Last Gleaming* (2008), *Dawn's Early Light* (2009), *Oh, Say Can You See?* (2010), and *In God is Our Trust,* (2011).

Laurie Lewis is a RONE Award Winner (*The Dragons of Alsace Farm*) and was twice named a New Apple Literary Award winner, winning Best New Fiction for *Love on a Limb*. She is a BRAGG Medallion honoree, and she was twice named a Whitney Awards and USA Best Books Awards finalist.

Laurie loves to hear from readers, and she invites you to join her VIP Readers' Club, or contact her at any of the following locations.

VIP Readers' Club:

https://www.laurielclewis.com/newsletter

Website:

www.laurielclewis.com

Twitter:

https://twitter.com/laurielclewis

Goodreads:

https://www.goodreads.com/author/show/1743696.Laurie_
L_C_Lewis

Facebook:

https://www.facebook.com/LaurieLCLewis/

Instagram:

https://www.instagram.com/laurielclewis/

OTHER BOOKS BY LAURIE LEWIS

Laurie (L.C. Lewis) invites you to read her other books

BOOKS WRITTEN AS L.C. LEWIS

Free Men and Dreamers

A sweeping War of 1812 historical romance saga detailing the triumphs and struggles of the first American-born generation.

Volume 1: *Dark Sky at Dawn*
(Best Books Finalist, USA Book News)

Volume 2: *Twilight's Last Gleaming*
(Best Books Finalist, USA Book News)

Volume 3: *Dawn's Early Light*

Volume 4: *Oh, Say Can You See?*
(2010 Whitney Award Finalist)

Volume 5: *In God is Our Trust*

BOOKS WRITTEN AS LAURIE LEWIS

Unspoken

Awakening Avery

The Dragons of Alsace Farm

(2017 RONE Award Winner, 2016 Whitney Award Finalist, 2017 New Apple Medallion Winner, BRAGG medallion Winner.)

Sweet Water

(2017 Readers' Favorite Award)

Love on a Limb

(2018 New Apple Winner for Best New Fiction)

www.ingramcontent.com/pod-product-compliance
Lightning Source LLC
Chambersburg PA
CBHW071533260626
47170CB00002B/613